## Praise for the Pickled & Preserved Mysteries

"A one-of-a-kind mystery with homemade food, small-town secrets, and winsome characters."
——Ellery Adams, *New York Times* bestselling author
of the Books by the Bay Mysteries

"This warm-hearted mystery . . . had me turning the pages late into the night. Encore!"
——G. M. Malliet, Agatha Award–winning author
of the Max Tudor Mysteries

"A charming new sleuth in a peck of pickles and murder."
——Connie Archer, national bestselling author
of the Soup Lover's Mysteries

"Hughes's second series entry . . . will delight fans of culinary cozies . . . Fans of Susan Wittig Albert's China Bayles series should enjoy this plucky heroine." ——*Library Journal*

"Will keep the reader guessing . . . A pleasing puzzle, *License to Dill* preserves Hughes's stature as a first-rate mysterian who specializes in homemade food and homemade homicide." ——*Richmond Times-Dispatch*

"If the first book is any indication of the direction this series will take, I say the author has a winner on her hands. It is a well-plotted, page-turning mystery." ——*MyShelf.com*

W9-CBS-934

# Scene of the Brine

MARY ELLEN HUGHES

BERKLEY PRIME CRIME, NEW YORK

BERKLEY
PRIME
CRIME

**An imprint of Penguin Random House LLC**
**375 Hudson Street, New York, New York 10014**

SCENE OF THE BRINE

A Berkley Prime Crime Book / published by arrangement with the author

ISBN: 978-0-425-26247-4

PUBLISHING HISTORY
Berkley Prime Crime mass-market edition / February 2016

PRINTED IN THE UNITED STATES OF AMERICA

10  9  8  7  6  5  4  3  2  1

Cover illustration by Chris O'Leary.
Cover design by Sarah Oberrender.
Interior text design by Laura K. Corless.

Penguin
Random
House

This one's for two brothers and sisters-in-law who have always been a special part of my life:

Ed and Anita Lemanski, and Ted and Janet Lemanski

# Acknowledgments

An author can research only so much online and through books. Sometimes discussions with experts in their fields are called for. First of all, a special shout-out to the men in blue who, besides working tirelessly to keep us safe, have always been so generous in sharing their expertise with me on various points of the law. It's very much appreciated, and any mistakes that slipped in are mine alone. I'm also grateful to Dianne Wienand Lemanski, who helped me better understand several points in the real estate business. Sheila Marchand was my go-to person on plants—both harmless and poisonous—and she's been great with helping me keep them straight.

Many thanks to my editor, Robin Barletta, for working closely with me to make this the best possible book, as well as the excellent behind-the-scenes team at Berkley. Of course, none of this would have started without the help and encouragement of my agent. Thanks again, Kim Lionetti.

I owe much to my first readers, the long-running Annapolis Critique group—Shaun Taylor Bevins, Becky Hutchison,

Sherriel Mattingly, Debbi Mack, Bonnie Settle, and Marcia Talley. Thanks to all for their excellent comments on my early drafts. All criticism was constructive, as it should be, and very gratefully received.

As usual, my husband, Terry, deserves the patience award for being a willing sounding board whenever I ran into story problems. He's continually acted not simply as a listener but also a solver and idea stimulator. Though some pickles improve by sitting undisturbed, my stories get better with a lot of tossing around. Thanks so much for participating in the catch and throw, Terry. Love you!

# 1

*B*ang!

Piper jumped at the noise. Then she smiled and shrugged. A little, well, a lot of noise in her pickling shop was more than fine with her. In fact, it was downright delightful. It meant she was on her way to getting a new front door to replace her old and cracked one. And not just any door. What Piper was having installed was a custom-made, absolutely beautiful, hand-carved door.

"Can you afford it?" Uncle Frank, ever practical, had asked when she'd described the creation to him and Aunt Judy.

"Amazingly, I can. Ralph Strawbridge quoted me a price that was not much above what I'd find in a Home Depot or Lowe's."

It all came about when Ralph, a relative newcomer to Cloverdale, visited Piper's Picklings for the first time, interested in trying one or two of Piper's specialty pickles. As Piper ran through the list of choices, she'd noticed that Ralph's gaze had shifted to the wooden plaque she'd finally hung on her wall. The plaque had come from Thailand, sent by her ex-fiancé, Scott, several months ago as he traveled the world in his effort to "find himself." Piper had held off on hanging the plaque, beautiful as it was, because of her extreme annoyance at the time with Scott, who was ignoring the fact that they were no longer a couple. But eventually it seemed a shame to keep such an exquisite piece hidden away in a closet.

Vegetables of all kinds had been carved into the wood—pineapples, squashes, beans, peppers, and more, along with delicately intertwining vines. The genial, forty-something man stared at it as if entranced.

"That is quite impressive," he'd said. When Piper agreed, he'd added, "How would you like something like that on your entry door?" Ralph had gone on to explain that he was a professional woodworker, specializing in custom-made furniture. "I noticed your front door was in pretty bad shape. I could make a new one for you and pick up the theme from that plaque."

As he described the door he could create for her, Piper salivated, so perfect did it sound for an entrance to her pickling shop. But she was sure anything of that sort would be way out of her budget.

"Not at all," Ralph assured her. "Believe me, this project would be as much for me as for you. A door of that type would be a terrific challenge. I'd truly love to tackle it." He then quoted her a price that astonished Piper, since it seemed to barely cover the materials.

"I look at it as good advertising," Ralph said with a smile. "It'll be my personal billboard, since everyone who comes through your door will likely ask where it came from."

"And I'll certainly tell them," Piper said, amazed at what had dropped into her lap.

They'd discussed details and eventually set a time frame, and within weeks, on that mild, late April day, Ralph Strawbridge had begun work toward installing his hand-carved door. Piper could barely keep from grinning ear to ear.

Her old door had come off, and Ralph called her over to inspect the doorjamb. "There's definitely wood rot near the bottom," he said, pointing to the areas on both sides. "I should replace the entire frame."

Piper nodded. "I remember you mentioned that possibility. Go ahead with whatever you need to do." Her several discussions with Ralph had convinced her he knew exactly what he was doing. She'd also carefully checked around before making a final commitment and found that in his few months in Cloverdale, Ralph Strawbridge had built a reputation for excellent work. The only surprising part was that he hadn't done a large amount of work—though it wasn't for lack of interested customers. He turned down three jobs for every one he took on; at least that was the impression Piper got. Apparently Ralph picked and chose only work that interested him, and Piper felt privileged to be one of the chosen few.

Having gotten Piper's go-ahead, Ralph jumped nimbly to his feet and scrambled through his tool box. His loose-fitting denims didn't camouflage a fit and trim body, a condition that seemed maintainable by the middle-aged only through consistent hard work or hours in the gym. Hard work was clearly Ralph's method, though judging from his obvious enthusiasm Piper doubted he'd call it work.

Ralph pulled out a pry bar and put it into position, ready to attack the door frame, but then stepped back as Sugar Heywood approached.

"Hey, there, Ralph," Sugar said as she stepped gingerly through the doorway. "It's good to see you! How're you doing?"

"Doing great, Ms. Heywood."

"Don't you *Ms. Heywood* me, Ralph. We shared too many cups of coffee in my kitchen for that." She turned to Piper. "Ralph made me the most beautiful cabinet."

"And Sugar made the best apple pie I've ever had," Ralph said, grinning.

"Oh, go on," Sugar said, laughing, but she didn't bother to deny it. Sheila "Sugar" Heywood was well known in Cloverdale as an excellent cook and a popular special events caterer. Piper was sure her apple pie fit Ralph's description perfectly.

"So, what in the world are you doing to Piper's doorway?" Sugar asked, and Piper jumped in with the answer, sure that Ralph would streamline his response, making the project sound like a simple repair job. When she finished, the attractive silver blond, Rubenesque-figured caterer looked properly impressed. "I can't wait to see that," she said. "Ralph is absolutely the best."

Ralph dipped his head in acknowledgment but looked ready to get on with his work, so Sugar said to Piper, "I'm hoping you have a few jars of those sweet cherries that you put up with brandy and red wine. I'll be making my almond cakes for Jeremy Porter's Realtors' dinner, and your cherries make the absolute perfect topping."

"I have plenty," Piper assured her. "Amy and I made a bunch last fall. There's two jars out front here and more in the back. How many do you need?"

"I'm sure I'll need at least a dozen."

Piper smiled and shook her head, thinking how Sugar was certainly her best customer, picking up all varieties of Piper's pickles and preserves depending on her latest planned menu. "That's great," Piper said, "but maybe you should think about making your own, sometime. It's easy enough, and I can walk you through the process as well as provide whatever equipment and seasonings you'd need. With all the farms around, including my uncle Frank's, you'd have no end of supplies of fresh fruits and vegetables. I'm just saying it might be more economical."

"Piper, you don't know how I'd love to. But with all the cooking I'm already doing, I just don't have a single spare minute in my day. Besides, with the great variety you carry, it's so easy to walk in and grab what I need. I make a point, by the way, to share exactly where a pickle or a jam came from whenever my clients or their guests rave about it—which is often."

"I appreciate that, Sugar. I've had more than one person come by because of that." Piper led Sugar to her back room for the brandied cherries.

As Sugar helped Piper pull the jars from a shelf and load them into a cardboard box, she said, "I know you're going to be over the moon with Ralph's door. He does

truly amazing work. And he's a fantastic guy, as well."
She paused until the screeching sound of nails being
pulled out of wood assured her Ralph was out of hearing
distance, then confided, "I would have been more interested in the man if he had a little more ambition."

When Piper looked over in surprise, she added. "Don't
get me wrong, Piper. I'm not a snob in any way whatsoever.
Heaven knows, I've worked my share of minimum-wage
jobs when we lived back in Texas and was glad for them.
But I made up my mind early on that I wouldn't let myself
get stuck. I intended to do a lot better for Zach's sake, and
in time I did."

Piper knew Zach was Sugar's twenty-year-old son.
"I've only known you since I moved to Cloverdale myself
last August," she said. "Your catering business seems to
be going great, but I take it, it wasn't always so?"

"Heavens, no. I started it only a few years ago after
scraping up enough money to get things going. I'm talking about waitressing, short-order cooking, and so many
other jobs that I can't even remember. But I *always* had
the goal of running my own catering business and to
make it the biggest and the best I could. I don't see any
point in not aiming high."

Sugar glanced toward the carpentry noises with a hint
of wistfulness. "Ralph is a great guy in many ways. But
with his skills, he could do so much more! I mean, he
turns down work right and left and spends three times
as long as any other craftsman on the jobs he does take.
He does wonderful work but he'll never get beyond
barely scraping by with working like that, which drives
me crazy. By comparison, look at Jeremy Porter. He

started out years ago selling little starter homes and now he heads his own real estate company. That really impresses me."

Piper counted the jars they'd loaded, then closed the flaps of the box over them, thinking about Sugar's comment. Jeremy Porter was a bachelor about Sugar's age, and highly successful, judging by the large house he'd bought a year or so ago when he moved to Cloverdale. The house was a historic mansion, built during the late 1800s by one of the area's railroad barons. Sugar had mentioned that she was catering a business dinner for Porter. But something about the tone of Sugar's voice and the look on her face when she mentioned him made Piper wonder if . . .

"Are you seeing him?" Piper blurted, then clapped her hand to her mouth. "I'm sorry. That just came out. It's none of my business."

Sugar grinned. "I am, and don't worry about it. I'm sure it's common knowledge."

"Then I'm the last to know." What had happened, Piper wondered, to the Cloverdale "news spreaders" who certainly hadn't missed a beat when Piper went on a first date with Will Burchett? Was there a virus going around that had struck half the population dumb? If so, was there a way to capture and hold on to it for future use?

"That's great, Sugar. I haven't met Jeremy Porter yet, but if you like him I'm sure he's wonderful."

"It's been a bit of a whirlwind," Sugar admitted, "but I'm loving it. I haven't dated anyone seriously for ages, what with trying to be a good mom to Zach as well as get my business going. But with Zach off in college now, I'm totally ready for a little *me* time."

Piper smiled. "How's Zach doing?"

"Wonderfully! He loves his major—botany—and it shows, 'cause he's made the dean's list every semester. Zach's home now on spring break. Which reminds me." Sugar picked up her box of brandied cherries and started walking toward the shop front. "I promised to pick up a couple of books being held for him at the library. Can you imagine?" she said. "Studying on spring break!" She rolled her eyes but her pride shone through.

Piper grinned, thinking there were worse ways to spend your time on a school break, some of which she might have actually tried herself eight or nine years ago, though nobody in Cloverdale needed to hear about that. She rang up Sugar's purchase and as the caterer hefted her box once again to leave, Ralph noticed and stepped over to gallantly take it from her. Piper watched as the two walked together toward Sugar's car, chatting and smiling and looking for all the world like a couple extremely comfortable with each other.

When Ralph returned, he told Piper he'd have to run out to get the wood for the new doorjamb. "Your doorway will have to stay open until tonight, so you might want to keep an eye out for stray dogs and such."

"I haven't come across any dogs with a taste for pickles yet," Piper said, "so I think we're safe. It's a perfect day for letting fresh air in, though." She breathed in appreciatively. "Springlike, but no insects to worry about yet. So an open doorway definitely works for me today."

"I'll be quick," Ralph promised, taking a moment to scribble down one or two things in a notebook and double-check a measurement. He then trotted briskly out and hopped into his truck.

Piper gazed after Ralph's truck, thinking about Sugar's comments on Ralph's work ethic. It was true he took his time. If Piper had had a simple handyman replace her old door with a new one, the job would likely have been done by now. But Ralph was a craftsman. She didn't mind putting up with the mess a little longer for him, convinced the wait would be well worth it.

As Ralph's truck disappeared down the street, Piper caught sight of her part-time assistant, Amy Carlyle, walking toward Piper's Picklings for her shift. Though she was some distance away, Amy's long red hair was unmistakable, especially as it caught the April sun and became a glowing torch. With her wide network of friends, as well as the town's sheriff for a father, there wasn't much that went on in Cloverdale that Amy missed, so the second she stepped through the doorway Piper asked, "Why haven't I heard about Sugar Heywood and Jeremy Porter?"

"You didn't know?" Amy slid her light cardigan off to reveal a pretty yellow blouse tucked into black slacks. The sensible black shoes she wore worked for both her job at the shop and Amy's later-on part-time job as an assistant chef at A La Carte, where she hoped to gain enough experience to eventually run her own restaurant. Sugar Heywood would approve of Amy's ambitious goals, though for the time being Piper thoroughly appreciated Amy's help in pickle preparation as well as sales.

"No, I didn't know," Piper said. "But since you did,

and probably half the town as well, I'm surprised it never came up."

Amy shrugged and slipped the loop of a green Piper's Picklings apron over her head. "Maybe because they're kind of old, so it doesn't seem like a really big deal."

"Old?" Piper repeated, surprised until she reminded herself that Amy was barely twenty-one. "Maybe to you they are," Piper conceded. "But I wouldn't exactly put them in that category."

Amy grinned. "Well, not *old* old. Not ready for retirement homes, certainly."

"'Retirement' is not a word in Sugar's vocabulary, no matter what her age. She's a highly driven person." Piper glanced toward her work-in-progress doorway. "Which is fine, but I hope it's not affecting her decisions in the romance department more than it should." When Amy raised her brows questioningly, Piper shrugged. "Never mind. It's really none of my business."

"Jeremy Porter's been to A La Carte a few times," Amy said. "He seems like an okay guy, but that creep who works for him, Dirk Unger—he's Porter's accountant or something—he can be a royal pain. They were in together last night, and Unger sent back a meal that was perfectly fine. He's done that more than once. The waitstaff get a lot of hassle from him, too. He's always pointing out little slips in their service, or things *he* considers slips, like not keeping the water glasses fully topped or pointing out a spilled drop of coffee on a saucer. I don't know if he's trying to impress his boss with his so-called knowledge of fine dining but he sure doesn't impress us."

"Uh-oh," Piper said. "Sugar said she's catering a

business dinner for Jeremy Porter. I hope for her sake that Dirk Unger won't be there."

"Would he criticize someone he knows his boss is dating?"

Piper shrugged. "I don't know Unger but he sounds like someone who might enjoy stirring up a little trouble." The shop's phone rang and as Amy went to answer, Piper had another thought. If Jeremy Porter kept someone like Unger close by, what did that say about *him*?

## 2

~~~~~

Ralph Strawbridge returned with the new wood for Piper's doorjamb and had been back to work, trimming and hammering, for an hour or so when Piper invited him to join her and Amy in a lunch break.

"We have leftovers from A La Carte—ratatouille with chicken."

When Ralph hesitated, Amy said, "There's more than enough for three, honest. You have to help us finish it up, or we'll be eating it again tomorrow and be thoroughly sick of it."

"I can't imagine getting tired of anything *you've* prepared," Ralph said, and Amy's cheeks glowed with pleasure.

Ralph set down his tools and followed the two to the back room, where Amy pulled a covered dish from Piper's refrigerator and slipped it into the microwave. Piper had a commercial kitchen in her shop's back area, which she used for putting up the dozens of varieties of pickles and preserves, often with Amy's expert help. As Ralph washed his hands, Piper opened up three folding chairs and Amy pulled out plates and forks. When the microwave dinged, Amy checked and stirred the aromatic stew, then decided to warm it for another minute.

"Oh," she asked Piper, "is there any of the French bread left?"

"Aha," Piper said. She did a quick search in a cupboard. "Yes!"

"Ratatouille *and* French bread," Ralph said, shaking his head as he wiped his hands. "I may feel compelled to significantly reduce my bill after such royal treatment."

"And what if we add some of Piper's pickled carrots to the mix?" Amy asked.

Ralph shrugged helplessly and mimed ripping up a sheet of paper, which brought laughs from Piper and Amy. The microwave dinged a second time, and Amy took out her dish, then set it on the counter for everyone to help themselves.

They ate quietly for a while, savoring the meal, until Ralph asked, "So, Amy, when you set up your own restaurant, will it be French?"

"I'm not sure," Amy said. She tore off a small chunk of bread and popped it into her mouth, chewing thoughtfully. "I suppose it'll depend on where it is. I love the cuisine, but A La Carte might have French locked up here in Cloverdale. Maybe I'd do better to choose something different."

He nodded. "I've noticed that places that offer good, fresh food in a hurry seem to be getting popular."

"You mean like Chipotle?" Piper said. She had eaten in one of their franchises at the Bellingham Mall recently and found it pretty good. "They say their food is local and sometimes organic. I liked it and it was very affordable."

Ralph nodded. "Chipotle does Mexican food but you could probably use the same idea with anything, Amy."

"I never thought about that," Amy said. "I'd always pictured my dream restaurant as 'fine dining' like A La Carte. But fresh and fast, as long as it's good, isn't a bad idea."

"Fine dining doesn't have to mean white tablecloths and a maître d'," Ralph said. "And it'd be a much lower initial investment as well as give you time to build a reputation."

"That could work for you," Piper said. "But what about Nate?" Nate Purdy was Amy's boyfriend and he'd been the nightly musical entertainment at A La Carte almost from the time Amy started working there. Piper had the impression that they had long-term hopes to continue that sort of teamwork.

Amy's pale brows pulled together delicately. "Nate and I have talked a lot about him performing in—and bringing his fans to—my imaginary future restaurant. That probably wouldn't work in a place where there'd be much less lingering over coffee. But Nate has been getting pretty good feedback on the demo he made. Maybe he'll want to move on to better things."

Maybe so, Piper thought, but "better things" in Nate's eyes probably didn't apply to Amy. Piper doubted he would let anything take him away from her for long.

"Well," Ralph said, "it's just one idea. A good cook—excuse me, *chef*—has plenty of options."

"Sugar Heywood has done well with her catering," Piper said, looking up casually at Ralph as she did. The soft smile that appeared on his face spoke volumes, at least to her mind, especially as he immediately hid it with a forkful of ratatouille.

After a moment of chewing, he nodded. "She's another excellent cook," he agreed, then added with a grin, "They seem to congregate here in Cloverdale, don't they?"

Amy laughed. "Good cooks go where they're appreciated. Nobody wants to spend hours on a perfectly seasoned dish and see ketchup get dumped all over it."

"Or have it sent back to the kitchen for no good reason," Piper said. "Like *some* people."

Ralph looked up. "Who would do that?"

"Amy said Dirk Unger sent his dinner back last night at A La Carte."

"The more fool he," Ralph said, shaking his head. "But I'm not surprised."

"Do you know him?" Piper asked.

"We've met. Jeremy Porter had me come to his house to discuss refurbishing the built-in bookshelves in his library. At the last minute, Porter couldn't be there and he had Unger take over." Ralph grimaced at the memory. "Big mistake. Those were beautiful carved mahogany shelves that I could have restored in time to their original glory. All Unger seemed to care about was the petty costs of every screw and nail and he made sure I understood he'd be overseeing the project and watching me carefully. His strong implication was that he assumed I would unnecessarily stretch the expense and cheat whenever I could. When Porter called later, he seemed surprised that I was no longer interested in the job."

"His loss," Piper said.

"Does Mr. Porter live alone in that big house?" Amy asked.

"He did at the time," Ralph said. "But I believe his mother and sister have recently moved in with him."

"Really?" Piper said. One more thing she hadn't heard about.

"I guess that's nice of him to bring his mom and sister to share that big place," Amy said. "A little odd, though. I mean, I can't wait to be on my own and he gives that up?"

Ralph made no comment and in a moment Piper heard "Yoo-hoo!" from the front of her shop. With no front door, she also had no working door jingle. She jumped up before Amy could. "I'll get it. I've finished and it sounds like Mrs. Tilley."

Amy nodded, knowing that Mrs. Tilley often had dozens of questions on any pickling project she had in mind, which built on previous questions she'd already put to Piper. It was easier for all if only Piper attended to her. As she left, Piper heard Amy ask, "More ratatouille, Mr. Strawbridge?" From the way Ralph had dug into his first serving, Piper was pretty sure what his answer would be.

"Hello, Mrs. Tilley," Piper said. "What can I do for you today?"

"What happened to your door, Piper?" Mrs. Tilley asked querulously, seeming to fear that Piper's front door had somehow been ripped off and carried away during the night. By whom, Piper couldn't imagine, considering the condition of the old thing, other than anyone desperate for firewood.

"Ralph Strawbridge is making me a new one, Mrs. Tilley. It's going to be beautiful."

"Oh! I'm so glad." She asked the expected questions about the door project, which Piper was happy to answer, and by the time they got around to the subject of pickling, Ralph had emerged from the back room, while sounds of Amy cleaning up could be heard.

"Mr. Strawbridge," Mrs. Tilley said. "I can't wait to see Piper's new door."

Ralph smiled, nodded, and wisely avoided further discussion by picking up his tools and getting busy. So Mrs. Tilley turned back to Piper with her questions about asparagus, which included pickling versus freezing—*both are good, and it freezes very well*—and the best length to trim the asparagus for pickling—*about four inches*.

When Mrs. Tilley finally decided what she needed from Piper's shop to get started and had gathered and paid for everything, she mentioned having run into Lydia Porter, Jeremy Porter's mother, on the way to Piper's Picklings.

"A lovely woman," she said, tucking away her credit card. "We met briefly at the Cloverdale Women's Club. She's just moved here from Albany, where she was head of the board of a private school. She mentioned her husband was one of the original Porters of Essex County, which I don't know anything about but it sounds quite impressive, doesn't it? And her own family included more than one governor, I believe. Or was it senator? Anyway, she intends to hold a tea at their home as a way to meet most of the residents of Cloverdale. Isn't that exciting!"

Piper nodded but wondered just who the "most" would include, considering the invitation would come from a person who made a point of mentioning her impressive ancestry at the drop of a hat.

"She asked me to recommend a local caterer. I'm afraid my mind went blank," Mrs. Tilley admitted. "It's been ages since I had occasion to hire one myself."

"Sugar Heywood is very good," Piper said and saw Ralph's face turn toward her with a smile.

"That's right! I forgot all about Sugar. I'll call Lydia the minute I get home and pass that on to her."

"I'm sure both Sugar and Mrs. Porter will appreciate it." Piper handed Mrs. Tilley her bagged purchases and wished her a good day. After the older woman had left, Piper said to Ralph, "I'm surprised Jeremy Porter's mother didn't already know about Sugar. After all, Sugar is catering a business dinner for him." Ralph seemed more interested in Piper's doorjamb than the communication between Jeremy Porter and his mother, so she left him to his work and went to her back room.

The lunch dishes were washed and put away and all traces of the recent lunch break removed except for one folding chair. Amy perched on it, curled over as she studied her cell phone. She looked up guiltily as Piper approached.

"Sorry. I got involved in some Internet searching after that bug Mr. Strawbridge put in my ear about fast gourmet dining. It's becoming quite a trend!"

"No problem. It's good to know about and study all possibilities. At least you have plenty of time before you'll need to make a decision."

Amy grimaced. "That's the truth. And who knows what the latest trend will be by the time I'm ready to take the plunge?" She tucked away her phone and stood up. "But first things first. Are we making anything today?"

Piper grinned. "Glad you asked. I came across a recipe for a lime jelly with herbs that looked interesting, so I picked up a bunch of limes. Would you like to get started on juicing them?"

"Absolutely." Amy snapped to work, as she usually did when food preparation was involved. She pulled out the limes from Piper's refrigerator bin and got busy juicing while Piper poured green apple pectin stock into a large preserving pan and gathered the needed sugar and herb sprigs.

Everything was mixed and coming to a boil under Amy's watchful eye, when Piper heard an unfamiliar male voice out front. Knowing the jelly preparation was in good hands, she went out front to see what was up. A rather scrawny but well-dressed man was talking to Ralph, and from the expression on his face Ralph wasn't pleased about it.

"Can I help you?" Piper asked.

The thin man looked over, his small but piercing eyes taking in Piper in an uncomfortably calculating way. "I was just telling Strawbridge here how delighted I was he found another job after the bookcase project with Mr. Porter fell through." He didn't look all that delighted to Piper, but before she could respond the lizardlike man held out his hand and introduced himself.

"Dirk Unger," he said. "I was just passing by, but now

that I'm here, perhaps you could explain to me exactly what a pickling shop offers?"

"I'd be happy to," Piper said politely, though she really wished she could simply put a Piper's Picklings advertising brochure into his dry hand and send him on his way. "My shop carries all the equipment and seasonings needed to pickle or preserve any vegetable or fruit. I also offer an excellent line of pickling cookbooks. Plus, as a help to anyone unfamiliar with the wide variety of pickles, jams, jellies, and preserves they can make or for anyone just wanting the occasional jar of a particular pickle or jam, I cook up an extensive selection on the premises." Piper gestured toward the shelves of colorful and carefully labeled jars.

Unger wrinkled his nose. "Is that what that smell is coming from the back?"

Piper stiffened. "We're in the process of making lime jelly with herbs."

"I thought it smelled terrific," Ralph said before banging at a nail.

"If you like boiled lemonade," Unger said. "Well, I'm sure you draw plenty of customers who do," he added with a placating smile, though Piper didn't feel the least bit placated. "Although I frankly can't imagine making a success of a business with such a narrow niche market. But then, Cloverdale . . ." He left his probably unpleasant thought unspoken.

Unger gazed around the shop as though inspecting it for spiders or rat droppings, and, disappointed at finding none, finally rubbed his hands together briskly. "Well, I'd best be on my way. It was interesting to meet you, Miss

Lamb." He spun around. "Good luck with the repair work, Strawbridge." And to the relief of both Piper and Ralph, he left.

After a moment, Piper said, "I understand why you turned down Jeremy Porter's bookcase restoration project."

"Uh-huh," Ralph said, then drove another nail into the doorjamb.

"I heard some of that," Amy said, appearing at the back room doorway. "Picture our poor A La Carte waiters trying to please a patron like him."

"Well, for his sake I hope he's an outstanding accountant," Piper said. "If he were working for Jeremy Porter as a Realtor, he'd send clients running for cover with people skills like that."

Piper thought of Sugar Heywood and hoped the caterer didn't need to deal with Unger. Then there was Porter's status-conscious mother . . . Piper shook herself. She was getting much too Cloverdalian, thinking about affairs that were none of her business. Best she stick to her pickles and jellies, at which thought she turned and marched back to the—to her mind—delicious-smelling limes.

# 3

~~~~~~~

The following day, Sugar dropped into Piper's Picklings. She seemed disappointed at first not to see
Ralph, who, after removing the plywood he'd used to
close Piper's doorway for the night, had returned to his
workshop to put finishing touches on Piper's new door.
But Sugar soon bubbled excitedly to Piper about her
latest catering coup—Lydia Porter's tea.

"It will be the event of the year and will be a huge
boost to my business," she said. "Lydia intends to invite
a huge crowd. She says it's to get to know the residents
of Cloverdale," Sugar said, then winked. "But I think it's
mostly to show off the house and what they've done
with it."

"If she's out to impress, she was smart to get you to
handle the food," Piper said.

"Thank you, Piper. I'm sure Jeremy played a big part

in that—the dear man. Tonight, you know, is his Realtors' dinner. I thought I had all my ducks in a row, but I suddenly panicked that I might not have enough of the brandied cherry preserves. I hope you didn't sell the last of those jars."

"Didn't sell a one. How many do you want?"

"Five more should do it. We can just pack them in this." She held up a brightly colored canvas tote and followed Piper to the workroom. As Piper pulled out the preserves from her shelf, wrapped the jars in protective paper, and loaded them into the bag, Sugar talked about the rest of her menu, which totally impressed Piper: filet mignon with béarnaise sauce, potato puffs, and stuffed artichokes, followed by Sugar's almond cakes and Piper's brandied cherries.

"Who gets to enjoy this fantastic spread?"

"Oh, it's all Realtors. This is a welcoming dinner, of sorts. Jeremy has been buying up most of the smaller agencies in the area. Stan Yeager has been one of the rare holdouts."

"Stan Yeager?" Piper knew Yeager, who had helped her find her own shop's premises, and had enjoyed working with him.

Sugar nodded. "I guess not everyone realizes the advantages of being under one large and stable business umbrella."

*Or is ready to give up their autonomy for promised security*, Piper thought but did not say. Sugar, she figured, was probably echoing Jeremy's words, which was understandable. Piper loved being an independent business owner and couldn't imagine selling out to some kind of bigger pickling operation. Not that the offer had ever come up.

"By the way," she said, leading Sugar back to the shop area, "Just to give credit where it's due, Mrs. Tilley recommended you to Lydia Porter for the tea." Piper didn't mention her own prompting, convinced she'd only hurried things up a bit. "Although I'm sure Jeremy added his own encouragements."

"That's good to know, Piper, thanks. I have little thank-you goodie baskets. I'll take one over to Mrs. Tilley." She grinned. "Jeremy will have to make do with filet mignon."

"I don't think he'll complain."

"Speaking of which, I'd better get back to my work." Sugar glanced at the partly finished shop doorway. "Say hi to Ralph for me when he comes back, will you?"

Piper promised, then waved good-bye as she reached for her ringing phone. It was Will Burchett, the Christmas tree farmer she'd been dating.

"I'm hoping you're free tonight," Will said, "and in the mood for a steak dinner."

"Wow! How do you do it?" Piper asked. "Read my mind, I mean. Sugar Heywood was just here and she had me drooling over the menu she's fixing, which happens to be filet mignon."

"Pure serendipity," Will said, laughing. "Or credit an old friend of mine who'd just called. He's passing through and wants to get together for dinner. With him, dinner out means only one thing: a huge steak. I suggested Chandler's. They have seafood, too, in case you or his wife would prefer that."

"That sounds great." Piper had heard good things about Chandler's, which was several miles out of town but considered to be well worth the drive. She asked about the couple she'd be meeting and learned that Matt Fleming was a former college classmate of Will's and that he and his wife, Jen, lived in Albany. Since Piper had lived in Albany for a few years until very recently, she felt sure she'd find things in common to chat about with Jen if Will and Matt got carried away reminiscing, which was likely.

They settled on the time and Piper hung up with a smile, looking forward to the evening. Though they'd been seeing each other for a few months, she and Will had been taking things slowly, particularly after Piper's ex-fiancé, Scott, had taken it into his head to move to Cloverdale. Though Piper had done her best to remain distant from her former fiancé—both emotionally and physically—circumstances kept defeating her efforts. Will had been amazingly patient, which Piper appreciated tremendously.

The rest of the afternoon kept her busy with customers—despite Dirk Unger's skepticism about her "niche" market—but she managed to work in a few pleasant thoughts about Will, speculations on what to wear that evening, and the taste of filet mignon.


Will picked her up at seven, looking great in "dress" denims topped with a dark tee and sports jacket. Will's summer tan had faded over the winter but would no doubt reappear as the weather continued to warm and he became active again in his fields. Piper looked forward to that, since it was the tan highlighting his amazing blue eyes last August that had first caught her attention. She had decided on a red sweater with a few sparkly threads running through, along with a black skirt and heels. She'd pulled her dark hair back loosely, adding a few twists secured by pretty barrettes. The appreciative look in Will's eyes told Piper she'd done better than okay.

On the ride to Chandler's, Will filled Piper in a little more about his friend. "We both started out in plant sciences," he said, "but Matt switched to a business major. He took a job as a market analyst, which means he travels a lot. I haven't seen him for, oh, I guess about five years."

Piper had friends she hadn't seen in quite a while, but with whom she'd managed to stay in touch through e-mail and social media. Will, she knew, was more of a face-to-face person than an online chatter, so she said, "You'll have a lot to catch up on."

When they drew near the restaurant, a couple about their age—he in a dark suit and tie and she in a dress and stylish shawl—were walking toward the entrance. "That's them," he said, and tooted his horn lightly. The two looked over, their faces lighting up as they recognized Will. They waited as Will parked and within minutes the four were exchanging greetings and introductions. Will had a few inches on Matt, Piper noticed, but Matt probably had several pounds on Will, possibly due to the difference in their occupations. Though Will ate like a horse, he also worked like one, and the balance of calories showed. Jen was blond, pretty, and, like her husband, very friendly. Piper looked forward to a very enjoyable evening. All four headed into the dark, wood-paneled restaurant, and Piper smiled as she caught delicious aromas of sizzling steaks and perfectly seasoned vegetables.

When Piper opened her menu, she stifled a gasp at the prices. She glanced at Will for some hint of direction but he and Matt were deep into "what have you been doing?" talk. When he finally glanced at his own menu, he never flinched, so Piper took that as a go-ahead sign to order what she liked. She hoped the Christmas tree business was flourishing.

As they waited for their food and between sips of wine, Piper learned that Matt and Jen were the parents of ten-month-old Dylan, safely ensconced at the moment with his maternal grandparents; that Matt was very satisfied with his job; and that Jen had left a teaching position to be a stay-at-home mom. "Just until Dylan's old enough for preschool," she explained. She had also jumped at the chance to accompany Matt on this trip. "I love Dylan to pieces," she said, "but I need a dose of grown-up talk once in a while."

Conversation slowed as their orders arrived—all four had chosen steak, and none, apparently, cared to be overly distracted while enjoying it—then picked up speed again at coffee time. As Will and Matt slipped into college reminiscences, Piper chatted with Jen about her own time in Albany, explaining how she'd worked in the tax office before deciding to chuck it all and open her pickling shop in Cloverdale. After answering a few questions about pickling, she brought up Lydia Porter. "She's a newcomer to Cloverdale, originally from Albany, where, I understand, she was connected to a private school. You wouldn't happen to know the name, would you?" From Jen's *just bit into something awful* expression, Piper judged she had.

"Lydia's in Cloverdale? My sympathies," Jen said.

"Uh-oh. That bad?"

Jen laughed. "Well, I might be exaggerating a tiny bit. I'm sure she has friends who think she's wonderful."

"But?"

"Well, she was on the board at the private school where I taught, Tedbury Academy. Her son and daughter had attended, and she did, too, many years ago, and it apparently was very important to her to maintain the school's image. This, to her, meant severely limiting who was or was not admitted. She didn't seem to care an iota about the academics. Lydia Porter was one reason I found it easy to leave when Dylan was born. Now that she's gone, I'll be much happier to return when the time comes."

"Honey," Matt interrupted, "what was the name of that guy who had that crazy party the night before graduation?" The conversation having been turned in a new direction, Piper listened to the story as all three contributed their own memories. She enjoyed the peek into Will's pre-Cloverdale days, though by the time the evening ended—reasonably early, since they all had a busy day ahead of them—what lingered in her mind was Jen Fleming's comments about Lydia Porter.

She had no reason to think Lydia's apparent snobbery would affect her one way or another. But in a town as small as Cloverdale, Piper didn't doubt it would affect someone, and the first person who came to mind was Sugar Heywood, simply because she was seeing Lydia

Porter's son. Sugar was a lovely woman and a successful entrepreneur. But she had worked her way to that position, pulling herself up by the proverbial bootstraps. This would impress a lot of people but Piper had a feeling Lydia Porter would not be one of them.

# 4

~~~~~

"It's beautiful!"

Piper gazed in awe at the door Ralph Strawbridge unloaded from his truck. He propped it against the outside wall of Piper's Picklings as he got ready to haul away the plywood that had covered Piper's doorway overnight. The lower half of the door had been carved in bas-relief, as Ralph had promised, with a variety of vegetables linked by vines, which then curled around and over the window on the upper half. A warm stain and glossy finish had highlighted each cucumber, apple, and bean to artistic perfection.

"So, you like it?" Ralph asked unnecessarily. A small crowd gathered, adding their appreciative "ahs." Piper could only nod dumbly, grinning from ear to ear as she took it all in.

"Hey, look at that!" a familiar voice cried, and Piper

turned to see Scott Littleton climb out of his red Volvo. "That's great!" He wove his way closer and studied the door. "You did this?" he asked Ralph, who nodded as he ran a clean rag over it, removing invisible specks of dust. A light of recognition appeared on Scott's face and he turned to Piper. "Isn't it a lot like—?"

"Yes, like the plaque you sent me from Thailand. That was what inspired Ralph."

"Wow! I'm honored. Not that I had anything to do with the plaque, of course, other than picking it out."

"It was a beautiful gift," Piper said. "And perfect for my shop." She continued to be pleasantly surprised by the hints of modesty she was seeing in Scott of late, a trait that had disappeared from the old Scott and one of the reasons their engagement had fizzled. His move from a major city to a small town seemed to be having positive effects, though Piper was still waiting to see if they were permanent.

Scott had set up a law practice in Cloverdale after resigning as assistant district attorney in Albany and had taken an office a single block away from Piper's shop. Piper had made clear at the time that she wasn't available for impromptu lunch dates or any other dates with her ex-fiancé, which had worked for a while. But proximity plus subtle changes in the man, along with Scott's clear ongoing feelings for her, had been putting a definite pull on her affections, while Will continued to make very strong tugs of his own. It kept her emotions in a swirl, which Piper dearly hoped time would help her settle.

Scott was dressed for work in a navy suit and tie that Piper remembered from his Albany days. He'd let his dark hair grow a bit longer, she noticed, which allowed a slight wave to form. As an assistant DA he'd kept it clipped much closer, which always seemed a bit severe to her. Piper shook herself at that point. Time to stop thinking about Scott's hair.

Scott checked his watch. "Better get going," he said. "Got a new client coming in."

As the new lawyer in town, Scott had been building his practice very slowly, so Piper was pleased for him. "Hope it goes well."

"Thanks. Love the door!" he said, then hopped back into his Volvo to drive the final block to his office.

The rest of the gawkers drifted away as Ralph seemed in no rush for the installation. "Can I get you coffee?" Piper asked.

"Maybe later," Ralph said, so Piper left him to his work and went back inside to set up shop. Within minutes, she was pleasantly surprised to see Aunt Judy's Equinox pull up in front.

Piper's white-haired, pleasingly plump aunt climbed out of her car, her attention immediately grabbed by the door. "Isn't that lovely!" she exclaimed as she gazed at it, careful not to get in Ralph's way while she took in all the details. "That door is going to be a town landmark," she said, finally slipping through the doorway and into the shop." When Ralph laughed, she said, "No, I mean it, Mr. Strawbridge. I've never seen anything like it anywhere. You'll be turning Piper's shop into a 'must see' stop for visitors to Cloverdale."

"If they also come in and buy Piper's pickles, I'll have done my job."

"Well, of course they'll do that. How could they not?" Aunt Judy said, smiling affectionately at Piper, who came over to give her a hug, gratefully aware that it was in Aunt Judy's kitchen that Piper had learned all about pickling and preserving in the first place.

Piper had spent many childhood summers on Aunt Judy and Uncle Frank's farm, while her archaeologist parents went off to far-flung and kid-unfriendly digs. It was the memory of those happy days along with her aunt and uncle's presence there that had decided Piper to move to Cloverdale, and though there'd been a couple of bumps in the road—some might call a murder or two major potholes—Piper hadn't come close to regretting it.

"I came to town this morning with a few errands to run," Aunt Judy said. "But before I left home, I heard from Emma Leahy."

Her aunt's face had grown serious. She looked thoughtfully at Ralph working at the doorway and drew Piper into her back room before continuing.

"Apparently there was a bit of a to-do at Jeremy Porter's dinner last night."

"The Realtors' dinner that Sugar Heywood was catering?" Aunt Judy's tone made Piper uneasy.

Aunt Judy nodded. "Emma's next-door neighbor's daughter, Ashley, was working on the waitstaff and caught it all."

"What happened?"

"Ashley said the dinner had gone perfectly. It was held in the Quince Lake Resort's banquet room, by the way. Everyone raved about the food and they were sending compliments back to the kitchen. When the speeches were over and things were breaking up, Jeremy Porter came back to the kitchen, full of praise for Sugar and what she'd accomplished. Lydia Porter walked back with him, and so did that awful man, Dirk Unger. Do you know Unger?"

"We've met, and I wasn't charmed."

Aunt Judy grimaced, agreeing. "Jeremy was apparently still in a speech-making mood, and he was going on and on, pretty much crediting Sugar with the success of the entire evening, which Unger didn't seem to like much. As Ashley put it, he stood there looking as sour as a pickle. Maybe he felt he deserved credit for some part in the dinner planning? I don't know."

"What about Lydia?"

"Lydia was quiet. Stiffly polite was the impression I got from Ashley. Anyway, Jeremy praised the waitstaff, too, but again threw credit for their well-trained performance back to Sugar. He said something like, 'How fortunate you all are to have a boss like Mrs. Heywood.' That's when Dirk Unger piped up to ask, 'Mrs.?'"

"Huh?"

"That was pretty much Jeremy Porter's response, and Unger said, 'Well, it's always been my impression that a woman needs to have been married—at least once—to be called Mrs. Jeremy Porter looked confused at that but Lydia Porter gasped. Sugar got tears in her eyes and her son, Zach, who'd been helping out, turned purple. He rushed over to Unger shouting in his mother's defense and looking like he might hit the man until others grabbed and held him back. Unger actually smiled then, like he'd gotten the reaction he wanted. Ashley described it as a grotesque smile."

"How awful."

"It was. A terrible man, poking his nose into something that was none of his business. But he clearly wanted to stir up trouble for Sugar."

"It upset her, obviously. But other than that, what did he hope to accomplish?"

"My guess is he wanted Sugar out of the picture. That he didn't want anyone to get in the way of his own influence on Jeremy."

"Would Sugar's history matter that much to Jeremy?"

"It will matter to Lydia," Aunt Judy said, "and from what I've learned, Lydia will see that it matters to Jeremy."

As Piper considered that with raised brows, they heard sounds of customers entering the shop. "I'd better let you go," Aunt Judy said. "I just thought you should hear the version that came from a reliable source, since you might get variations of the story throughout the day. Plus, if Sugar comes by and seems upset, you'll understand why." Aunt Judy slid the strap of her purse back onto her shoulder. "Maybe it won't turn out as bad as we fear."

Piper nodded and managed a smile, though her hopes weren't high.

She dealt with her customers, who thankfully chatted only about pickling and the new door that was being installed, which helped to distract Piper. But about an hour later the concerns Aunt Judy had raised heightened as Zach Heywood walked into the shop, looking grim.

The lanky twenty-year-old nodded politely, though with a tight face, to Ralph Strawbridge, then did the same to Piper.

"My mom asked me to tell you she won't be needing the dozen jars of plum jam she ordered."

Piper remembered Sugar's plans to make scones for Lydia Porter's tea and to set them out with clotted cream and plum jam. Canceling the jam was a bad sign.

"She hopes that doesn't cause a problem," Zach added. He flipped his straggled hair impatiently out of his eyes, which, despite his mild words, were blazing.

"It's no problem at all," Piper said soothingly. "You can tell your mom if she wants to talk anytime, I'm here."

Zach nodded, appearing to think that over. "It won't be right away. She's kinda upset."

"I'm sorry to hear that. If it's from what I think it is, it's very unfair."

"They're jerks!" Zach suddenly burst out. "All of them. And that Unger guy is the worst. That the Porters keep a snake like him around at all makes them just as bad."

Piper saw Ralph Strawbridge look over with concern before she turned back to the younger man.

"My mom's a great person, okay?" Zach said, still agitated. "And she's worked extremely hard all her life. That Unger would bring up something like—" He banged his fist against Piper's counter, making her jump. Two women who'd been about to enter the shop stepped back. Ralph walked over at that point and draped a friendly arm over Zach's shoulders.

"Why don't we go get a cup of coffee at the deli," he suggested. When Zach hesitated, Ralph said, "The walk there will be good for both of us." Zach exhaled, then nodded, and the two left, passing the women, who seemed frozen in place. "Ladies," Ralph greeted them, smiling disarmingly as Piper watched, grateful for his aid.

Ralph had obviously gotten to know Zach enough to earn his trust, possibly during his cabinetmaking time at Sugar's, and he clearly held Sugar in high regard. He wasn't going to like the tale of Dirk Unger's despicable behavior the night before, which Zach, no doubt, would share with him.

Piper was sure she'd see an angry workman return from this coffee break. The only question was to what degree.

# 5

~~~~~

When Ralph came back, Amy had arrived for her shift and both she and Piper were busy with customers. He returned to his work without saying a word, and Piper's glance in Ralph's direction caught only a tight set to his jaw. If he was angry—which he must have been—he was holding it all in and thankfully not taking it out on her door.

Customers continued to admire the beautiful door and Ralph acknowledged their compliments but without pausing in his work, which most seemed ready to attribute to his admirable focus and professionalism. Around midday, though, business in the shop calmed and Ralph laid down his tools after Amy had gone into the back room.

"How would you feel about running over to see Sugar for a minute?" he asked Piper.

"You mean now? I'm not sure she'll be in the mood for company."

"She wouldn't be for most people. But you know what happened, right?" Piper nodded, and Ralph said, "Sugar won't feel the need to hide it from you. Zach says she's pretty upset but maybe you can show her that the sensible people in her life won't care a whit. She'll need that."

Piper thought for a moment, at first wondering why Ralph didn't go himself. But not having access to his inner thoughts or being inclined to pry, she nodded and reached back to untie her apron. "I'll see what I can do." As she chucked the apron and pulled on her light cardigan, she asked, "How was Zach when you left him?"

"Better. When we left the deli he said he was going over to a friend's."

Amy reappeared from the back holding a box of spices and Piper asked, "Mind taking over for a while?"

"No problem. Nate's stopping by soon, so he can pitch in if things get busy again. And if it gets super busy," Amy added with a grin, "we'll just press Mr. Strawbridge into duty."

Ralph smiled. "If it gets to that point, I'll just barricade the doorway. Problem solved."

Amy laughed along with Piper, who grabbed her purse. "Call if you need me," she said, then headed out the back to the alley where her hatchback was parked. Once in the car, she pulled out her cell phone to check Sugar's address. She debated a moment about calling first but decided not to risk being put off. Piper put the key in her ignition, not exactly sure how she was going to handle the visit but asked herself, *What would Aunt*

*Judy do?* The answer she got was that Aunt Judy would take along something homemade and edible. Piper ran back inside and grabbed a jar of orange and lemon marmalade, which she knew Sugar particularly liked. It was a minuscule start, comfortwise, but Piper hoped for further inspiration as she drove.

Sugar's house was a pretty two-story on a quiet road just outside Cloverdale that had been built, she'd once told Piper, around 1850. Its white siding and black shutters were in pristine condition and aged oak trees flanked each side, their budding leaves looking fresh and green, while white blooms of a string of pear trees could be seen along the back. Piper went up the three front steps under a short overhang and tapped the shiny brass knocker on the door twice, then waited. She spotted the curtain at one of the front windows twitching and in a moment heard the click of the lock turning.

"Piper." A wan-looking Sugar, her blond hair hanging limply, peeked through a narrow crack. "I'm pretty rotten company today."

"I didn't come to be entertained, Sugar. You had a rough time last night. I thought you could use a little cheering up." She held out the jar of marmalade.

Sugar smiled weakly and opened the door wider to take the jar. "Thank you. Got anything for a battered ego?"

"I'd say more than your ego got trampled," Piper said, stepping through the doorway as Sugar waved her in.

"Oh, Piper," Sugar said, her face suddenly crumpling. Piper reached for her friend and hugged tightly, feeling the older woman tremble, then gradually calm. "I'm such a fool," Sugar said. She pulled back and wiped her eyes before offering a wan smile. "Come on back," she said with a toss of her head. "I can at least offer you coffee and cake. Leftover almond cake from last night. Lydia didn't want it."

"Lydia is an idiot," Piper said, following Sugar down the hall and past a tidy living room to an enormous kitchen that had been fully updated with gleaming stainless steel appliances and granite countertops.

"With that I'd have to agree," Sugar said, smiling more widely. "But catering her tea was going to be such a fantastic boost to my business, which, I hate to admit, is going through a bit of a slump. Word will get around now that I've been dropped. It wasn't for food-related reasons but I can't exactly go around explaining that, can I?" She sliced a piece of cake and poured a mug of coffee for Piper, who carried both to the huge center island.

"Sugar," Piper said, slipping onto one of the stools, "this is the twenty-first century. Attitudes have changed."

"For some, maybe. But definitely not Lydia." She shook her head. "What hurts me most, though, is Jeremy. I was really starting to care for him." Sugar sank onto a stool across from Piper, gulping back more tears. "I thought he felt the same. But he hasn't offered any support whatsoever. I've been dropped like a hot potato." She managed a wry smile. "Ironic, since my twice-baked potatoes were just about his favorite thing."

"Do you think his nonsupport is because of Lydia?"

"Maybe. I did see a subtle change in him after she and his sister, Mallory, moved in. Before that, Jeremy was this very smart, strong businessman with a tender side to him, qualities I happen to love. And when he said his mother and sister were moving in, I got the impression it was his idea and that he was stepping up to help family members who depended on him. Admirable, right? But later I caught hints that the move was more their idea than his. And I noticed Jeremy deferring to Lydia on decisions he should have been making himself."

"It sounds like he's deferred to her as to who should or should not be in his life."

Sugar nodded. "And that's hard to take, Piper. Jeremy was the first man I let into *my* life after all these years. I thought I was choosing so wisely. Look how that went!" She wiped at her eyes again. "I obviously don't have a lick of sense where men are concerned. And my business is probably shot to heck because of it. I might as well just pack up and move on. Start all over someplace else. Poor Zach, stuck with such a mess of a mother."

Piper jumped in to bolster Sugar up as best she could, reminding her of the wonderful job she'd obviously done with Zach and assuring her that her business would not only survive but thrive because of the excellent reputation she'd earned. It didn't appear that any of what she said was truly sinking in.

Sugar had just dissolved into more tears when Piper heard the front door open. Sugar quickly wiped her face and blew her nose.

"Mom?" Zach called.

"In here, Zach." Sugar jammed her tissue into a pocket, but she couldn't hide the ravages on her face.

"Mom, I—" Zach stopped at the kitchen doorway at sight of Piper. "Oh! Hi."

"Piper and I were just enjoying some almond cake," Sugar said, jumping up from her stool and putting on a wide smile, which Piper was sure didn't fool Zach for a moment. "Did you want some? I have lots." When Zach shook his head, she asked, "A sandwich? I have—"

"Mom, I'm not hungry!" Zach cried, then immediately looked ashamed. "Sorry. I didn't mean to yell." He turned to Piper and in a much milder tone said, "Thanks for coming to see my mom."

Piper smiled. "We had a good talk." She checked her watch. "But I'm afraid I've got to get back to the shop now and relieve Amy."

"Take some cake to Amy," Sugar said, quickly wrapping a generous piece in foil as Piper carried her mug and plate to the sink. She walked Piper to the front door. "Thank you for coming," she said. "I'll try not to be such miserable company next time."

"Just go easier on yourself, okay?" Piper said, giving Sugar a final hug. "There's a lot of us who really care about you, you know."

Sugar nodded, even smiled brightly, but Piper knew the false cheer would disappear once the door had closed.


Piper drove back, feeling down, but her spirits lifted when she drew close to her shop and saw that her brand-new door had been fully installed. She could barely scramble out of her car fast enough.

"Is it all done?" she asked Ralph, who stood back, studying his handiwork.

He nodded, looking satisfied. "All done and ready to go."

"Isn't it gorgeous?" Amy asked. She and Nate had come out to join a small crowd of admirers.

"I think you should have a grand opening celebration for this fantastic new door," Nate said, grinning.

"It truly deserves it," Piper said. "Will you provide the music?" she asked, only half joking. A celebration actually sounded very good to her after the sad hour she'd just spent with Sugar, which reminded her of the foil-wrapped almond cake and sent her back to her car. "Sugar sent this for you, Amy," she said, handing it over.

"How is she?" Ralph asked.

Piper winced. "Not so great, but I'm hoping the worst is over. Zach is with her."

"What's going on?" Emma Leahy asked, pushing through the crowd. "Well!" she said when she saw the object of interest. Piper's best customer, an enthusiastic gardener whose entire wardrobe seemed to consist of faded overalls and oversized shirts, took in Ralph's creation for several moments, then turned to the craftsman. "You've outdone yourself, Ralph!"

Ralph dipped his head in acknowledgment. "Thank you, ma'am."

"We think there should be a grand unveiling," Amy said.

"But it's never been veiled," Ralph countered.

"You know what I mean," Amy said, laughing. "Bring

everyone here at one time to see it, now that it's done. What do you think, Piper?"

"I like that idea the more I think of it. How quickly can we put something together?"

Amy instantly turned "chef," and Piper could fairly see food images flash through her head. "With a little help, we could have it ready by tomorrow night, which happens to be Nate's and my night off from A La Carte."

"Wonderful!" Emma said. "I'll pitch in and also spread the word."

"Ralph," Piper said, "you'll be the guest of honor. Does tomorrow evening work for you?"

Ralph laughed. "Pretty much any evening would work for me."

"Perfect!" Piper turned to Amy. "Let's get the ball rolling."

# 6

~~~~~~

Piper gazed at her transformed shop, impressed with how well they'd put together their last-minute party. Amy had the brilliant idea of duplicating the carvings in Piper's new door with actual fruits and vegetables and had made a beautiful center display of cucumbers, pineapples, beans, and strawberries encircled by freshly washed leafy vines. She'd also cut up chunks of fruit to be dunked into a delicious cream cheese dip.

Aunt Judy contributed bite-size meatballs in a spicy sauce in an electric warming pot; Emma Leahy and Joan Tilley, following Amy's recipes, had made platters of yummy appetizers; and Piper had prepared trays of a variety of cheeses and crackers along with selections of pickles. Lots of pickles.

Piper had hesitated over approaching Sugar for something sweet but decided the distraction might be good

for her. Her thought had proved right when Sugar immediately offered to whip up one of her delicious cakes—
an offer Piper definitely couldn't refuse.

Notice of the party was spread by word of mouth, and
people began arriving around five thirty. Gil Williams,
who owned the new and used bookshop next door, was
one of the first. He'd exchanged his regular brown,
elbow-patched cardigan for a more festive Kelly green
sweater and had smoothed down his unruly white hair.

"Quite impressive," he said after a long, critical exam-
ination of Piper's new door. "Perhaps I should think
about sprucing up my own place. What theme would you
suggest?" he asked Ralph. "Works of Shakespeare or
selections of classic mysteries?"

"Mysteries," Amy jumped in to answer. "It would fit
both you and your shop."

Gil lifted a questioning eyebrow but Piper knew
exactly what Amy meant. Gil had been extremely good
at helping her puzzle out solutions to more than one
too-close-for-comfort crime. Plus he'd managed to keep
his own life a bit of a mystery, generally disappearing
at the end of his workday with only an occasional hint
as to how he filled the remaining hours.

"Come get something to eat, Gil," Aunt Judy called,
waving him over, and he genially obeyed, making room
for new arrivals at the doorway. Uncle Frank had driven
in from the farm and was handling the drinks. He ran
through the choices for Gil as Aunt Judy piled meatballs
onto a paper plate and pointed out other goodies.

Amy's longtime friends Megan and Érin arrived
together, Erin explaining that Ben Schaeffer, her

boyfriend as well as Megan's brother, would be late. They had brought pizza rolls and crab dip with crackers and Amy shifted trays on Piper's counters to make space.

Piper was a little disappointed when Zach walked in carrying a sheet cake his mother had made. The cake was gorgeous—chocolate letters spelling out congratulations to both Ralph and Piper atop swirling waves of creamy white frosting—but Piper had hoped Sugar would arrive along with it.

"Mom asked me to offer her regrets," Zach said. "She just wasn't up to going out."

"Please tell her we miss her," Piper said. "You'll stay a while, though, won't you?"

Zach looked ready to say no but Amy, Megan, and Erin collectively pressed him to try their particular culinary treats and he found himself holding a paper plate that was being rapidly filled.

"Got a pickle for a hungry man?"

Piper had been facing Zach and hadn't noticed Will coming in. "There's plenty more than pickles," she said with a smile. "I'm glad you could make it."

"My fertilizer delivery arrived early, so I had time to clean up."

"*Extremely* glad to hear it," Piper said, grinning. "Manure can be—"

"Not *that* kind of fertilizer," Will said, laughing. "The chemical type." He reached for a roast beef and cheese wrap that Amy had sliced into finger-food size and downed it in two bites.

Before he could reach for another, Piper asked, "Mind starting with the appetizers? The crowd is really growing and I'm not sure we'll have enough for everybody. Timing this for the dinner hour might not have been the best idea."

"No problem," Will said agreeably, but as he headed for the crab dip, two of Aunt Judy's lady friends walked in with more food and Piper relaxed. She cleared more pickling equipment away to make room.

The party quickly moved into high gear. People arrived to marvel over Ralph's door, then circled through the shop to chatter about it as they picked up food and drink. Plates loaded, they gradually eased out to the side-walk to make space for others, lingering there. Piper greeted Stan Yeager, the Cloverdale real estate agent who'd helped her find the premises for her shop.

"Quite a get-together you've got here," Stan said.

Piper liked Stan, even when he jumped to cringeworthy conclusions about her, such as assuming she and Will were ready to tie the knot and buy a house together. "I'm amazed and delighted with the turnout," she said, looking up at the lanky Realtor. Piper thought his eyes appeared a bit sunken and shadowed and hoped those possible signs of stress weren't business related. Sugar had mentioned that Stan was one of the few resisters of Jeremy Porter's buyout offers. Porter's mega-realty operation moving into the area couldn't help but affect Stan's small office.

"Never one to pass up a party," Stan said with a grin that seemed slightly forced. He selected one of Piper's cheese-and-pickle-topped crackers and had just popped it in his mouth when Emma Leahy tugged at his arm.

"Stan! What can you tell me about the old Hopkins place going up for sale?"

Piper watched Stan struggle to answer without choking as the two edged away in the continuing flow of the crowd. She heard the strum of a guitar in her back room and lit up. Nate had jokingly agreed to entertain but Piper hadn't dared to hope he was serious. Apparently he was, as the door to the back opened and Nate's clear tenor voice rang out with a rendition of the eighties song "Celebration."

To her amazement, most of the crowd, whose ages ranged from early twenties to way past sixty, quickly joined in. Nate carried it on for several verses, finally ending to claps and cheers. It was the perfect way to top off the party!

Nobody would let Nate stop there and he was besieged with requests, which he cheerfully responded to, gradually moving through the crowd and out onto the sidewalk. It was marvelous and Piper saw grins on every face within view.

Things suddenly quieted, though, as sirens sounded. Heads swiveled to watch flashing lights in the distance, but as the lights faded away, attention returned to the party. Only Aunt Judy's expression remained worried, and she made her way over to Piper.

"Where do you suppose that ambulance was heading?" When Piper shrugged helplessly, she added, "Old Mr. Winkler hasn't been too well lately. I hope he hasn't taken a sudden turn."

"No, Judy," Emma Leahy leaned over to say, then pointed to a middle-aged woman in a paisley dress. "Patsy Winkler is over there. She'd certainly have heard if it was her father."

Aunt Judy nodded, only partly soothed. Piper knew her aunt's mind was running over a mental list of vulnerable Cloverdale residents. To distract her, since there was really nothing she could do, Piper asked, "How are your meatballs holding out? They've been pretty popular."

"Oh! I meant to bring out more from your refrigerator. There's been quite a few new arrivals. I'll do a quick warmup in the microwave." Aunt Judy scurried off and Piper hailed the next guests who'd made it into the shop, needing to raise her voice over the singing, as all thoughts of the sirens were forgotten.

Ben Schaeffer arrived and before locating Erin made a point to advise Piper that the noise level of her party might be a violation of a Cloverdale ordinance. Besides his insurance agency work, Ben took his volunteer auxiliary officer duties highly seriously, which had sometimes strained Piper's patience. That evening, though, Piper simply smiled and pointed out Amy's father, Sheriff Carlyle, who was gamely swaying to the music along with his daughter and her friends.

"I think we're good, Ben, but thanks. Chicken wrap?"

Ben helped himself without further comment and left to work his way toward Erin.

Piper waved at Will, who'd been caught in a far corner of the shop, and indicated the still-brimming trays of food, signaling that he should come get his fill. He nodded but as he began winding through the crowd, Piper caught a familiar voice. Scott Littleton was heading her way from the opposite direction. Will had been wonderfully patient about giving Piper time to sort out her feelings but a face-to-face meeting with her former fiancé in such close quarters might be asking too much. Piper slipped out from behind her counter to intercept Scott.

"Hey, there you are!" Scott had changed from his lawyer suit and tie to more casual wear and Piper recognized the plaid shirt she had given him when they were still a couple. Had he purposely chosen it? she wondered. Then she reminded herself it had become a favorite of Scott's ages ago and decided he'd probably long forgotten its original source.

"Quite a shindig this turned out to be!" Scott said, raising his voice above the din. "I never heard of a grand opening for a door—hey, a grand door-opening!" He laughed at his little joke. "But it certainly drew a crowd."

"I'm not sure if it was interest in Ralph's door that brought everyone. For some it may have been interest in our food. But either way, it's turned out to be a lot of fun."

"Speaking of food . . ." Scott began, and Piper glanced back to see Will standing near the sandwich trays, his back to them.

"Start with Amy's fantastic dips," she advised Scott, firmly turning him to the opposite side of the shop. "Then work your way around."

As Scott followed her suggestion, Piper headed over to Will, who by then had loaded his plate. As he turned at her shoulder touch, she said, "Let's step outside for a minute."

"Fine with me."

Piper grabbed a plastic cup of iced tea and led the way to a spot that was close enough to enjoy Nate's music but quiet enough to talk without shouting. Piper took a deep breath and felt her adrenaline level, which had momentarily spiked at Scott's arrival, level out.

"How long do you suppose this will go on?" Will asked. He bit into one of Piper's crisp dill pickles.

"Probably until the food runs out." Piper grinned. "Maybe we shouldn't have put out quite so much?"

"If it gets to be a problem, I'll be happy to help it disappear."

They listened as Nate finished his latest song, then heard the sound of metal tapping on glass—the universal signal for attention. As the crowd quieted, Megan Schaeffer's voice rang out.

"It's time to cut the cake," she announced. "Piper, where are you?" she asked. "Want to come do the honors?"

"Go ahead, Megan. Or Aunt Judy is an expert cake cutter, if you'd rather not." Piper called from her doorway. If Sugar Heywood had come, she would have asked her to cut it and reap the compliments she richly deserved for her culinary creation. Piper suddenly realized she hadn't seen Zach since shortly after he arrived. He must have slipped out early without her noticing.

Megan nodded. "Okay, we'll collectively cut it in a moment. But first I propose we all raise our glasses in a toast to Ralph Strawbridge and his absolutely beautiful hand-carved door!"

"Hear, hear!" several voices called out, and Piper, along with many others, raised her glass in tribute to Ralph. Although all the glasses were filled with iced tea or sodas, the enthusiasm reached champagne height.

"Speech!" someone called, and others echoed that,

chanting and clapping in rhythm until Ralph laughingly gave in.

"Thank you all," he said. "And thanks to all the wonderful ladies for this excellent spread." After the cheers that followed had died down, he added, "But none of this would have happened without Piper Lamb, who commissioned the door in the first place, and who—"

A cell phone rang, causing Ralph to pause and dozens of heads to turn in its direction. Piper saw Sheriff Carlyle lift his phone to his ear. The crowd remained silent, watching as the sheriff's face turned grim. He said a few words, then pocketed the phone and rapidly made his way out of the shop without comment. All eyes followed as the sheriff jumped into his parked car, then sped off, his lights flashing.

"Oh, dear," Aunt Judy quietly voiced what everyone was likely thinking. "Something must be very wrong."

# 7

After Sheriff Carlyle made his dramatic exit, the party continued on but in a much more subdued manner. The cake was cut and distributed, Nate's lively music morphed into softer ballads, and former revelers hummed along softly. As the cake disappeared, so did the partygoers, one by one. Piper was sure the thoughts of many were on the emergency that had called the sheriff away, as were hers.

The suspense lingered until the next morning when Piper rose early to finish cleanup. Leftover food had been distributed or refrigerated the night before and trash gathered and hauled off, but shop countertops needed polishing and merchandise had to be returned to its proper place. Piper was retrieving a box of canning jars from her back room when she heard taps at her alley door. She raised the shade to reveal Gil Williams on the stoop. Piper quickly turned the lock.

"I just learned what happened last night and thought you'd want to know," he said, stepping inside as Piper opened the door.

"What is it?" Piper asked. Gil's look was grim and she braced herself.

"The ambulance we heard rushed Dirk Unger to the hospital. Unfortunately, he died there."

"Gosh, I'm sorry to hear that. But why was the sheriff involved?"

"From what I understand, Unger at first appeared to be suffering from cardiac arrest. But later they came to suspect poison."

"Poison!" Piper backed toward a stool and sat down. Her thoughts raced. "Any chance it could have been accidental?"

Gil shook his head. "I don't have any details. I imagine more testing and investigation needs to be done."

"Yes." Piper looked up at Gil worriedly. "But if it turns out to be murder . . ." Piper couldn't voice what she most feared.

"No use worrying until all the facts come out," Gil said. He rubbed his hands together as though they'd suddenly become cold and Piper felt chilled as well. "I'll let you know if I hear more."

"Thanks, Gil." Piper let Gil out and relocked her back door. She turned away, feeling stunned by the news, and wondered if she should call anyone. When Gil first mentioned poison in connection with Unger, her thoughts had instantly flown to Sugar Heywood. Unfairly, surely, but if Piper's thoughts had gone in that direction, others' would have, too.

If last night's suspense was bad, Piper was sure the next round of waiting was going to beat that by a mile.

Piper had opened up for business and was idly leafing through her invoices when she noticed a woman standing outside her new front door. After several moments the woman, whose apple-red cheeks echoed her overall roundish shape, walked in, calling out a cheery "Good morning!"

Piper, whose mood had been stuck at gray, suddenly felt like a bit of sunshine had peeked through the clouds.

"I missed the party last night," the woman said, "so I came by to see the new door for myself. I love it! I'm Tammy Butterworth, by the way," she said, extending her hand.

"Hi, Tammy." Piper introduced herself, then asked, "Are you new to Cloverdale?"

"I am!" Tammy exclaimed, as if Piper had made an impressive deduction. "Jeremy Porter made me an offer I couldn't refuse, so I picked up and moved here."

"You're a Realtor?"

Tammy's burst of laughter was infectious and Piper couldn't help joining in, though she had no idea what she was laughing about. "No, dear," Tammy said. "I don't sell houses. I clean them!"

"Ah!"

"I cleaned Jeremy's other house, so when he wasn't happy with the cleaning staff for his new house in

Cloverdale—Jeremy's very particular—he asked if I'd come and do the job. I was in the mood to relocate, so I did. Not as a live-in," she said, seeming anxious that Piper understand that. "Uh-uh. I have my own place. And I take other jobs, too. Homes, offices, you name it."

"I'll keep that in mind in case anyone is looking for help."

"Thank you, sweetie! Now tell me, what kind of shop is this? I never heard of a pickling shop."

Piper was happy to oblige and happier, too, to have an obviously receptive listener as she ran through her list of pickles, preserves, and the means to produce them.

"How lovely!" Tammy declared when Piper had finished. "I've done a little canning but no pickling of any kind. I'm going to try it! Where do I start?"

Piper pulled out a couple of cookbooks that explained the basics of pickling, along with offering many great recipes, and let her new acquaintance look them over. As Tammy browsed, Piper decided the woman must not have heard about Dirk Unger and speculated that it might not have been her day to clean at the Porter house. But to Piper's surprise, as Tammy flipped a page in one of the cookbooks she said, "A shame what happened to Mr. Unger, isn't it?"

"Yes. It was. I just heard about it an hour ago."

"Oh, I heard it last night."

"You did?"

"Uh-huh." Tammy reached for the second cookbook. "Mallory Porter—she's Jeremy's sister—called to say I shouldn't come in today and why. Which is why I had time to come here!" She smiled brightly at Piper, clearly not too broken up about Dirk's passing.

"Did Mallory Porter know what happened?"

"You mean that he might have been poisoned?"

"Uh, right."

Tammy nodded. "That was why she canceled my cleaning. She said the police were going to be there asking a lot of questions. She wasn't too happy about that."

"Unhappy about the questions or about Unger's death?"

Tammy laughed. "The questions, definitely. Neither of the women—Lydia or Mallory—liked Mr. Unger. They were always after Jeremy to get rid of him. But for whatever reason, he never would. Well, now that battle's over, anyway." She held out one of the cookbooks. "I'll take this one," she said. "And I should probably get new jars and lids and stuff. I'm going to try the pickled beets. I loved the ones my mother used to make."

"A good choice." Piper helped Tammy gather the items she needed, thinking the whole time about what the woman had said. There were a thousand questions forming in her head, but before she could get any of them in order, it was time to ring Tammy's items up.

"Why don't you leave your number with me," Piper suggested, wanting to keep in touch with this woman. "In case anyone is looking for a cleaner."

"Sure!" Tammy scrambled through her purse and pulled out, to Piper's surprise, a pack of business cards. The card she handed Piper had a cartoon drawing of an apple-shaped woman—obviously Tammy Butterworth—wielding a mop, along with her contact information. Piper turned the card over to see a QR code along with a website address.

"You have a website?"

"Doesn't everybody?" Tammy asked, to which Piper winced.

"I've been meaning to," she admitted.

"Oh, you should get one up, honey! You have no idea how much business you could be losing without one. I can recommend my web designer. Her link's on my home page."

"Thank you," Piper squeaked. She handed over Tammy's purchases, which filled two large bags.

Tammy took off and Piper gazed after her, feeling properly chastised for her lack of good business practice. She'd been working, off and on, on putting together at least a makeshift website herself, but had made little progress, with the multiple distractions of her new life in Cloverdale getting in the way. She comforted herself with the fact that she did at least have flyers printed up, which she had given away at the previous summer's Cloverdale fair. Piper had reached for her cell phone to pull up Tammy's website when Aunt Judy walked in, holding Jack, her black-and-white mixed-breed, on a leash. Months ago she and Uncle Frank had taken in Jack as a skinny, fur-matted stray and gradually rehabilitated him into the healthy and lovable dog he now was.

"You don't mind my bringing Jack into the shop, do you?" Aunt Judy asked, unnecessarily.

"Of course not!" Piper bent down to ruffle Jack's fur as he yipped happily at the sight of her, his tail wagging furiously. "How's my most favorite dog in the world?"

she asked, more of Jack than her aunt, though it was Aunt Judy who answered.

"He's fine but he needs his booster shots. I'll walk him over to Dr. Rhodes in a minute but we wanted to stop in and say hello."

Jack yipped at that, as though agreeing, then calmed and sat obediently at Aunt Judy's bidding.

Aunt Judy's face sobered. "You've heard, perhaps, about that man who worked for Jeremy Porter?"

"Dirk Unger? Yes. Awful news."

"It is, and I'm very sorry for him, despite the kind of person he seemed to be. But I'm most concerned at the moment for Sugar Heywood."

Piper nodded. "She was my first thought when I heard about it, too."

"Surely—"

"No, I don't think for a moment that Sugar could have done anything so terrible. But the connection is unavoidable after what Dirk Unger did to hurt her the other night."

"But since poison is usually taken in food," Aunt Judy said, "would that eliminate Sugar? She would hardly be fixing a meal for that man."

"Pretty unlikely, yes, but there are other methods. At this point, though, not knowing what the poison was and how it acts means we can only make guesses, which is next to useless."

"You're right." Aunt Judy reached down to pat Jack, who'd started squirming. "Oh, how I wish Sugar had come to your party last night. I completely understand why she couldn't bring herself to do so but it might turn out to have been a bad mistake."

Piper hoped they were unnecessarily worried, and Aunt Judy took Jack off to the vet's, leaving Piper to wonder how long it would take to pinpoint the cause and circumstances of Dirk Unger's death—and how many theories and accusations she would hear before the truth was finally uncovered.

# 8

<br>

Piper began to lose count of the number of people who stopped in to discuss Dirk Unger's death. She looked forward longingly to Amy's arrival, which would allow Piper to escape to her back room for a while to make pickles—always a stress-easing as well as productive activity for her. When Amy walked in, however, her first words kept Piper rooted to the spot.

"I've heard from Kendra, one of our kitchen staff. Daddy's been questioning all the A La Carte people."

"Really!"

Amy stowed her purse under the counter. "It was my day off so I didn't know that awful man, Dirk Unger, had lunch at A La Carte yesterday." She wrinkled her nose. "Despite his obviously low opinion of everything we fixed."

"Does that mean your father thinks that's where Unger

was poisoned?" Piper's hopes for Sugar escaping suspicion rose. On the other hand, this was the restaurant where Amy worked part time, and she needed the job.

"As usual, Daddy didn't let me in on his official business, but it doesn't sound that way. Kendra said he was most interested in knowing if Unger had taken food home with him."

"And had he?"

"No. He never does, and he didn't yesterday. Thank goodness! I mean, can you imagine if the poison could be traced to food from A La Carte's kitchen?"

"It would certainly ruin the restaurant and put a lot of people out of jobs. The poison, though, could have been slipped in by anyone, like whoever Unger was dining with or someone stopping at his table." The multiple possibilities ran through Piper's head, though the images of all the evildoers had fuzzy blobs for faces.

"I know! How unfair would that be? But at least we seem to be off the hook."

Piper agreed. "From your father's questions, it sounds like Unger's poison needed to be consumed fairly close to the time he became sick," Piper said. "So it must have been ingested with his dinner or at least around dinnertime." She still couldn't see that implicating Sugar, though it didn't definitely rule her out, either. Stranger things had been known to happen than a victim accepting food out of the blue from a person they'd hurt.

At that thought, Piper decided it was time for her to take a break. "I'm going to work on the carrots I have in the back."

"Want any help?"

"Not on the carrots. If you'll take care of things out here, that'll give me the downtime I need right now. I've been dealing all morning with speculations on the poisoning. I'm most happy to turn that over to you for a while."

"Fine with me. I'll just play super dumb when the subject comes up."

Piper smiled, knowing that act wouldn't fool many, but she wished Amy luck and headed on back. Her project that day was spicy carrots and she looked forward to the peeling and chopping ahead. It was one of the first recipes she'd learned in Aunt Judy's kitchen and making it always brought back the proud feeling she'd had as a ten-year-old after helping process several pounds of Uncle Frank's organically grown vegetables (and snatching several tasty bites of the fresh carrots in the process).

Piper turned on her iPod, propped safely out of the way on an upper shelf, choosing a calming Gilbert and Sullivan song, "I'm Called Little Buttercup," and hummed along as she pulled her carrots from the refrigerator and checked her supply of vinegar and spices. By the time she reached the chopping stage, her playlist had moved on to the operetta's "We Sail the Ocean Blue," and she found her knife strokes keeping time smartly with the music.

She had brought her vinegar, water, and spice mix to a boil and was ready to add her carrot sticks when she heard a commotion in the shop. Piper recognized Sugar Heywood's voice and instantly stopped what she was doing and turned off her stove.

Amy leaned in through the dividing door. "Ms. Heywood wants to—" she began.

"Send her in," Piper said, grabbing a towel to wipe her hands and turning off her music.

"Piper, I'm so sorry to bother you." Sugar rushed past Amy, visibly upset. "I just didn't know where to turn."

"What's happened?"

"It's Zach. They've taken him in for questioning!"

"Zach? Why?"

"It's that stupid poisoning of that stupid man, Dirk Unger. Just because Zach is a botany major and the poison came from some odd plant he might know about, they think he could have done it."

Piper's head was swirling. She hadn't considered Zach at all. But Zach had been furious with Dirk Unger on behalf of his mother, she reminded herself, so Sheriff Carlyle's reasoning might be understandable.

Sugar had been pacing, her words tumbling over each other, and Piper opened out two of her folding chairs and directed her friend to sit down and take a few deep breaths.

"First things first," Piper said. "What poison are they talking about?"

"It a plant called bloodroot. I never heard of it before but it grows wild everywhere. Zach is always out walking, looking for any interesting plants. Everyone who knows him knows that. But he's not looking for poisons! He'd never want to kill anybody, no matter what."

"Bloodroot," Piper said. "How did they come up with that?"

"Apparently they tested the food in Unger's kitchen. They found it in his leftover salad."

"Do you know how it works?"

Sugar shook her head helplessly.

"Hold on," Amy said from the doorway. She was typing rapidly into her iPhone. "I'm pulling it up now."

They waited as Amy did her search. "Here it is. Bloodroot. It's an herb with thick roots and red juice. Grows mostly in woods. It has white flowers and all parts of it are poisonous."

"What are the symptoms?"

"Let's see. Just touching it causes rashes. But if you eat it, it causes violent vomiting, then cardiac arrest. Wow! Who knew something like that was around?"

*A botany student might know,* Piper thought. *But who else?* "How quickly does it act?" she asked.

Amy scrolled, mumbling incoherently as she read. "Ah! Here it is! One to two hours."

Piper thought back to when they heard the sirens. What time was that? Seven thirty? Eight? She wasn't sure.

"Zach was here last night when he brought your cake, Sugar. That was around five thirty. But I don't think he hung around long. Did he come back home?"

"Not until late, maybe one in the morning. I was asleep, but I heard him come in. He said he was at his friend Justin's, watching a movie."

"Good. That's an alibi." As long as Justin can say Zach showed up there early. "Were you alone all evening?"

"Me? No. I wasn't up to coming to your party, as upset as I was, but my next-door neighbor, Ginnie, stopped in after Zach took off with the cake. We ended up baking cupcakes for Ginnie's grandkids who were coming over the next day."

*That covered Sugar's alibi,* Piper thought, *assuming*

*Ginnie concurred.* Zach's alibi, on the other hand, was still pending.

"Did you call a lawyer for Zach?"

Sugar looked up in surprise. "No. Should I have? I didn't even think of it. I don't even know of one."

"I think Zach should have someone with him."

"But he's not guilty!"

"All the more reason. A lawyer will look after his rights. Scott Littleton's office is right down the street. I can vouch for him."

Sugar hesitated, then said. "You're right. I should talk to Littleton. Maybe he can get this whole ridiculous thing straightened out and over with. Thank you, Piper. I knew you were the right person to come to." Sugar had calmed considerably, now that she had a sense of direction.

"Piper's had plenty of experience—" Amy started to say until Piper shot her a look. She had far too much experience with past murders. She sincerely hoped Sheriff Carlyle would speedily arrest the proper culprit of this latest crime and let her stay happily out of it.

Sugar hurried out, having been pointed to Scott's office. A customer walked in almost immediately after, and Amy waited on her, leaving Piper to return to her spicy carrots. She turned on her stove but left her iPod off. There was far too much to think about.

*Could Zach have done anything so terrible?* Piper didn't know him well, but the few times she'd met him he'd always struck her as a levelheaded person, or as levelheaded as twenty-year-olds could generally be. He obviously was very protective of his mother and had been furious over Dirk Unger's action after the Realtors' dinner.

It seemed to Piper, though, that if Zach had been angry enough to kill Unger, he would have done it immediately, or very soon after—violently and person-to-person, rather than secretively by poison. Poison just didn't seem like a young man's weapon of choice. However, Zach was a student of plant life. Could that have offered a special intellectual satisfaction that made it appealing?

Piper shook her head. She was thinking much too far ahead. The sheriff was simply questioning Zach. Hopefully, Sugar's son could verify his actions and whereabouts during the critical time. And that would be the end of it. Piper added the carrots to her simmering vinegar mixture, then left them to check on her jars in their water bath.

The jars of spicy carrots had been filled and sealed and were cooling when Piper heard an unfamiliar voice carrying from the front of the shop. In a moment, Amy appeared at the doorway.

"There's a lady who would like to speak with you," she said. From the pucker of Amy's brow, Piper guessed it wasn't a customer wanting pickling advice. A salesperson? A charity donation request?

"Who is it?" Piper asked.

Amy paused, glancing back to the front of the store, then whispered, "It's Lydia Porter. Jeremy Porter's mother!"

# 9

Piper took a moment to gather herself before stepping out to meet Lydia Porter. She glanced down at her apron, which had become spotted with spicy-carrot splashes, but let it stay. If evidence of Piper's hard work offended Jeremy Porter's mother, so be it. She could deal with it.

"Miss Lamb," the silvery-coiffed, short but somehow still imposing woman said, holding out her hand. "Lydia Porter. I'm so pleased to meet you."

In a blue Chanel-styled suit, heels, and a string of pearls, Lydia Porter appeared dressed more for an elegant lunch than a visit to Piper's shop. Piper shook her hand, which wouldn't have surprised her if it'd been white-gloved, and responded cordially. What was Lydia Porter doing there at a time like that? Mrs. Porter quickly illuminated her.

"I wanted to personally invite you to my tea. Somehow yours was not included in the invitations that were sent out. I'm here to rectify that unforgivable oversight."

"You're still holding the tea?" Piper asked, surprised.

"Oh, yes. I so want to get to know Cloverdale and its residents."

*And carefully cull the ones who don't meet your standards?* Piper badly wanted to stand up for Sugar Heywood but decided to hold off and listen. Amy had gone into the back room but left the dividing door open and was probably all ears herself.

"I understand from one of the ladies at the Cloverdale Women's Club that you recently moved here from Albany?" Lydia asked.

"That's right. Several months ago."

"Albany is my family home as well," Lydia said with a satisfied smile. "You may know of my uncle, Congressman Wardell Smyth?"

"Um . . ."

"An extremely effective representative for our state during the Roosevelt and Truman administrations. He was seriously considered to be Harry Truman's vice president but then Alben Barkley, you know . . ." Lydia's voice trailed off, hinting at possible political machinations that had insidiously blocked Congressman Smyth's much-deserved political rise.

Piper nodded as sympathetically as she could manage, still puzzled as to what had brought about this personal invitation to Lydia's tea.

"Your parents, I hear, are renowned archaeologists." Lydia said, smiling.

*Ah! That was it.* Piper was tempted to respond that no, she had been raised by two high school dropout hippies whose commune, in addition to decrying anything governmental, still enthusiastically practiced free love—just to see the look on Lydia's face. But in fairness to her parents, she nodded. "They've had some success in their field."

"And are they in the area?"

"Sadly, no. They are currently on a dig on one of the Greek islands."

"How disappointing. I would have loved to meet them as well."

Would that affect Piper's invitation? To find out and possibly put Lydia on the spot, Piper asked, "When is your tea?"

"This coming Sunday," Lydia answered smoothly, apparently still willing to welcome a simple pickling shop proprietor. "I did put it off a few days," she said, and Piper expected the reason to be Dirk Unger's death until Lydia explained, "We've had to have a few renovations done on the house. Not too surprisingly, things took much longer than promised to get done." She laughed deprecatingly. "One can never rely on guarantees from the working class, can one?"

"Actually, I've had very good experience, lately. Ralph Strawbridge installed my new front door two days ahead of his own deadline."

"Yes, well . . ." Lydia glanced vaguely at Piper's door but was clearly unimpressed.

Piper could contain herself no more. "I was sorry to

hear about Mr. Unger's death. That must be very upsetting to your family."

"Oh, yes, terribly," Lydia said, appearing quite unruffled. "Jeremy relied on Dirk quite a bit. But nobody is irreplaceable, of course. I'm sure the entire situation will be sorted out very soon." Lydia turned toward Piper's shelf of preserves. "While I'm here, I should pick up a jar of your lovely brandied cherries. Oh, there they are!" She plucked a jar from its spot and handed it to Piper to ring up, having smoothly changed the subject to something more "tasteful." Piper, however, was not to be deterred.

"Sheriff Carlyle," she said, carrying the cherries toward her cash register, "will certainly discover the truth of the matter—in time. As the people who knew Mr. Unger best, your family must have been able to provide him with good information about the man's movements on the day he died."

"Oh! Heavens!" Lydia laughed and flapped a hand. "Hardly. At least not Mallory or myself. Mallory, of course, is my daughter. You'll get to meet her at the tea," Lydia said, as though that were an added treat for Piper to look forward to. "Neither of us had much to do with Dirk Unger. He was Jeremy's employee." Her pinched lips as she said that confirmed Tammy Butterworth's claim of battles with Jeremy over the man.

Piper was eager to pursue the topic more but her shop door opened at that moment, admitting Mrs. Tilley, whose face lit up like a Christmas tree at the sight of Lydia Porter.

"Lydia, imagine finding you here! You poor, dear thing. What a terrible time you all must be going through. How are you holding up?"

*Quite well,* Piper thought, but Lydia Porter shook her head and sighed as Mrs. Tilley twittered away, full of sympathy for Lydia's imagined distress. Amy emerged from the back at that point and caught Piper's eye, rolling hers in exasperation. The two waited silently, Piper beginning to wish she could ease the pair out and onto the sidewalk as the exchange continued.

Finally Lydia Porter said, "Well, I must be going. There are one or two more stops I need to make concerning my tea."

"I hope you found a replacement caterer as good as Sugar Heywood," Piper said.

"Oh, Sugar couldn't do it?" Mrs. Tilley piped up, apparently not up to speed on all the recent developments. "What a shame. She really is the best around."

Lydia Porter's eyes narrowed but she quickly regained her composure. "Actually, I've found someone in Bellingham who came with the highest references. I'm positive he . . ." She took Mrs. Tilley's arm at that point and walked her out of the shop as she enthused over her new caterer, leaving Piper and Amy to stare wordlessly.

"My gosh!" Amy said as Ralph Strawbridge's beautiful door closed behind the pair.

"She's quite the unique individual, isn't she?" Piper said.

"Unique? She's awful! Sugar is lucky to be out of her reach."

"I agree. I'm not sure Sugar is ready to see that, but she has worse things to think about."

"You mean about Zach? That should be cleared up by now, though, don't you think? I mean, Daddy must just be eliminating people, 'cause no way could a nice guy like Zach do anything so awful."

"How well do you know Zach?" Piper asked. She had to admit that her own good opinion of Zach was based on fairly brief interactions along with anecdotes shared by his not-unbiased mother.

"Zach was a couple of years behind me in school, so we weren't good buds or anything. But he dated the younger sister of one of my friends for a while and I used to see him at her house a lot." Amy paused a moment, considering. "He was quiet but always friendly. He liked to talk about plants all the time, even then. Allie's mom, I remember, would ask him to check her gardens for poison ivy 'cause she was sensitive to it but could never spot it herself."

"Allie is the younger sister?"

"Uh-huh. A cute kid but kind of immature at the time—even for fifteen. She dumped Zach in a flash after they'd been going together for most of the year when someone on the football team took an interest in her."

"How did Zach handle that?"

Amy grew somber. "Pretty hard, actually. I remember Jessica, Allie's sister, telling me that Zach still came over to the house, asking to see Allie. When she wouldn't talk to him, he'd stand on the sidewalk out front for hours, looking at the house and I guess hoping she'd come out. Jessica felt sorry for him but eventually her dad had to have a firm talk with him." Amy winced. "I guess that sounds a little creepy, huh?"

"Well, he was what? Fifteen? What teenaged boy hasn't acted a little goofy over a girl at that age? Or am I rationalizing?"

"No, you're probably right. I don't know why I brought that up when you asked me about Zach. Everything else about him was fine. Great, actually. He was terrific in science, you know, and he tutored kids who weren't so good in it."

"Did he finally get over Allie?"

Amy shrugged. "I don't know. He didn't date anyone after that. But Jessica told me he brought flowers to the hospital."

"Hospital?"

"Yeah. When Allie had appendicitis. Or they thought she did. It turned out it wasn't her appendix after all. I'm not sure they ever figured out exactly *what* it was. But she was okay. Anyway, it was nice of Zach to bring her flowers, don't you think?"

Piper wasn't able to comment because at that moment Will walked in, coincidentally holding a beautiful bouquet of flowers. He grinned sheepishly as Piper's eyes widened.

"Don't give me too much credit," he said. "These came from a neighbor, Marguerite Lloyd, thanking me for pulling her car out of a ditch last week with my tractor. She grows them," he said, looking down at the lovely bunch of white lilies mixed with pink carnations. "In her greenhouse. I thought you'd appreciate them more than I would."

Piper took the bouquet he held out and buried her nose in it, inhaling the lovely perfume. "Thank you!" she said, delighted, even knowing they'd been regifted.

"I'll get a vase," Amy said. She turned toward the back, then stopped. "Are there any down here?"

"I have a couple upstairs. In the kitchen broom closet. Top shelf."

Amy scooted up the stairs to Piper's apartment as Piper leaned over her counter to give Will a thank-you kiss. "This makes my day, which hasn't been the greatest up until now."

"The Unger thing," Will said, nodding.

Piper told him about Zach being taken in for questioning because of the poison that had been used. "Sugar's pretty upset about it, of course." She heard faint noises of Amy's scrambling through her broom closet, then a muted cry of "Hah!" In a moment Amy trotted back down to the shop carrying a green vase that Piper immediately recognized. It was the vase that had held the huge bouquet of roses that Scott sent her last August. He'd ordered them while traveling through Thailand, timed to arrive on the anniversary of their first date—a highly romantic gesture of a kind he'd never managed to come up with when they were actually engaged.

Could she put Will's flowers in Scott's vase, Piper wondered? Oh heck, she decided, it was just a vase. Scott had never seen it, and Will had no notion of its origin. And they were actually Marguerite Lloyd's flowers, if you wanted to be totally picky. Piper took the vase to the back and half-filled it with water, then arranged the lilies and carnations in it.

"Beautiful!" Amy cried when Piper carried them back to the shop. "They'll look wonderful right next to the cash register, don't you think?"

"Yes—" Piper began, then looked up as her shop door opened. "Oh! Scott!"

Scott Littleton walked in, looking very lawyerly in a dark suit and tie and holding a brown leather briefcase. "Piper," he said, "I just came from—" He stopped, seeing Will standing there, looking outdoorsy in his usual rolled-sleeve shirt and jeans. "Oh. Hi!"

Will acknowledged Scott with a faint smile and a nod.

The four stared awkwardly at each other for a moment until Amy asked, "Did everything go okay with Zach?"

"Um, well enough," Scott said then turned to Piper. "I wanted to thank you for sending me the client."

Piper felt Will's gaze swing toward her. "I just thought Zach should have someone watching his back," she said.

"Absolutely. Your father," Scott said to Amy, "knows his job, no question. And I'm sure he's not out to pin things on anyone who's not guilty. But evidence can be misconstrued and suspects can blurt out information they're not required to give unless someone's there to advise them."

"But Zach's totally covered, right? He has an alibi."

Scott paused, then said, "I can't get into that, Amy. But rest assured, I'll do my best for him." He suddenly noticed the filled vase Piper held. "Nice flowers."

Both Piper's and Amy's gaze automatically turned to Will, and Scott said, "Oh. Well, then. Hey, look at the time! I'd better get going. Nice seeing you all!"

He turned and hurried out, and as the door closed behind him another silence ensued. Then Will said, "It's good Zach got a lawyer. Let's just hope he won't need him for very long."

Piper smiled and nodded. Will was being his usual wonderful, understanding self. Scott's hesitations, however, and lack of reassurances on Zach's situation hadn't totally filled her with confidence that Zach wouldn't be needing him for long.

# 10

~~~~~~

Later that afternoon, Piper was propping open her new door to let in the fresh spring air when she spotted Sugar and Zach heading her way, their expressions strained.

As they drew close, Sugar said, "Zach hasn't been arrested or charged. Your lawyer friend, Mr. Littleton, was a big help with that. But they've instructed Zach not to leave the area."

"Why?" Piper asked, bringing the two into her shop. "What's causing the sheriff to be so suspicious?"

"Zach's alibi has a big hole in it. He was at his friend Justin's to watch a movie, as he said. But he didn't get there until eight."

"Zach, you dropped off the cake for the party here around five thirty, then stayed a while. But I'm afraid I have no idea for how long."

"It doesn't matter," Zach said. His dark tee, worn over cargo pants, featured a stylized skull. Perhaps not the best attire for answering questions from authorities about a murder, but he surely hadn't anticipated that when he'd dressed that morning. "I already told the sheriff I hung around the party only about fifteen minutes. I wasn't in the greatest mood and I didn't want to be a drag. So I left and just walked around for a while. When I got tired of that, I went over to Justin's."

"Did you run into anybody you knew while you were walking?" Piper asked.

When Zach shook his head, Sugar said, "It looks bad, doesn't it?"

"Not necessarily," Piper said, trying for an upbeat note that she wasn't totally feeling. "There's still the matter of getting the bloodroot into Dirk Unger's salad. I doubt if you'd knocked on Unger's door, Zach, that he'd have welcomed you."

Zach snorted. "Not hardly. And no way would I go there, if I even knew where it was. Unger was the last person I wanted to see."

"So to get the bloodroot into his house—the address surely must be easy to find out—you'd probably have to break in. I didn't hear anything about smashed windows or doors at the place."

Sugar heaved a great sigh, looking at her son, who squeezed her shoulder. "Zach might not have needed to break in. Unger was a careful man with finances and accounting, but it seems he could be absentminded with his keys, so much so that Jeremy kept a spare set of the man's car and house keys. Jeremy told the police that

Unger often hated to admit he'd misplaced his keys once again and would simply leave his house unlocked until he found them again. Jeremy knew that was the case when Unger asked him to drive when they went someplace together."

"And was that the case on the day he died?"

Sugar nodded. "The two of them went to Bellingham on business after lunching at A La Carte. Jeremy drove because Unger claimed he'd left his car home and walked to the office to get some exercise. Unger actually hated exercise."

"But that's a good thing," Piper said, still straining for optimism. "If Unger's house was left open, anyone could have slipped the bloodroot inside."

"But how many others were mad enough at Dirk Unger to want to kill him?"

"That's what we need to find out," Ralph Strawbridge said, walking through the open doorway and surprising the three. "If Zach is going to get out of this mess," Ralph continued, "he's going to have to come up with proof that someone else did Dirk Unger in."

"Oh, he has to get out of this," Sugar cried. "And soon! Spring break will be over in a few days. He can't be missing classes. His grades would drop. He'd lose his scholarship!"

"Mom, I'll be okay. Don't worry! I can keep up with most of my classes online," Zach said, but Piper was thinking that Zach would lose a lot more than a scholarship if he were charged with murder. She suspected Sugar—and maybe Zach, too—couldn't yet bring themselves to admit the seriousness of his problem.

Ralph, though, had to be aware of the dangers. Gently turning Sugar's thoughts from angst to action, he asked, "Who can you think of that would have wanted Dirk Unger dead?"

Sugar didn't answer, looking bewildered and thrown for the moment by having to switch focus from her son's innocence to someone else's guilt.

"Anybody who met him," Zach offered unhelpfully.

"What about a Realtor?" Piper asked. "Jeremy Porter's realty business was gobbling up smaller offices and probably hurting the ones that held off."

"But why kill Unger over that?" Sugar asked. "Why not Jeremy?"

"Good question," Ralph said. "But Piper's suggestion still merits looking into. Anyone in particular?"

Piper frowned as an unwelcome thought came to her. "Stan Yeager, for one."

"Yes!" Sugar cried, eager now to pitch in and much less concerned about precisely who to point the finger at as long as it wasn't her son. "Stan was one of the very few who didn't sign on with Jeremy, which I thought at the time was foolish. How could his small realty office survive against Jeremy's huge, multi-area agency?"

"Stan did look pretty bleak when he arrived at the party last night," Piper admitted.

"What time was he here?" Ralph asked.

Piper had to think. "Later in the evening. I remember that Nate brought out his guitar right after I spoke with Stan. And it was after Nate had sung a few songs that we heard the sirens. So Stan must have arrived around seven."

"That gives him time to have gone to Unger's house," Sugar said eagerly.

"Unless someone can vouch for Stan's whereabouts before he arrived," Ralph said.

"Wait," Zach protested. "I don't want some other innocent guy getting in trouble just to get me off the hook!"

"We're not going to get anyone in trouble who doesn't deserve to be, Zach," Ralph said. "What we aim to do is to find the actual murderer by narrowing the field. You're in considerable danger, Zach, and you should realize that. You can't just sit around and hope for the best."

"Ralph is right," Piper said. "And I promise we won't jump to any conclusions. Stan is just one person I thought of. There must be more. It could be someone Unger antagonized before he came to Cloverdale. I don't know much about Unger other than his job. He lived alone. Was he ever married?"

Sugar shuddered. "I can't imagine but I suppose anything's possible."

"Jeremy would know. Could you find out about Unger's past from him?"

Sugar's face showed how awful that would be for her, though she said, "If it would help Zach—"

Zach stopped her. "There's gotta be some other way."

Piper thought a moment before smiling. "There might be." She pulled open the drawer where she'd dropped Tammy Butterworth's business card. "This lady," she said, waving the card, "just might be able to help us out." She explained what she knew about Tammy and her connection to Jeremy Porter.

"Perfect!" Ralph said. "You find out as much as you can from her, Piper. Sugar, how about you and I look into Stan Yeager's whereabouts yesterday before he showed up at the party? And keep thinking about anyone else who might have had reason to murder Unger."

"You guys can't do all the work," Zach protested. "What can I do?"

"You should probably check with Scott Littleton," Piper said. "He might have important advice about what you should and shouldn't be doing right now."

"She's right, Zach," Sugar said, looking much better for having a definite goal. "Let us get started on this. There'll be other ways you can help."

Zach didn't look totally happy with that but he agreed, at least for the time being. Piper was a bit surprised at how quickly she'd let herself be drawn in but couldn't imagine saying no to her friends in need. The three took off, and Piper studied Tammy Butterworth's card, wondering how best to ask a pile of invasive questions of this new acquaintance without sending her running for cover.

Piper was still considering the question as she pulled up to Aunt Judy and Uncle Frank's farm after closing up shop for the day. Besides spending time with two of her favorite people, she had come for the fresh-picked asparagus Uncle Frank said he had ready for her. Any stop at the farm, of course, automatically included an invitation to one of Aunt Judy's home-cooked meals, which particularly worked for Piper that evening. She hoped to discuss Zach Heywood's situation with the two and get their input, something that rarely failed to clear her own thoughts.

As she climbed from her car, Jack raced across the lawn to throw himself at her, making Piper grateful once again that the dog's genes included no Great Dane. Thirty or so pounds of super-excited dog were enough for her to deal with, and she did her best, enjoying the frantic, tail-wagging enthusiasm until Uncle Frank whistled Jack off.

"A person would think you were the one filling his food bowl every day, the way that dog dotes on you," Uncle Frank said, leaning down to peck Piper's cheek.

"I'd be flattered if I didn't know he greeted just about everyone who comes here like that," Piper said, laughing.

"Not everyone. He holds back on strangers and watches for cues from us on how to react. He's not one to be won over by a piece of steak."

"Then he's a good watchdog," Piper said, scratching Jack's ears as she walked with her uncle toward the white clapboard farmhouse, which was aging but kept in the best possible shape by her hardworking uncle and aunt. She picked up the earthy smell of freshly turned fields, and, as she climbed the porch steps, caught the aroma of something tasty simmering on the stove drifting through the screen door.

Aunt Judy bustled out of the kitchen, dish towel in hand, as they stepped indoors. "I hope you like what I made tonight," she said, hugging Piper. "It's called sweet, sticky, and spicy chicken. I've never made it before but Emma Leahy recommended it."

"It smells terrific. Anything I can do?" Piper asked as she followed her aunt back to the kitchen.

"Sit down and relax. I'm just waiting for my rice to be done."

"I'll go wash up," Uncle Frank said. "Be back in a minute."

Aunt Judy stirred and tested the contents of various pots and within minutes let Piper help her set bowls, the chicken platter, and her ever-present pickle dish onto the table.

"These are the pickled beets you helped me put up last fall," Aunt Judy said, pulling up her own chair and passing the dish to Piper.

"One of my favorites," Piper said, forking two slices to start with and reminded of Tammy Butterworth, who planned to make some herself. She asked her aunt if she'd met Tammy, explaining the woman's connection to the Porters.

"No, I haven't," Aunt Judy said. She handed the platter of spicy-glazed chicken strips to her husband.

"These aren't real hot, are they?" he asked, gazing at them suspiciously.

"Just a tiny bit, Frank. The brown sugar balances it. Don't worry."

Piper smiled, knowing her uncle's strong preference for familiar dishes. Her aunt, though, enjoyed experimenting in the kitchen and had needed to develop good coaxing skills to ease her husband out of his comfort zone.

"Tammy does cleaning?" Aunt Judy asked, helping herself to a spoonful of rice. "I guess that's why I haven't run into her. Most people I know do their own."

"The Porters might take up a major part of her time." Piper tasted the chicken strips and nodded encouragingly to her uncle, who then carefully cut a small piece for himself. "I'm hoping to talk with Tammy," Piper said. She gave her aunt and uncle a rundown of the latest developments on Dirk Unger's murder.

"Oh, I'm so sorry to hear that Sugar's boy is caught in the middle," Aunt Judy said. "I just can't imagine that nice young man doing anything so awful. But I'm afraid I can see Sheriff Carlyle's side of it."

Uncle Frank nodded. "The boy's got a big problem. Motive and opportunity. Add in evidence and Carlyle won't need to look any further."

"That's why we're checking into it ourselves." Piper said. "Great chicken, by the way, Aunt Judy."

"By *ourselves*, you mean . . . ?" Uncle Frank asked.

"Sugar, Ralph Strawbridge, and me. At least, so far."

"Piper, do you think you should?" Aunt Judy asked. "Remember what happened the other time you got involved."

"Strawbridge?" Uncle Frank reached for his water glass. "How does he figure in this?"

"As a friend to Sugar and Zach," Piper said. "I've gotten to know him pretty well as he worked on my shop door. There's more to Ralph than woodworking. Sugar, I suspect, has greatly underestimated the man. Anyway, he and Sugar are going to check out some things together and I promised to try to pump—that is, question—Tammy Butterworth about Dirk Unger's past."

Piper had decided not to mention their interest in

Stan Yeager for the time being. "Is there anyone else you think we should look at?" she asked.

Piper didn't expect names from Aunt Judy, who tended to believe the best about everyone until proven indisputably wrong, but she waited as Uncle Frank mulled over her question.

"What about that greenhouse lady?" he finally said.

"Who?"

"Oh, Frank," Aunt Judy said, "she couldn't possibly—"

"Judy, I'm just saying there might be something going on there. I saw them—her and Unger—arguing pretty heatedly the other day. "

"But—"

"Arguing where?" Piper asked, interested. "And are you talking about Marguerite Lloyd?"

"That's her. Couldn't think of her name. It was, oh, let me think, about a week ago. The day I stopped at TopValuFood to pick up that laundry soap for you, Judy. I was walking back to where I parked my truck at the far end of the lot, when I heard their voices. Loud. They were over in the next row, so I didn't hear all of what they were saying. I could see them all right and Ms. Lloyd was fit to be tied, that was pretty clear."

"How about Unger?" Piper asked.

"Well, now that I think of it, it was pretty one-sided. Guess you can't call it an argument, then, can you? The Unger fellow was mostly taking it in, and when he did answer her it was much quieter. But whatever he said to her wasn't calming. She screeched and stalked away. He stayed where he was, looking smug."

"Smug?" Aunt Judy said. "That would infuriate anyone, especially if they were mad to begin with."

Piper agreed, but the attitude sounded typical of Unger. "So you didn't catch what it was about?"

Uncle Frank shook his head. "Only something about him poking his nose into her business."

"Her greenhouse business?"

"Marguerite does landscape design as well," Uncle Frank said. "Maybe it was that. Could she have been hired to do Jeremy Porter's place?"

"Possibly," Piper said. "And you're right, it bears looking into. But," she assured her aunt, "I'll be as discreet as possible. Promise."

"I know you will, dear." Aunt Judy's brow puckered. "And I want Zach to be cleared as much as you do. I just don't want it to be anyone I know."

"It'll have to be someone," her husband pointed out, patting her hand. "Look at it this way: If it's a person you know, wouldn't you rather find out instead of going along thinking they're something they're not?"

"I suppose," Aunt Judy said doubtfully, and perhaps to cheer her up, Uncle Frank reached for her platter of sweet, spicy chicken and forked a second helping onto his plate. It seemed to work, as Aunt Judy smiled.

Piper decided they'd had enough talk of murder for the night and asked Aunt Judy about how Jack's visit to the vet had gone. But as her aunt answered in some detail, Piper made a mental note to look into "the greenhouse lady's" business very soon.

# 11

~~~~

Piper was just ringing up her first customer of the day—Mrs. Hendrickson, who'd developed a fondness for Piper's tea jelly and had stopped in for two more jars—when she saw Scott's red Volvo pull up outside.

"Thank you, Mrs. Hendrickson," Piper said, handing the bagged jars over. She watched the purple-jacketed woman pause at the door to trace a finger lightly over Ralph Strawbridge's carvings as Piper had seen so many people do. *Would that wear down the bas-relief in time,* she wondered, *like stalagmites that became rounded and polished from the touch of countless tourists?* She'd have to run that by Ralph. But for the moment she was more concerned with what Scott might be carrying in a large, oddly shaped brown bag.

"Morning!" Scott called, as he maneuvered himself

through the door. He was obviously on his way to his office, dressed once more in a dark suit and tie, though different ones from the day before.

"Good morning. What in the world do you have there?"

"You're not going to believe this," he said, holding on to his package, which didn't appear at all heavy. "Remember back in Albany when we were looking through that antique shop? It was that Saturday afternoon when we'd gone to get your ring resized?"

"Ye-es," Piper said slowly, remembering that period early in their engagement when she'd thought everything was going so wonderfully. *What,* she wondered, *had Scott done with the ring that she'd returned to him?*

"Well, do you also remember the painted cat you fell in love with but that I talked you out of getting because I thought it was silly?"

Piper didn't have to think hard on that. She quickly flashed on the seated cat made out of papier-mâché. It had been decorated whimsically in rainbow colors, and she'd loved it at once but had eventually agreed with Scott that it was impractical. Would she have given up so easily now? Highly doubtful, but the question was moot as Scott slid a near-identical creation out of his bag.

"Voilà!"

Piper gasped. "Where did you find it?"

"An antique shop over on Maple Street. Do you know it?"

Piper did. The shop had previously been owned by Alan Rosemont, the amateur bagpiper whose body had ended up in her pickle barrel. That had happened a few weeks before Scott moved into Cloverdale and she'd never mentioned it, or the rest of the story, to him.

"I haven't been there since the new owner took over," she said.

"You should check it out. Great stuff. Anyway, I spotted this and instantly thought of you. Do you still like it?"

Piper loved it but she hesitated to say so. "You bought it for me?"

"Of course!" Scott said, laughing. "I don't think it would exactly fit in at my law office, do you? Seriously, I always felt a little bad about talking you out of the other one. I shouldn't have done that."

He held the cat out to her, but Piper shrank back. "Scott, I can't accept such a gift from you. Though it was very thoughtful. I'm sure it was much too expensive."

"Not at all! Please take it. No strings attached, I promise! Even if the shop would take this little fellow back, I don't want to. He needs a good home." He gave the colorful cat a comically mournful look. "He was fading away in a dark corner in that shop, with nobody to love him."

Piper felt her lips twitch. "Well, I suppose I could find a space for *her*—I'm sure it's a her—as long as she stays quiet."

"Oh, silence is guaranteed."

Piper reached for the cat. "Thank you, Scott. But no more gifts, okay?"

"I thought you could call him Dill-bert," he said. "But since he's a she . . ."

"Dill-lilah, maybe?" Piper said, grinning.

"Or Jelly-an?"

Piper groaned. "Isn't it time for you to open up your office?"

"Probably, just in case somebody calls. No early appointments but Zach Heywood should stop in a little later." He grew somber. "I need to explain a few things to him, like the seriousness of his situation."

"He doesn't seem to quite get it, does he? But what twenty-year-old really believes anything bad could happen to them? That happens only in the movies or to somebody else."

Scott nodded. "Well, I'll do my best to get through. He's a smart kid, and a good one, I think." He glanced at Piper's clock. "Enjoy, um, whatever you decide to call her," he said, gesturing toward the cat. His smile reappeared.

"I will, Scott. And thank you." Piper watched as he hopped back into his sporty car and took off. Scott might be causing complications in her life but he was a very good lawyer and he obviously cared about his client. She was glad she'd sent Zach Heywood to him.

Piper looked at the pretty painted cat he'd left with her and sighed, unsure if she'd done the right thing by accepting the piece but at the same time smiling inanely over owning it.

"He got it, you know, because Will gave you those flowers," Amy said after hearing the tale behind Piper's gift. She grinned wickedly. "Now we'll see how Will tops papier-mâché."

"There won't be any competition. Will probably

won't even notice the thing." Piper had moved the cat around experimentally to several different places in the shop, ending up at an area near the window, but began to have second thoughts about the spot. Perhaps tucked slightly behind the canning and pickling jars would be better?

To end a discussion that was making her a tad uneasy, Piper asked Amy if she knew anything about Marguerite Lloyd, landscaper and source of Will's bouquet.

"Not much. Why?"

"It's just a stab in the dark, but Uncle Frank overheard her having a heated argument with Dirk Unger. I'm scrambling around for anyone other than Zach who might have had a grudge against the man."

"I can't imagine what Unger would have had to do with a flower lady. Maybe it had something to do with the Porters?"

"That was our guess and one of the things I hope to find out from Tammy Butterworth."

As Amy started cutting up the asparagus Piper had brought back from the farm, Piper called the cell phone number printed on Tammy's business card and asked if she could meet with her for a few minutes.

"Sure thing. How about now?" Tammy suggested. "I'm cleaning the Harpers' place. I can talk and work at the same time.

"Won't the Harpers mind?" Piper asked.

The infectious laugh that Piper remembered bubbled through the phone. "They're down in Florida. They rented the place out while they were gone for the winter but they're heading back soon and want it spruced up. There's people in and out doing repairs, too. You might as well join the crowd."

With Amy around to watch the shop, Piper took off in her hatchback, driving through town for about ten minutes before pulling up to the redbrick ranch home that Tammy had directed her to. A black van with "Reyes Heating and Air Conditioning" lettered on its side occupied much of the driveway, its opened doors and miscellaneous equipment blocking the way, so Piper parked on the street and followed the curved walkway to the front door.

She rang the bell but got no response. Assuming the vacuuming noises she heard inside were the reason, she opened the unlocked door and spotted Tammy, her back to her, bobbing her head in time to whatever was coming through her earbuds as she energetically pushed a vacuum cleaner over a thick beige rug.

"Hello!" Piper yelled from the doorway, then stepped in and eased over to the woman's line of vision.

"Hey!" Tammy said, reacting not with a start as Piper had feared, but with a delighted smile. She pulled out her earbuds and shouted over the noise of her vacuum. "You found it. Great! Give me one minute to finish here, okay?"

Piper nodded and backed out of the way. She watched as Tammy worked, sliding aside hassocks and lifting floor lamps with a balletic grace that brought visions of *Swan Lake* to mind despite Tammy's decidedly round figure. The ongoing smile on the woman's face hinted at real joy in her task, something Piper could say she experienced during her pickling efforts but hardly ever while cleaning.

"There!" Tammy said, finally cutting off the noise. She snatched up the cord and began winding it around the holder. "So, what can I help you with?"

"It's about Dirk Unger's murder," Piper said. "I'm wondering if it might have something to do with his past and if you could tell me anything about that?"

Sudden loud pounding overhead pulled both heads upward.

"They're working on the air-conditioning in the attic," Tammy cried over the din. "Let's go to the kitchen." She led the way through a polished wood–filled dining room to the other end of the house. As they reached the bright white-and-black tiled room, she said, "I haven't been in here, yet, so I'll just get on with my work while we talk, all right?"

"Sure," Piper said, watching Tammy pull cleaning supplies out of the white-painted cupboards. She automatically asked if she could help, as she would have if it were Aunt Judy's kitchen. Her offer, however, prompted genial laughter.

"No, dear," Tammy said with a look that said Piper might be the expert on pickling but Tammy Butterworth was the professional on setting houses straight. "Dirk Unger's past," she said, mulling over Piper's question as she filled a small bucket with hot, soapy water. "Let's see. He's worked with Jeremy for years but I think he started out some place in Ohio. Couldn't tell you exactly where, though."

"Was he ever married?"

"Married?" Tammy squeezed a sponge into the bucket and began swiping at the black-speckled granite countertop. "Good question. I have no idea. I can't picture anyone falling in love with him, can you?"

"No," Piper admitted. "Or him caring enough about someone else. What about before he and the Porters moved to Cloverdale? Did he make any enemies, anyone who might have followed him here?"

"To kill him, you mean? Probably a whole lot of people hated him. Dirk did Jeremy's dirty work for him—firing people, stuff like that. He was good at it. Enjoyed it, most likely." She rubbed at a particularly sticky spot on the counter.

"Does anyone stand out?"

Tammy paused, shaking her head. "Sorry, sweetie. They probably all hated him equally. A bunch could probably have filled a bus and ridden over as a group to do away with him." She cackled brightly. "I didn't see anything like that around, did you?"

Piper shook her head. This wasn't getting her anywhere. She decided to move on, as did Tammy, who, finished with her countertop, grabbed a bottle of stainless steel polish. "Someone," Piper said, "overheard Unger in an argument with Marguerite Lloyd a few days before he died."

"The woman with the landscaping business?" Tammy asked.

"Yes. Do you know if she was hired to work on the Porter property?"

Piper's hopes sagged as Tammy once more shook her head.

"Nope." Tammy poured polish liberally onto a cloth and smoothed it over the refrigerator door. "Lydia balked at Jeremy getting the yard dug up this year, though he wanted to. She didn't want the mess during her big tea. But," she added, rubbing at the door, "I think she wanted to keep Marguerite Lloyd in her good graces for the future, so Lydia passed her name on to the Fortneys. The wife apparently wants to do something special with their lot."

The name Fortney rang a bell with Piper but she couldn't immediately think why. "How did Lydia know the Fortneys?"

"Oh, Lydia's been busy getting to know everyone in Cloverdale—and everything about them." Piper thought back to how Lydia knew about Piper's parents' occupation and was sure that was true.

"Now," Tammy said, pausing thoughtfully, her rag limp in her hand. "That might be the reason for the problem between Lloyd and Dirk."

"What would?"

"The Fortneys. I overheard Dirk arguing that Lydia should recommend a different landscaper to them. Don't ask me why. His own place is surrounded by concrete and ground cover. He certainly didn't care one way or another about gardens or who plants them."

*Probably not,* Piper thought, *but he did care about influence and control.* Piper didn't know how that applied to Marguerite Lloyd, but it bore looking into.

Booms suddenly sounded overhead as the air-conditioning work apparently moved over the kitchen.

"Sorry, dear," Tammy shouted as the racket continued.

"I'll need to clean the floor here next. If you want to keep talking, you'll have to do it from the dining room. And raise your voice."

"That's okay," Piper yelled back. She'd gotten enough information from Tammy to chew on for a while. "I should get back to the shop. Thank you!"

Tammy nodded and slipped her earbuds back into place, a beatific expression filling her face as she then reached into the closet and pulled out a mop.

# 12

~~~~

"Oh, Corinne Fortney is my old friend!" Aunt Judy said when Piper called to ask.

"I thought the name sounded familiar."

"Yes, I'm sure I must have mentioned her. I was so pleased when I heard they were moving back to Cloverdale. That was around the time you were setting up your shop, so I'm sure you had plenty of other things to occupy your mind. Corinne and I were good friends all through school. But after she married Lou, they moved to Chicago for his job. We always kept in touch but it's not like seeing someone every day, is it?"

"Did they get their place landscaped lately?"

"You know, Corinne was talking about that, but I don't believe they've gone ahead with anything."

"Any idea why?" Piper asked.

"Actually, no. Corinne seemed very excited about the plans."

"Want to find out what happened?" Piper explained about Marguerite Lloyd possibly being the landscaper in question.

"Well, that's interesting. Of course, I wouldn't want to pry," Aunt Judy said. "But if Corinne doesn't mind talking about it . . ."

Piper was pretty sure any friend of Aunt Judy's would be likely to open up about most anything. Which was exactly why she'd enlisted her aunt's help.

Aunt Judy said she'd see about arranging a visit to the Fortneys, and a grateful Piper got back to her business at hand, which was finishing up what Amy wasn't able to do on the pickled asparagus before leaving for A La Carte. Piper ladled the blanched asparagus tips, pickling spice, and vinegar mixture into hot canning jars.

She'd filled and sealed the jars and returned them to the canning pot for a final boil when the bell on her shop door jingled. Piper set a timer and went out front to find Ralph Strawbridge.

"How did it go yesterday?" Piper asked, sure that Ralph had come to report on what he and Sugar had discovered—if anything—on Stan Yeager.

"I think you may have given us a good lead," Ralph said, and Piper felt an internal wince.

"Oh?" she asked, determined to keep an open mind.

"Sugar and I talked with several of the people with businesses near Yeager's office. Those who noticed agree it was five thirty when he closed up and left on Wednesday, the day of the murder."

"And he didn't show up at the party here until close to seven."

"Right. Of course, he could have simply gone home first. But Sugar knows one of his neighbors pretty well, a woman who walks her dog on a regular schedule. So we arranged to be strolling down her street at the right time to run into her."

Piper's timer went off. "My canning jars," she explained. "Come back with me while I finish up." Ralph followed her and opened a folding chair for himself as Piper began lifting her jars of pickled asparagus from the canning pot with a pair of tongs, setting them, one by one, on a folded towel.

"Looks good. When can I try one?" Ralph said.

"Not for a while," Piper said, smiling. "They need to sit here quietly for twelve hours, first of all, and I happen to think they taste better for being stored a few weeks. But that's just me. It could be that I just like to admire them for a while." She grabbed another jar with her tongs. "So what happened with Stan's neighbor?"

"Well, Sugar was great. I know how worried she is about Zach, but she managed to put on a happy, no-cares-in-the-world face and called out to Monica—the dog-walking neighbor—as soon as she came within sight. Monica looked surprised but happy to see Sugar, and even better, didn't seem aware of Zach's situation."

"How did Sugar explain her interest in Stan's comings and goings?" Piper asked, continuing with her jars.

Ralph smiled, clearly impressed with Sugar's ingenuity. "After a couple of minutes of chitchat and fussing over Monica's dog—one of those little dust mop ones—Sugar suddenly looked toward Stan's house and said, 'Oh, I guess we're too early. I don't see any car in the Yeager driveway. Or is that his car parked at the curb?' Monica glanced over and said, 'That's not Stan's car. He drives a black Audi.'"

"She's right," Piper said. "That's what Stan drove me around in when we were looking for a shop for me. What time of the day was this?"

"A little before five thirty, when we knew Yeager would likely still be in his office. Monica knew that, too, and mentioned that he rarely got home before five forty-five, which was when she was usually heading back on her dog walk."

"So I assume Sugar found out if Stan had come home at that time on Wednesday?"

"She did. I got lost in the convolutions of the conversation at that point but it eventually came out that Stan's wife has been out of town for a few days, visiting a daughter, and Monica had a last-minute thought to invite Stan over for dinner that evening. But she didn't see his car in their driveway until eight."

"Which is when he must have come home from my party and Dirk Unger was either dead or dying."

"Correct."

"So there's a period of time—between five thirty and seven—when Stan could have gone over to Unger's place and planted the poison."

"Yes, unless he can prove he was elsewhere," Ralph said. "We did check with nearby restaurants but he hadn't stopped in any of them."

"That sounds awfully close to Zach's problem—not having an alibi."

"It does. But Monica also strengthened Yeager's motive. His wife, it seems, had told Monica that Stan suspected Dirk Unger had stolen some of his clients and he was furious about it."

Piper listened, aware of a sinking feeling as Ralph's report worsened things for Stan. She liked the Realtor, who had his quirks but had always seemed honest and well meaning. That didn't necessarily rule out the possibility of murder. She'd sadly come to realize that desperate circumstances could bring out a dark side in people. Piper thought of Uncle Frank's words, that it would be better to know the truth—

"Wait!" she said, suddenly thinking of something in Stan's favor. "What about the poison? Bloodroot. Stan isn't a nature person. How would he know about such a plant?"

"I don't know," Ralph admitted. "Except there are ways of finding out such things, Piper. Books, the Internet, asking an expert . . ."

Piper sighed. "You're right. It just seems too foreign for Stan, though, don't you think? If he wanted to kill Dirk Unger, an obscure poison like bloodroot doesn't seem like his first choice."

"Neither would bludgeoning or stabbing, I'd say. And I'm guessing Stan isn't particularly big on guns."

Piper shook her head. "I've heard him argue for more gun control, actually."

"So perhaps poisoning would be Yeager's most likely

choice. And choosing a poison that comes from a locally growing plant means no record of purchase, you know."

Piper nodded, though she still couldn't picture Stan tramping through the woods or being able to identify the right plant. She could see Zach doing that, however, which put her back exactly where she didn't want to be. She sighed again.

"You and Sugar have come up with good information, Ralph. Stan Yeager will stay high on our list of suspects for now." She told him about the argument Uncle Frank witnessed between Unger and Marguerite Lloyd. "Tammy Butterworth gave me a lead on what that argument might have been about." She explained about Aunt Judy's friends, the Fortneys. "I'll see what I can learn from them."

"Sounds good. We'll keep working on Stan," he said, folding his chair back up and leaning it against the wall. "Maybe we'll find something that will clear him," he added, and Piper smiled. Ralph had picked up on her reluctance to see her likable Realtor as a murderer.

"It'll be whoever it is," she said. "And I'll deal with it. The important thing is to prove it wasn't Zach, who we know it isn't."

"Amen to that." Ralph said, leading the way out to the front of the shop. "Nice cat," he said as he passed by Scott's papier-mâché gift, which Piper had thought was tucked inconspicuously among her canning supplies.

Apparently, the brightly colored creation was not as unnoticeable as she'd hoped. Would Will ask where it had come from? Should she offer the information before he asked? She'd promised herself to be open and honest with

Will but would her reporting a silly little gift from Scott be blowing its importance out of proportion? If it was truly unimportant, though, why had she started hiding it?

Good question, and one she promised herself to examine—soon.

# 13

~~~~~

Aunt Judy called with an invitation to dine that evening with the Fortneys.

"Corinne said she and Lou have reservations at A La Carte. She insisted they'd truly love for us to join them. Frank, too, of course, but Frank has a lodge meeting. What do you think?"

Piper was delighted with the opportunity to talk with the couple, so Aunt Judy said she'd pick Piper up at six forty-five. By six forty Piper had changed into a simple beige dress with a softly flaring skirt dressed up with a pretty necklace and heels. A La Carte, she'd learned early on, was not a "casual dining" spot. When she spotted her aunt's Equinox coming down the street, Piper grabbed a light coat and trotted down the stairs to meet it at the curb.

"Thanks for setting this up, Aunt Judy," Piper said as she climbed into the blue SUV, the color chosen by her aunt and the model by her uncle with his wife's safety in mind. So," she said, buckling up, "tell me about the Fortneys. Why did they move back to Cloverdale?"

"You look very nice," Aunt Judy said first with a smile, putting off Piper's question until she'd checked her mirrors and pulled forward. "Lou retired. He liked Chicago but Corinne had had her fill of big-city living. They both still have family and friends here so she convinced him to come back to Cloverdale." Aunt Judy slowed at an intersection and signaled for a right turn. "Lou likes to get his own way, for the most part, and Corinne is probably the only person who can sway him."

"What kind of work did he retire from?"

"A supervisor in some kind of manufacturing plant—I think. You can ask him about it if you want but it might get him going for quite a while. Just warning you."

Piper grinned. "I'm more interested in what they've been up to in Cloverdale than Chicago."

"Probably wisest to stay with that."

Aunt Judy turned onto A La Carte's street. It was lined with parked cars. "A busy night," she said, tsk-tsking, and crept ahead, catching a spot that a gray Impala was just vacating. "You'll probably have to listen to a lot of reminiscing by us old folks," she said as she cut her engine and pulled out her keys.

"That's fine," Piper said. "If it puts the Fortneys in a relaxed and confiding mood, they may be open to sharing a lot more by the time they catch up to the current times."

"And a little wine won't hurt, either," Aunt Judy added with twinkling eyes and a grin.

They walked the block to A La Carte and passed by its

hanging baskets, filled at that time of year with blue and
yellow pansies, then under its blue canopy to enter into
the reception area of the restaurant. Aunt Judy informed
the hostess that they were meeting with the Fortneys.

"Oh, yes," the young woman said, recognizing the
name. "They're already seated." She picked up two large
menus and led Piper and her aunt into the large dining area
made cozy with wood ceiling beams and a brick fireplace.
Piper was reminded of her first visit to the restaurant as
she began to wind her way between the white-cloth-topped
tables. Nate had been in danger of losing his performing
job then and Piper and Will had urged everyone they could
think of to come and show their support for the singer. It
had turned out to be a rousing good time—and a significant
boost to Piper and Will's budding relationship.

"Judy—over here!" A woman about Aunt Judy's age
called and waved to them, and Aunt Judy waved back.

A tall and imposing man rose as they approached, nap-
kin clutched in one hand, and Aunt Judy begged, "Lou,
please sit down." She introduced Piper to the two and they
took their seats in an exchange of greetings.

"Did your aunt tell you we've known each other since
kindergarten?" Corinne Fortney asked Piper. From a
distance, the woman's strikingly golden hair color and
stylish dress had subtracted at least ten years from her
presumed age and set her apart from Aunt Judy and her
other friends. But close up, Piper saw a grandmotherly
smile and warmth that matched her aunt's and explained
their long-lasting closeness.

Lou Fortney, on the other hand, with his serious
frown and somewhat overbearing manner, made any

rapport with Uncle Frank doubtful, and Piper wondered if the "lodge meeting" had been on her uncle's calendar or had popped up suddenly.

Corinne launched into a story that sent Piper's aunt into girlish giggles, which Piper found amusing, the story having to do with squirt guns sneaked into a high school classroom. Polite questions about Piper's pickling shop followed, and after everyone had studied their menus and ordered, Aunt Judy asked Lou how he was enjoying his retirement and return to Cloverdale.

"It's been interesting," he said, drawing a deep breath. He then commenced a detailed account of the sale of their home in Chicago and their search for the perfect place in Cloverdale, a story that included all the features Corinne wanted in a house, some he thought were unnecessary or that he'd insisted on, and what they eventually settled on.

Their food had arrived by the time he wound down, and as Lou fell silent for a moment in contemplation of his plate, Piper grabbed the chance to ask, "Was Stan Yeager your Realtor?"

Lou instantly scowled, and it was Corinne who answered. "We started with Mr. Yeager but we switched to—oh, there he is!" she said, her attention caught by movement near the entryway. "Look, Lou. There's Jeremy Porter now."

All three turned in that direction and Piper recognized Lydia Porter walking behind the hostess and ahead of a man who must have been Jeremy. Since Piper had only heard about Jeremy up to that point, she studied the man with interest.

Jeremy Porter was taller than his mother but below average for a man. His bearing, however, gave him a commanding air, enhanced by his well-tailored suit. Thick, dark hair framed even features and a squared jaw, and Piper could understand Sugar Heywood's attraction to the man beyond the career success that she'd so admired. A taller, somewhat gangly woman trailed behind the others.

"Who is that with the Porters?" Piper asked.

"That's the sister, Mallory," Corinne answered.

"Ah." Piper remembered Lydia mentioning her daughter. She watched as Jeremy's sister stumbled slightly in her efforts to keep up with the others. Mallory obviously had garnered whatever height genes were in the mix but had missed out on much of the poise and bearing. She was very well dressed, however, though Piper thought the style of the expensive-looking suit she wore leaned more toward Lydia's generation than Mallory's.

As the trio were seated several tables away from the Fortneys, Corinne said, "Don't they all look nice. I always think it's a good sign of a man's character when he treats his mother well, don't you? Bringing her and his sister to Cloverdale to live with him surely was a generous thing to do."

From what Sugar had told Piper, the idea had been mostly Lydia's, but she simply nodded. "You said you switched from Stan Yeager's agency to Porter's. Were you unhappy with Stan?" she asked.

"Well, after what Mr. Unger told us about him . . ." Corinne said, turning back to her food and poking a fork into her garden salad.

"What in the world could he have said against Stan?" Aunt Judy asked, sounding shocked. "I've known only good things about him."

Corinne hesitated, as if unwilling to upset her friend further, but Lou Fortney obviously had no such reservations. "Unger warned us that Yeager had several complaints being looked into by the Realtors' Code of Ethics board."

"What!" Aunt Judy's fork clattered to her plate. "I can't believe that."

"It's true," Corinne said. "Mr. Unger showed us a printout of the complaints."

"No way were we going to deal with someone like that," Lou said.

"Did he give you the printouts?" Piper asked and the twin head shakes were her answer. *Was Unger above faking such reports,* she wondered? It would be simple to churn such things out of a computer. Obviously, the Fortneys hadn't investigated further. How many other potential clients might Unger have pulled away from Stan Yeager in that way? She agreed with Aunt Judy that Stan's realty ethics were highly unlikely to have been compromised. He'd been conscientious to the letter when she'd dealt with him. No wonder Stan had looked so strained, if he'd been losing clients like that. Would he have known of the causes?

Corinne changed the subject to their food, raving over it, and Aunt Judy credited Amy, who likely had a part in its preparation. "Amy also helps Piper out part time," she said, which brought the conversation to pickling, a subject Piper was normally most happy to discuss. That night, however, she answered questions more perfunctorily, her thoughts still on Unger and Stan Yeager.

Their conversation stopped as Nate Purdy was introduced and stepped onto the small stage to begin his nightly performance. As he strummed his guitar to do a final tuning, Piper heard Aunt Judy explain Nate's relationship to the chef she'd just mentioned. Corinne's eyes danced at the tale of young romance but Lou simply huffed and returned to his roasted duck à l'orange. The women at the table, along with an obvious majority of the room's diners, greatly enjoyed Nate's music, which began with French folk songs and moved on to a variety of popular songs. Piper spotted Amy standing at the kitchen door, clearly never tired of listening to her boyfriend's music.

When Nate finished his set he rose to take a break, promising to be back in a few minutes. The waitress appeared with dessert and coffee and Aunt Judy asked the Fortneys about their landscaping plans. "I remember you were working on them with someone. Have you made any decisions?"

Corinne's face fell a bit. "We were talking with that lovely woman, Marguerite Lloyd. Lydia Porter recommended her to us. Ms. Lloyd is very knowledgeable, obviously, and she made perfectly wonderful suggestions."

Piper waited for the *but* . . .

"Would have cost too much," Lou said flatly. He shoved a forkful of apple pie into his mouth and glanced around, daring anyone to contradict him.

Corinne sighed. "It would have, I'm afraid. I didn't see it at first—it really was a wonderful plan and I was absolutely in love with it. But Mr. Unger pointed out the significant bite it would have made in our retirement savings and how we would be wiser to invest the money in something he recommended. He *is* an accountant—or was, I should say—so we respected his opinion."

Unger again, Piper thought.

"We can't be putting that kind of money into flowers," Lou said. "Have to think of the future. I should have seen that myself but Corinne was so happy with the idea . . ." Lou Fortney's face softened for the first time as he looked at his wife.

"No, we needed to be practical, Lou. Mr. Unger convinced me of that."

*That must have been what Marguerite Lloyd was so upset about in the TopValuFood parking lot,* Piper thought. She had known exactly what had changed the Fortneys' minds. *Why did he do it, though,* Piper wondered? Did Unger have something against Marguerite or did he simply delight in upsetting people's lives in general?

Corinne talked about what she might do herself for a little garden and the dinner gradually wound down. Bills settled, they gathered their things to leave. As the four wound their way toward the exit, Lydia Porter looked up and called, "Corinne!"

Corinne instantly veered over and the others followed, Lou looking impatient. But Piper was glad of the chance to check out Jeremy at close range.

"So you took my advice on this restaurant," Lydia said, looking smugly pleased.

"You were so right, Lydia. The food is wonderful!" Corinne said, gushing just a bit. *What was it about*

*Lydia,* Piper wondered, *that brought that reaction from some women?*

"Lovely to see you again," Lydia said, nodding to Piper and Aunt Judy. "May I present my son, Jeremy, and daughter, Mallory?"

Jeremy rose and extended his hand, seeming delighted to meet them, though in a polished, businesslike way. Mallory nodded and responded with something that was half greeting and half cough. She then pulled out a tissue and blew her nose.

"My condolences," Piper said, "on your employee, Mr. Unger."

"Yes, yes, thank you," Jeremy said. "Very sad."

He actually did look a bit sad, more so than his mother had at the shop. Piper was about to say more when Lydia broke in.

"Mallory absolutely loves your brandied cherries, Ms. Lamb. Don't you, Mallory?"

Jeremy's sister looked up, just a bit startled. Had Lydia kicked her under the table? "Hmm? Oh. Yes. Yes, they were good. You'll have to tell me how you make them."

Mallory looked the least likely of anyone Piper knew to try making her own preserves, but she smiled. "I'll be happy to if you'd like to stop in at the shop sometime."

Lou cleared his throat loudly at that point. "Shouldn't hold you all up from your dinner."

Corinne and Aunt Judy immediately agreed, as did Lydia.

"Yes," she said. "I'll be happy to finish and be gone before that *musician* reappears." The eye roll and dismissive sniff she added said everything about her opinion of Nate and his performance.

Piper saw Aunt Judy draw an indignant breath and gave her arm a *let it go* squeeze. Besides, the surprised look on Corinne's face probably said enough. There was a flurry of good nights, and Piper nudged her aunt away with Corinne and Lou following closely behind.

"How could anyone not appreciate Nate's musician-ship?" Aunt Judy huffed in the car after they'd waved their final good-byes to the Fortneys.

"Lydia should be more careful about voicing that opinion if she wants to stay in the good graces of most of Cloverdale," Piper said.

"She strikes me as someone who expects to impose her own opinion on the rest of the world." Aunt Judy turned her key in the ignition. "What a dislikable, pomp-ous woman! I surely hope she doesn't influence too many on that point."

"I wouldn't worry about it. Dirk Unger, on the other hand, definitely swayed Corinne and Lou's opinion on Stan Yeager and Marguerite Lloyd, didn't he?"

"Yes, and that was very surprising. He surely must be wrong about Stan. And as far as the landscaping goes, I'm reasonably sure that Corinne and Lou could have afforded most anything Marguerite designed. Corinne has talked about cruises they planned to go on and new furniture they were ordering—and she was never one to puff things up to sound grander than they were. Corinne had been so excited over her garden plans."

"And Lou looked like he genuinely hated to see her disappointed. How did Unger manage to change their minds?" Piper asked.

Aunt Judy shrugged her bewilderment. "Hypnotism?"

Piper smiled, though in a way it didn't seem so far-fetched. Cobras hypnotized their victims, didn't they? And Dirk Unger had been definitely snakelike, at least to Piper's mind. The question was, which of his victims had struck back with his or her own venom?

As Aunt Judy pulled away from the curb, Piper asked, "Can you tell me how to get to Marguerite Lloyd's green-house? I've decided to pay her a visit tomorrow."

# 14

After Piper got home, she turned on her laptop and did an online search for the Realtor's Code of Ethics, looking for any legitimate complaints that might have been made about Stan Yeager. She discovered that complaints were not made public but were handled privately, first by a grievance committee, then by a board. She didn't know if Dirk Unger had access to such information—possibly through Jeremy—but she highly doubted that any such valid complaints existed, especially multiple ones, as Corinne had claimed. Stan Yeager surely would not remain a licensed Realtor if that were the case, and she'd seen his framed certification on his office wall.

While she was online, Piper searched Marguerite Lloyd's name and was led to her greenhouse website. A basic site with photos of flowers and landscaping ideas, it gave Lloyd's professional background, which included time spent working in Springfield, Ohio. That was interesting, since Tammy had said Dirk Unger started out in Ohio before joining Jeremy Porter. Of course, Ohio was a big state, but it was a connection, and the only one between the two that Piper had found so far.

What could she learn by talking to the woman? She wasn't sure, but Piper thought of one person who might help her break the ice. She grabbed her phone.

"Will," she said when the familiar baritone voice answered the call. "Feel like taking a break tomorrow?"

"Sure," Will said, sounding pleasantly surprised, then more cautiously asked, "What's up?"

"Just covering all the bases," Piper assured him. She told him about all she'd learned lately concerning the Dirk Unger murder—which sounded depressingly meager as she spelled it out.

"Do you know much about Marguerite Lloyd?" she asked.

"'Fraid not. I've passed by her place, of course, but never had a reason to stop in. The only time I met her was when I pulled her car out of the ditch."

"Hopefully she'll still feel grateful enough to chat a good long while, and ideally about things connected to Dirk Unger."

"So I'm to be your shill?"

Piper grinned, hearing the dry humor behind the question. "Nothing underhanded. Simply a friendly discussion."

"Uh-huh. What time do you want this interroga—um, friendly discussion—to take place?"

"One o'clock works for me."

When Will agreed that that worked for him, too, Piper said she'd swing by his place at that time. As she ended the call, she hoped Marguerite Lloyd would be a major breakthrough in her efforts to save Zach from a murder charge. Stan Yeager was looking more and more likely as a substitute candidate, and she hated that. Ms. Lloyd, however, was unknown to her, which allowed Piper to put her in that position much more comfortably.

She went to bed with high hopes, though her sleep that night became restless as familiar faces peered at her through prison bars. Will? Uncle Frank!

In the morning she blamed her odd dreams on the rich meal and wine of the evening before.

At precisely one o'clock the following day, Piper turned into the driveway marked by the familiar sign: "Burchett Tree Farm and Christmas Shop." As she followed the graveled drive between rows of lush evergreen trees of varying sizes, she thought of her first visit there when Will had given her a private tour of the place. She'd learned more that evening than she'd ever dreamed there was to know about Christmas trees and their care and feeding. What impressed her most at the time, though, was Will's obvious excitement over his place. It was a longtime dream that he'd studied and saved for, the realization of a goal reached on a very direct path. It was a special person, she felt, who was able to do that, and within a minute that special person came into her view as she neared the parking area.

"How about I drive," Will called, crunching over the stones toward her as she slowed to a stop.

Since Will knew the way better, that made sense, so Piper climbed out, waving to Tomas, Will's new employee, whose tractor pulled a trailer full of equipment toward the fields.

"How are things going with the farm?" she asked as she and Will headed for his green van.

"Pretty well. The rainy spring has been good for the trees. For the weeds, too. But Tomas has been working hard to keep them under control."

Piper loved the year-round Christmas-y scent that filled Will's acres and she breathed in deeply before climbing into the van. "My tree is thriving, too," she said, referring to the potted spruce tree Will had surprised her with the previous August, which had decorated the sidewalk near her front door ever since. Thinking of that gift reminded her of her latest one—the papier-mâché cat from Scott. When Will started his van and shifted into gear, she drew a second deep breath and said, "I have something to confess."

Will glanced at her, then back at his rearview mirror as he executed a neat Y turn. "You poisoned Dirk Unger?"

"Nothing that drastic." Piper smiled. "Scott picked up something at the antique shop over on Maple Street. For me. And I accepted it." She saw Will's brows jiggle and his lips purse as he considered that. Piper pushed on, describing the ornamental cat and giving the story behind it. "He guaranteed no strings attached and that's how I took it."

Piper waited as Will drove silently on. He came to the end of his driveway and stopped, checking for traffic. Instead of pulling out, though, he looked over at her.

"It sounds like Scott wanted to make amends for an action he regretted."

Piper nodded.

"Very decent of him."

"Mmm-hmm. Does it bother you very much? I mean, about me keeping it?"

Will looked back at the road and pressed on his gas pedal, pulling out in a smooth, steady way, then said, "As long as you don't set the thing next to my spruce tree." Piper smiled. "On the other hand, it's papier-mâché. Maybe a good rain would melt it? What do you think?"

"I think that would be a shame. For the artist who created it, that is."

"Ah, yes, the artist. Not that he'd know, of course." Will reached for Piper's hand and squeezed it. "I appreciate your mentioning it, I really do. I'm not crazy about your former fiancé bringing you gifts but I'm not about to rant and rave or sulk or do other stupid stuff. You're with me now and that's what I care about the most."

Piper squeezed his hand back and added her second one on top for good measure before letting go so he could steer properly. Her heartbeat had picked up a bit and she was happy to say nothing for a while as she watched the green countryside fly by.

"Marguerite Lloyd's place is down that way," Will said, breaking their comfortable silence and pointing to a side road to the right.

Piper nodded and quickly reorganized her thoughts. She still hadn't figured out what to say to Lloyd. How could she learn what she needed from the woman?

"I thought maybe I'd buy a plant or a bouquet for Aunt Judy," she said. "I can't pretend I need landscaping."

"Me neither." Will navigated the turn and followed the narrow road. "Could you be writing up something about the place for the women's group your aunt belongs to?"

"The Cloverdale Women's Club? That's a great idea! Aunt Judy's always mentioning one thing or another that she's read in their newsletter. I'm not a member. But if I happened to join soon, who's to say they wouldn't appreciate a nice article like that?"

"I'm sure they'd love it."

"You're a genius, Will Burchett," Piper said and leaned over to plant a kiss on his cheek, causing the van to waver briefly over the yellow line.

"That's what they all say," Will said, grinning as he straightened his wheel. A sign announcing "Lloyd's Landscaping" came into view and he slowed for the entrance.

A short, paved driveway brought them to a wide parking area in front of a greenhouse. Piper noticed a few broken windows in the greenhouse patched with wood, though the tables of blooming seedlings inside looked fresh and healthy. A worker dragged a watering hose between long rows of potted shrubs outside, while another unloaded bags of mulch from a truck onto a small mountain of additional bags. A scattering of customers browsed through the greenhouse and Piper took a step toward it after climbing from the van until Will called her attention to a structure on the right. "That looks like an office. Why don't we check there?"

They walked over to a trailer perched on cinder-block

stilts. Portable stairs led to a center door that had been propped open. Will trotted up the stairs and leaned in.

"Hey there, Ms. Lloyd. How're you doing?" He waved to Piper to come on up.

"Will Burchett! Great to see you again."

Piper joined Will in the narrow trailer to see a slim woman in her fifties getting to her feet behind a paper-strewn desk, her steel gray hair pulled back into a pony-tail. If Piper had run into her on the grounds, she might have taken her for one of the employees rather than the owner, dressed as she was in jeans and a T-shirt topped with a loose, rolled-sleeve shirt. The firm set of her jaw, however, along with a look that spoke of dozens of thoughts being juggled, signaled "boss." Marguerite Lloyd squeezed around her desk to give Will a welcom-ing hug that included a few robust back slaps.

"This man was my rescuer," she said, turning to Piper as she held Will by the shoulders. "There I was, stuck in a ditch with no working cell phone, thinking I was in a ton of trouble, when he suddenly appeared around the bend like a guardian angel and pulled me out."

"Just happened to be in the right place at the right time. Ms. Lloyd, this is Piper Lamb. She'd like to write up something about your nursery for the Cloverdale Women's Club."

Marguerite Lloyd gave Piper a speculative look, then grinned and held out her hand. "Nice to meet you, Piper." She gave her hand a solid shake. "I thought I'd met all the women in that club. You must be a newcomer."

"My aunt Judy has been a member for years," Piper said, skipping over the fact of her own nonmembership.

"Lamb! Right. Judy Lamb. So you're her niece? I heard somebody connected to her had moved into town. Sure, if you want to give my place a little publicity, I'm all for it! What do you want to know?"

The phone on the desk rang and Marguerite Lloyd reached for it. Piper scrabbled through her purse for the small notebook she usually kept there, along with a pen. Marguerite rattled off a few plant names into the phone, then said, "Send Patty over to handle the phone here. I'm going to be busy for a few minutes." She hung up and turned back to Piper. "This is your first time here, right? Let's take a look around the grounds while we talk."

They tramped noisily down the metal steps, Marguerite quickly taking the lead and chattering away, giving Piper answers to questions she hadn't yet thought to ask. "Bought this place ten years ago," she said. "From old Seth Higgins. Guess you didn't know him—way before your time. He handled it mostly as an offshoot of his farm. I expanded things a lot after I took over." She ran through details of the inventory she'd added, the landscaping services she offered, and the number of employees she'd eventually hired.

Piper scribbled in her notebook as Marguerite walked them through the greenhouse and out into the field of potted shrubs, talking steadily the whole time. When she paused at one point for a breath, Piper interjected, "Would you say your landscaping service is the major part of your business or the garden supplies?"

"Landscape design is my passion." Marguerite's eyes flashed in confirmation. "I like to concentrate on that."

"Your website says you got started in Springfield, Ohio."

"You've done your homework," Marguerite said, pleased. "Yup, that's where I learned a lot of what I know about this business. The rest came just by doing."

She chattered on about the approach she took to her landscape design, which was to incorporate as many indigenous plants as possible. "Some clients get fancy ideas from magazines about what they want and I have to explain to them why certain plants just won't work here. You have to consider the soil and the temperatures. Some plants will survive but only with nonstop watering or winter wind protection. Do they really want to get into all that, I ask? Usually they'll have second thoughts and change their minds."

"One of my aunt's friends, Corinne Fortney, was talking about landscaping her property," Piper threw out casually, as she wrote in her notebook. "Last I heard, her plans were on hold. Was she someone who wanted the wrong plants?" Piper looked up to catch Marguerite's reaction.

The landscaper's face darkened. "You'll have to ask Mrs. Fortney about that." A worker was unloading trays of seedlings onto a nearby table when one was accidentally knocked to the ground. "Watch what you're doing!" Marguerite snapped, causing the woman to look up, red-faced, then scramble to rescue the fallen seedlings.

"I just can't abide carelessness," Marguerite grumbled to Piper as they continued on.

"You moved here from Springfield, Ohio?" Will said, jumping in. "I remember hearing that Dirk Unger, the guy who worked for the Porter group, came from there. Did you happen to know him?"

Piper held her breath, sure that the answer would be a resounding no, no matter what the truth might be. To her surprise, Marguerite growled, "Dirk Unger! That slimy, scheming, two-faced . . ." She stopped to collect herself. "Yes, I knew him and hoped never to run across him again. Then he popped up here in Cloverdale! I—"

At that moment a second employee ran up from behind with news of a problem—an apparent mix-up on an order. Piper felt he probably would have waited on it if he'd been aware of Marguerite's current mood. "For God's sake!" she exploded at the hapless young man, who jumped two steps back. "Can't I rely on a simple, blasted thing—?" She glanced at Piper and stopped to draw a deep breath, hands on hips.

"I can't talk anymore," she said to her. "Come back tomorrow if you need more for your story." Marguerite began to stalk away, then turned to order, "Don't come. Call. After six."

Piper and Will stared as Marguerite charged toward the greenhouse, her employee following a safe eight or ten feet behind.

After a moment, Will asked, "Think you'll call?"

Piper stared at the doorway Marguerite had just stormed through. "Maybe I'll just e-mail. Or text."

Will nodded.

"Good choice," he said.

# 15

<hr />

Piper and Will had returned to the parking lot and were heading toward his van when Piper caught sight of a familiar figure walking toward them.

"Hello there!" Emma Leahy called out, looking for once appropriately dressed in her usual grass-stained clothing. "What brings you two here? Planning to grow something more than Christmas trees, Will?"

"Not for now," Will said.

Piper hesitated about what to share until she remembered how helpful Emma had been when dill farmer Gerald Standley had been under suspicion of murder. Where, though, would Emma's loyalties fall in this case? With Sugar Heywood and her son, Zach, whom she might know only in passing, or with the owner of a business that occupied an important chunk of Emma's life? There was one way to find out.

"We're here because of Zach Heywood. Did you know he's become a suspect in Dirk Unger's murder?"

"No! Why on earth?"

Piper ran through Sheriff Carlyle's reasons for focusing on Zach. "Those of us who know him can't believe Zach is guilty, but it's looking bad for him. We need to discover who's really responsible for the murder and soon. Sugar is frantic."

"I'm sure! But, but . . . you're looking *here*?"

Piper explained why Marguerite Lloyd could have a motive. "During the brief time we spent with her today, her bitterness toward Unger was clear. You know her better. Would you say she's capable of acting on it?"

"Oh! My." Emma stared for a while, considering the question. Piper understood the delay. Who, after all, easily moves a person they've known for years from their comfortable Master Gardener slot to that of possible murderer? She watched as Emma's expression slowly changed from stunned to analytical.

"Marguerite does have an awful temper," she said, to which both Will and Piper easily agreed. "And it doesn't cool down in any kind of hurry, from what I've seen. I've known her to banish a customer for life when one of his kids accidentally tipped over the water garden display. It did make a terrible mess, but still . . ."

"That's the kind of aggravation that good business-people learn to deal with," Will said. "And in a way that doesn't lose them customers."

Emma nodded. "Marguerite probably hurt herself more that day than the accident had cost her. She's had other, bigger losses lately, too, ones that were out of her control. Storm damage, for one. See those broken panes on her greenhouse? That's one of the more visible signs, and something I would think she'd have fixed right away if she could afford it. But with the recent slump in the economy, her kind of business suffers. Gardens are considered by some to be a luxury," Emma said with a look that signaled that definitely wasn't the case with her. "If money gets tight, flowers get dropped from many a budget."

"Which is probably why she was so upset with Dirk Unger when he derailed her landscaping prospect with the Fortneys," Piper said, glancing at Will. "It could have been desperately important to her, financially."

"I could see her becoming mad enough over that to consider murder," Emma said. "Maybe," she qualified.

"Being a plant person, she'd know about bloodroot," Piper pointed out.

Emma agreed. "But with Marguerite's temper, I guess I'd expect her to do something like whack Unger over the head with a shovel right away, not wait for an opportune time to poison him."

"She might have a temper," Will said. "But she's not stupid. She wouldn't want to end up weeding prison gardens for the rest of her life because of a man like Unger."

Both Emma and Piper nodded thoughtfully at that, Piper picturing Marguerite Lloyd carefully harvesting bloodroot from the woods and chopping it up to blend unnoticeably into a salad. Would that have given her satisfaction enough to rein in a preference for immediate action? At this point, Piper didn't know.

Piper thanked Emma for her helpful input, and she and Will took off. During the drive back to the Christmas tree farm, they tossed around the pros and cons of Marguerite being a serious suspect, ending up with agreeing to keep her, for the time being, as a "maybe" until more information turned up.

"Thanks for coming with me," Piper said as she switched to her own car at Will's. "I hope you don't feel it was a big waste of time for you."

Will leaned into her open driver's-side window to give her a lingering kiss. "Actually, I was considering stirring up a few innocent people as suspects, just so we could do this more often."

Piper grinned. "I'm sure we can come up with better reasons to get together than that." When Will looked inclined to lean down again, she quickly turned her ignition. "After business hours," she said, laughing, and put her car into gear. She waved at Will's disappearing reflection in her rearview mirror as she drove down his driveway.

Back at her shop, Piper found Gil Williams talking with Amy. He brightened at the sight of her but still looked serious.

"I was just telling Amy what I learned from one of my customers," the bookseller said.

"I have a feeling it's not good," Piper said, slipping off the light jacket she'd worn to Marguerite Lloyd's place.

"Well, it definitely won't help Zach with the situation he's in." Gil sighed and ran a hand through his white hair, mussing it more than it had been to start. "Zach, it seems, has a history of violence."

"Uh-oh."

"An altercation took place this past winter at his college. I don't know the details—my customer's daughter is at the same school, which is how he learned about it—but it's likely on the boy's record."

"Maybe it wasn't his fault," Amy said. "Maybe he was simply in the wrong place at the wrong time and got pulled into the middle of something."

"And maybe we should ask Zach about it," Piper said. "Whatever happened, though, I agree, Gil. If it's on his record it'll be one more strike against Zach for the sheriff."

"Oh, shoot!" Amy said. "I'd say I'd talk to Daddy about it, but I can't, really. I mean, I can try, but I won't get anywhere."

"Let's find out exactly what happened first," Piper said. "I'll get in touch with Zach."

"Good," Gil said. "Sorry to be the bearer of such news but I thought you should know. I'd better get back to my shop."

He took off and Piper placed a call to Zach Heywood's cell phone. It went to voice mail so she left a brief message asking him to call back. Customers walked in as she disconnected so she put concerns about Zach on hold as she returned to her world of pickling and preserving, a place that was much more predictable and to which she could more usually count on having all the answers.

By closing time, Piper still hadn't heard back from Zach, so she called Sugar to see if he was at home. He wasn't, and Piper asked Sugar to tell him to get in touch without explaining why. She wanted to hear Zach's explanation of the "altercation" directly from him, not from Sugar—assuming she knew about it. If she didn't, Piper would insist to Zach that he tell his mother immediately, before she heard about it from someone else— like the sheriff.

Piper was on the verge of locking up when she saw Scott's Volvo pull up to the curb. What now? She watched closely as he climbed out but spotted no suspicious-looking package. Perhaps he had something to share about Zach's case.

"Hi," Scott said as he walked in. "I wasn't sure you'd still be here." He looked tired, minus his jacket and tie and with the sleeves of his rumpled white shirt rolled up untidily.

"One more minute and I wouldn't have been. Hard day?"

Scott shook his head. "Just filled with tedious, time-consuming details. Part of the job description. Lunch, unfortunately, got lost in the muddle, so I'm starved. I was heading for a quick dinner when I saw your store lights still on. You know how I hate dining alone. Can I talk you into joining me?"

Piper was on the verge of declining. She had no plans

and Will had already told her he would be busy with work that evening, but— Her phone rang. She quickly checked the display. It was Zach.

"Zach!" she said, excited to finally hear from him.

"We need to talk. Where are you now?"

"I just left the library."

Piper thought fast. Scott should hear what Zach had to say, too. "Head over to Niki's," she said, referring to a small restaurant within walking distance of the library. "I'll meet you there in a few minutes with Scott Littleton."

Scott's eyebrows shot up and he suddenly looked a lot less tired.

Zach agreed and Piper disconnected, then turned Scott toward the door. "Give me a minute to close up," she said. "I'll explain all on the way over."

Niki's was a small, family-run restaurant that offered great Mediterranean-style food in a casual setting. It was usually crowded and noisy, which was perfect, Piper felt, since Zach needed to be able to talk freely without fear of being overheard. A few bites of good food couldn't hurt, either, as far as loosening him up. When Scott pulled into a spot across the street from Niki's, they saw Zach waiting near the door, hands in pockets and shifting his weight uneasily.

Scott sighed. "Why do clients think it's okay to keep things from their lawyers?"

"Wait till you hear the whole story," Piper said, opening her door.

"Right. That's what Ted Bundy said."

Piper rolled her eyes and climbed out.

A young hostess met them near the door and Scott requested the empty table at the back. When their waitress appeared with water, they ordered quickly, Zach hesitating until Scott said, "My treat." Piper waited until the sandwich and wrap platters arrived, then asked Zach to explain what had happened at college to put a black mark on his record.

"But," Scott cautioned, "realize what you say right now won't be considered confidential, okay?"

"Okay. But the whole thing was one stupid mistake," he said, before biting a significant chunk out of his gyro.

"Just start at the beginning," Scott said when Zach reached for his Coke and took a gulp. Zach nodded.

"We were at a basketball game, in the stands. My buddy Tom and me. The game was winding down and it was pretty clear we were going to lose, so people were talking to each other instead of watching. These jerks in back of us had been making a lot of noise the whole time, trying to top each other with lame jokes and trash talk. For some reason they started going on about a girl I know from chem class. Missy. She's my lab partner, a great girl, and she didn't deserve any of what they were saying. After putting up with it for a while, I turned around and asked them to cut it out."

"How did they react?" Piper asked.

"Like the goofballs they were. Plus I think they'd been drinking. I should have known and saved my breath 'cause they thought it was hilarious to ramp it up even more. And louder."

Piper could see the anger in Zach's eyes as the scene ran through his head.

"At that point I should have just got out of there. Tom wanted to split. I don't know what I thought I was going to accomplish by getting into an argument. Missy wasn't a girlfriend, you know? But she was a girl I thought needed standing up for. I mean, what if all that got back to her? How would she feel?"

"So how did the fight start?" Scott asked.

Zach shook his head helplessly. "I don't even know. Somebody's soda got knocked over somebody else's pants. I swear it wasn't me that did it. Plenty of yells and pushes. Punches thrown and pretty soon it's one big brawl. Security runs over and before I know it Tom and me are under arrest."

"What about the others?" Scott asked.

"A couple of them were grabbed, too. The rest scattered. I felt really bad about Tom. None of it was his fault."

"Any injuries?"

"Cuts and bruises. Somebody twisted an ankle."

Scott nodded. "So you were arrested. What was the charge?"

"Assault. Second degree. It was all wrong but there was nothing I could do about it. I just wanted it over with, so I pleaded guilty. Got a sentence they called probation before judgment. That meant I could go right back to school."

Scott nodded. "PBJ is not classified as a conviction, so you got off lightly, but it does go on your record.

Zach looked from Scott to Piper and back. "I thought

that was the end of it. I never told my mom. How did you find out?"

"You're not the only person from Cloverdale who goes to that school," Piper said. "It might not have ever been mentioned but people are more aware of you now. You should tell your mother, or someone else will."

Zach winced but nodded. "I wish I'd never come home for spring break."

Piper wished he'd never gone to that basketball game, either, but such thoughts were just wasted energy. Though Zach's explanation, that he'd been standing up for a friend, was better than if he'd been out for some sort of revenge, the fact remained that he had an arrest for violence resulting in bodily harm on his record. She didn't know precisely how that was going to affect his situation, but it couldn't be good.

They finished up at Niki's and Scott told Zach to show up at his office with Sugar on Monday. He promised to do so and hitched up his backpack to walk glumly off. Piper was stepping into Scott's Volvo when her cell phone signaled a text message. It was from Will. She waited until Scott closed her door to read it.

"Work done. Bushed. Just saying hi + thinking of U. What R U up to?"

Scott got in on his side and she slipped the phone into her pocket. She buckled up and listened as Scott talked about Zach's statement, even discussed it with him at some length as he drove back to her place. Had Zach told the whole truth of the matter? They could only hope so.

But a large part of her mind lingered on Will's question and how she would answer it. He'd been great about the papier-mâché cat, saying all he cared about was that Piper was with him then. Now she was with Scott, had just shared a dinner with him. It was, of course, to talk to Zach. But here she sat with her ex-fiancé as Will waited to hear what she was up to. What could she say that wouldn't sound like excusing and overexplaining? How understanding could she expect the man to be?

# 16

~~~~

Piper checked herself in her bedroom mirror. She'd ruffled through her closet for half the morning, trying to decide what was appropriate to wear to Lydia Porter's tea. *Who goes to afternoon teas, anymore?* If it weren't for her efforts to clear Zach Heywood, Piper wouldn't. It was too nice a Sunday afternoon.

She didn't doubt Lydia would get a good turnout. Curiosity to see the inside of the Porters' redecorated mansion would draw many. A few, like Mrs. Tilley, might be impressed enough with Lydia to feel honored at the invitation. The rest, like Aunt Judy, would attend out of courtesy. Piper was showing up to learn what she could about Dirk Unger, though she expected to expend a pound of effort for any ounce of reward.

She adjusted the lacy shrug she'd slipped over a sleeveless, full-skirted cotton dress. Would that do for blending in properly while trying to dig up dirt—metaphorically speaking? Piper sighed and grabbed her purse to make her high-heeled-careful way down the stairs, hoping the food would at least be good. That brought thoughts of Sugar Heywood, who *should* have catered the event, causing Piper to double her determination to make the most of the afternoon.

Piper thought about Will during her drive to the tea. She'd tried to reach him the night before after Scott dropped her off. But apparently Will's claim of being bushed was accurate, as her call had gone to voice mail. She intended to try again after the tea, when she might have more to talk about besides what she'd been up to the previous evening.

Piper turned onto the Porters' street and saw she wasn't the first to arrive. Cars lined both sides of the wide, tree-lined avenue and women in their spring finery ambled in pairs or groups toward the mansion. Piper parked and joined the parade, admiring the Victorian-era house up ahead. A Queen Anne style, she guessed, with multiple turrets and dormers jutting from the upper floors. The wraparound veranda made Piper salivate, picturing herself sipping lemonade in one of its green-painted rocking chairs on a warm summer evening—preferably minus the current owners. Wide stairs led up to that veranda, and she climbed them to reach the double front doors, trimmed with beautiful stained glass.

A young woman dressed in a black uniform and white frilled apron and cap, looking as though she'd stepped straight out of a 1940s film, invited guests into the grand foyer. Piper entered and joined many others in gaping about shamelessly. The foyer's gleaming oak paneling, graceful staircase, and muraled ceiling offered much to swoon over, though a second uniformed maid did her best to move everyone along to the huge dining room at the left of the foyer, relieving guests of the few wraps that had been worn on that mild day.

Lydia Porter stood just inside the opened pocket doors of the dining room, draped in flowing lavender silk and pearls, her silver hair coiffed and sprayed into immobility. Mallory occupied the space beside her, and she towered several inches over her petite mother despite low-heeled shoes but possessed little of her mother's bearing and poise. Her expensive-looking cotton dress could have been draped on a headless mannequin for all the presence she projected. She was, however, dutifully greeting each guest passed on to her by Lydia, in between coughs and sniffs.

"Miss Lamb." Lydia addressed Piper at her turn, smiling. "I'm delighted you could join us."

"Piper, please," Piper said politely, adding something about her pleasure over being there, which she hoped sounded sincere.

"I'm sure you and Mallory will have lots to talk about," Lydia said, smoothly moving her along to her daughter, who gave Piper a weak smile and a limp handshake. What Lydia imagined they could have in common Piper had no idea, but she returned the smile, came up with more appropriate things to say, and got out of the way of the next guest.

Funneled toward a beautiful extended mahogany dining table, she was in turn handed a delicate china cup of

tea by yet another uniformed woman, asked if she pre-
ferred sugar or lemon, and waved on to choose any of
an amazing selection of cookies, pastries, and tea sandwiches. Properly and efficiently dealt with, she was then
left to her own devices to wander about, sip, or visit.

She chose to explore for the moment, not having yet
come across familiar faces and interested in investigat-
ing the rooms that had been made available. She crossed
the hallway to a large living room, its walls painted a
dusty red brightened with white trim. The room was
filled with chatting women perched on new-looking
Victorian-style sofas and chairs or standing about on
the polished oak floor or oriental area rug. Piper wound
her way through, admiring an occasional table or mirror
that might have been genuine antiques, and came to a
second, smaller sitting room, just as attractive and just
as crowded.

She strolled back into the hall and, heels clicking on
the wood floor, followed it down to a library, which
reminded her of the unpleasant experience Ralph Strawbridge had with Dirk Unger when he'd been asked to
refurbish the built-in shelves there. From the looks of
them, Jeremy Porter hadn't found a replacement craftsman, as the shelves, though dotted with books and small
statuary, looked dull and worn. That, and the darkness
produced by too-heavy draperies, hadn't inspired any
guests to linger despite the scattering of chairs, and Piper
was about to leave when a voice out of the gloom startled her.

"Sad, isn't it?"

Piper peered more closely and saw a thin woman

sitting in the shadows at the far end of the room. The woman stretched her hand toward a lamp beside her and switched it on. "Come, sit with me a moment."

Curious, Piper moved forward, noting as she did that the woman appeared to be in her late seventies. Her navy blue dress with a white lacy collar looked more funeral-appropriate than tea party, as did her subdued, slightly sad manner.

"Frances Billings," she said, holding out a thin, age-spotted hand.

"How do you do," Piper said, taking the hand and introducing herself.

"I'm afraid I startled you, speaking out as I did," Ms. Billings said. "It's just that your expression seemed to mirror my own thoughts. You see, I used to own this place."

"Oh!" Piper scoured her memory but couldn't find *Frances Billings* anywhere in it. Wouldn't Aunt Judy have known and mentioned her?

"I haven't lived in it for many years," Ms. Billings said, as though reading Piper's mind. "Warmer climates, I find, are better for my health. But the house was in my family for many years. It was built by my grandfather in 1880."

"It's a beautiful house," Piper said.

"Yes." Frances Billings glanced around with wistful eyes. "And this was my favorite room when I was a child. But it requires much upkeep, as you can see. I had hoped to find these lovely shelves restored to their original glory, but the library seems to have been put on low priority. That, and the kitchen."

"I haven't seen the kitchen but if this were my house, that would have been my first project." Piper explained her love of pickling and preserving. "This library would have been a close second. The man who made a beautiful new door for my pickling shop was approached about refurbishing this room. Unfortunately for the Porters, they delegated Dirk Unger to oversee the project and Ralph couldn't see himself answering to the man."

"Unger!" Ms. Billings shuddered. "Horrible man. If I'd known he would be as involved with the house as he was, I might have reconsidered selling, even with my limited choices."

"He seems to have been universally disliked. Except," Piper corrected herself, "by Jeremy Porter."

"Yes, well, I noticed that Unger could be affable enough when it was to his advantage. And indispensable. Even Lydia, with her obvious distaste for the man, found him occasionally useful." Ms. Billings waved toward the bookshelves. "Those books? They weren't collected by the Porters. Dirk Unger had them carted in to fill these shelves, to make the room more library-like."

"So they didn't come with the house?"

"Oh, no. I had to sell my family's fine books long ago, along with most of the furniture, though I managed to keep a few things for the memories. No, Dirk Unger, I was told, snapped these up for a song at some estate sale. Whatever he paid was too much. A lot of rubbish, in my opinion. But then I doubt Lydia looked too closely."

Piper got up to take a look. There were quite a few clothbound books that at first glance appeared old and impressive. Few of the titles or authors, however, were familiar. The newer ones appeared to be book club editions of celebrity tell-alls or flash-in-the-pan bestsellers. Sorting also seemed to have been according to size and color. Piper found *Airport* next to a book on photography, and several *National Geographics* lined up beside *Know Your Digestive System*. Her gaze stopped at a tome titled *Healing Plants*, and she slid the slim paperback out. A quick check of the index found no listing for bloodroot. She returned the book to its slot.

"Definitely an odd mix," Piper said, "which looks a lot more interesting from a distance than close up."

"Much like some people," Ms. Billings said with a small smile. "Speaking of which, I suppose I should go back and do my duties as a guest." The older woman struggled a bit to pull herself up, and Piper went over to lend a hand. "Thank you, dear. It was good talking to you. I'll be fine now." To prove it, she walked steadily out into the hallway.

Piper watched from the doorway until the woman turned into the dining room, then headed back to the living room, where she ran into Mrs. Tilley.

"Piper!" Mrs. Tilley cried, setting her cup carefully back into its delicate saucer. "Isn't this the most elegant event you've ever been to?"

Piper could see that Mrs. Tilley, whose cheeks were glowing and eyes shining, thought so. "There's certainly a lot to admire," she said.

Mrs. Tilley's head bobbed. "The house! The food! Although"—she lowered her voice—"I have to admit that

Sugar Heywood's pastries are better. What a shame she wasn't available."

*Yes, wasn't it*, Piper thought.

Another woman, possibly late fifties and wearing a cream-colored silk suit, had strolled over to them, looking as pleased as Mrs. Tilley but in a more muted way. She took a sip of her tea and nodded approvingly. "Perfectly brewed," she pronounced. "Leona Pennington," she said to Piper, holding out a well-manicured hand. "I believe you're Judy Lamb's niece?"

"Yes, Piper Lamb," Piper said, shaking the hand. "And you're the president of the Cloverdale Women's Club, aren't you?" She managed to smile as she said it, though her thoughts flew back to Leona's cold treatment of Denise Standley a few months ago when the Standley family needed all the support they could get.

"I didn't realize you two hadn't met," Mrs. Tilley said. "You should come to one of our meetings, Piper. And Leona, you have to stop in at Piper's shop. She puts up the most wonderful pickles and preserves."

"I have a very delicate stomach, I'm afraid," Leona said. "But do come to our meetings with your aunt, Piper. We could use some young blood." She laughed lightly, her gaze flicking toward Mrs. Tilley as though to indicate it was their companion and not herself who qualified as aged. Leona Pennington, in Piper's opinion, wasn't that far behind, and Piper didn't much like her condescension toward sweet Mrs. Tilley. She was thinking that her own stomach might be too delicate to join any club that Leona Pennington ran, when a voice rang out from Piper's left.

"Aha! Ms. Lamb. How's that article for the women's club coming?"

Piper turned to see Marguerite Lloyd, wearing a long-skirted outfit that afternoon, though she'd stayed with the no-fuss ponytail. Piper stifled a gulp.

"Oh? What's this about?" Leona immediately asked.

"Piper, here, was out to my place getting info for your newsletter. You didn't know about it?" Her eyes narrowed as she looked back at Piper.

"It was a last-minute idea," Piper quickly explained. "I thought club members would enjoy learning more about Marguerite's gardening and landscaping business."

"Excellent!" Leona said. "Send it to me by Wednesday so I can edit it in time for our next newsletter. I'm delighted you'll be joining us."

"Well, I—"

"She should send it to *me*." Emma Leahy came up behind Piper, startling her, and in more ways than one. "I'm in charge of the club's newsletter and I handle all the editing. I doubt Piper's stuff will need much but we'll see."

Besides her interruption, seeing Emma in an actual dress had put Piper at a momentary loss for words. Did Emma Leahy have a life beyond gardening for which she possessed up-to-date, feminine clothing? The thought boggled Piper's mind.

"Of course," Leona said, smiling smoothly at Emma, referring to her newsletter editorship.

Marguerite continued to study Piper closely. "What were—?" she began, but Emma stepped in again.

"I saw Judy out in the garden," she said to Piper. "She was wondering if you were here."

"I'll go find her," Piper said and excused herself quickly to step away, letting out her breath once she'd exited the room. If her aunt was truly in the garden and Emma hadn't simply thrown that out as a means of rescue, Piper was very glad. She felt in need of fresh air and a welcoming face.

Piper found the door leading to the backyard and stepped out into mild air and brilliant sunshine. After a moment's blinking, she scanned several strolling women, their tea dresses adding as much color to the garden area as the flowers, and in the midst of them was Aunt Judy. Piper headed on over.

"Oh, there you are," Aunt Judy said, catching sight of her from her spot next to Corinne Fortney. "You look very nice. I hope you're enjoying yourself?"

"I am now," Piper said, giving her aunt a quick peck on the cheek and a cheery greeting to Corinne. "I just broke away from Leona Pennington."

Aunt Judy gave Piper a knowing smile. "I've warned Corinne about Leona, since she plans to join the club. And maybe," she added with a twinkle, "I can talk her into running for club president when Leona's term expires."

Corinne laughed. "One step at a time, Judy, dear. Let me at least learn the way to the club's meeting room before I try to take over its leadership." She finished off the sugar-dusted cookie she'd been holding and licked her fingers.

"I met an interesting woman in the library," Piper

said. "Frances Billings. She said she had owned this house."

"Frances is here?" Aunt Judy said, her eyes widening. "You know her?"

"I *knew* her. She was somewhat older, though, and it's been years. Frankly, I thought she might have died."

"She said her grandfather built the house."

Aunt Judy nodded. "He'd made his money in railroads, then chose Cloverdale to settle down in. I had the impression the fortune dwindled quite a bit during the next generation. It must have been sad for Frances to give up the house."

"She seemed to be soaking up old memories when I came across her but I don't think she minded getting the place off her hands."

"I should find her and say hello," Aunt Judy said, looking toward the house. "Do you remember her, Corinne? She was Frances Kingsley before she married."

"Only vaguely," Corinne admitted. "But I'll be glad to come along with you. Did you want to go back inside, Piper?"

"I'll catch up with you both later," Piper said. She had spotted someone she wanted to speak with.

She waved the two off, then stepped toward a rose garden, pretending interest in two blooming bushes that looked to have been planted decades ago. Lovely as they were, her concern was with the person seated on the stone bench nearby. After taking in the bushes from various distances and mumbling words that might have been taken for knowledgeable comments on the plants, she turned and smiled at her target.

"Taking a break from all the hand shaking?" Piper asked.

Mallory Porter fairly jumped, as though being addressed without her mother beside her was a startling event. "You're that pickle woman, aren't you?" she asked, then looked away, as though that settled things.

*Well,* Piper thought as she drew a deep breath. *This should be fun.*

## 17

"Yes, I have a pickling shop," Piper said, smiling as if Mallory hadn't just pronounced *pickle* as she might have said *mealworm*. "Not everyone's into pickles, though, I get that. I'm not much into teas, to tell the truth. But I have enjoyed seeing this house. You must love living in it."

Mallory shrugged but was at least looking directly at Piper. "It's big. Probably the biggest house in town."

"It definitely is," Piper agreed. "And historic," she said, but catching no sign of interest from Mallory on that point, quickly went back to big. "You could probably fit half the town in the house if you opened up the second floor."

"My bedroom and sitting room are huge. I'm decorating them both in lavender." She coughed twice. "But my allergies are bad here."

"I'm sorry. Should you be out in the garden?"

Mallory shook her head. "Not the flowers. It's the house, because it's so old. Dust and stuff. Mother says it will get better once she has the basement and attic thoroughly cleaned. She wanted the downstairs done first. For the tea, you know."

"Well, then, at least you can enjoy the garden. While it lasts, that is. I understand there are plans for replacing things eventually?"

Mallory shrugged. "I guess so. That Lloyd woman, I suppose. Dirk didn't like her but he won't have anything to say about it anymore, will he?"

"Mind if I sit?" Piper asked, and Mallory obligingly pulled her skirt out of the way. "Why didn't Dirk like Marguerite Lloyd?"

"Oh, it went way back." Mallory dug into a pocket for a tissue and blew her nose. "Somewhere in Ohio. I heard him telling Jeremy about it. Jeremy thought it was pretty funny."

"Funny? Why?"

"Because it made Dirk look dumb, which doesn't—didn't—happen much." Mallory gave Piper a sly look. "Jeremy acted like Dirk was a good friend but I don't think he really liked him that much."

*Hmmm.* "So what made Dirk look dumb?"

"Well," Mallory said, thinking, "Dirk was working for a big landscaping company out there, in the office. He and Marguerite butted heads too many times, so Dirk started watching for a way to get rid of her. He thought he spotted her ripping off the company. Something about ordering more plants and stuff than she needed for landscaping jobs. He figured she was selling the extras on the side."

"Was she?"

"I don't know. But Dirk went to the owner thinking he'd get her fired. But it turned out Marguerite and the owner were pretty tight." Mallory leaned closer to Piper and whispered, "I think they were sleeping together."

"Uh-oh. So I guess his boss didn't want to hear anything against Marguerite."

"That's what Jeremy was laughing about. That Dirk put his foot in it. Dirk ended up being let go, eventually. That's why he told Jeremy the story in the first place—to explain why a super-duper accountant like him lost that job."

"That must have been hard for him to admit," Piper said.

"But Dirk said he still came out on top."

"How?"

Mallory sniffed noisily, then swiped at her nose. "Dirk fiddled with Marguerite's orders. He canceled important plants, which caused holdups on Marguerite's landscaping projects. And he substituted real expensive plants for the ones she ordered and made it look like it was her mistake, like, maybe the Latin names were close to each other and she'd mixed them up. But his parting shot— that's what he called it when he was telling Jeremy—was cluing in the boss's wife about what Marguerite and the boss were up to."

"Wow. Dirk Unger wasn't someone to cross lightly, was he?"

"Uh-uh. Could be why Jeremy never fired him, even

though Mother was always pressing him to." Mallory seemed to suddenly realize how that sounded. "But Dirk couldn't hurt Jeremy like he did the boss in Ohio. Jeremy's too smart for that."

Piper wanted to pursue that but Lydia's voice suddenly sang out. "There you are!" She was closing in on them rapidly across the lawn. "I should have known you two would find each other. Unfortunately, I'm going to have to steal Mallory away."

Mallory obediently stood, her expression suddenly bland.

"I hope you're enjoying my little party," Lydia said to Piper, to which Piper was about to reply when Mallory burst out with a series of loud coughs. That drew Lydia's disapproving attention. "Really, dear, couldn't you have taken something for that earlier? And sitting out here in the garden certainly couldn't have helped."

"Mallory felt the garden was less of a problem than the house," Piper said, coming to her companion's defense. Even though Mallory didn't seem upset, Piper found Lydia's lack of sympathy for her daughter bothersome.

"I feel better out here," Mallory agreed, once she could speak. "I like the roses. I hope Marguerite Lloyd doesn't dig them all up."

"I don't know what Marguerite will want to do," Lydia said impatiently. "We haven't discussed it at any length. Now come along, Mallory, I need you inside. Please excuse us," she said somewhat stiffly to Piper, who nodded.

As they walked away, Piper heard Mallory say, "Maybe you shouldn't have Marguerite do the garden, Mother.

Dirk had a lot of things against her, you know. We were just talking about that." Mallory's head inclined toward Piper and Lydia glanced back, looking less than pleased.

Piper couldn't hear Lydia's response to Mallory but from the stiffness of Lydia's back and the tightness of her grip on Mallory's arm she guessed it wasn't particularly approving. Why, though, would Lydia care that Piper knew what had gone on between Dirk and Marguerite? Perhaps there was more to the story than Mallory let on? If so, how could Piper find out?

Puzzling over that, Piper walked back toward the house, thinking she'd catch up with Aunt Judy and Corrine Fortney. When she stepped inside, she heard a surprisingly deep voice standing out in that very feminine gathering, and she followed it to its source. Jeremy Porter had made an appearance at his mother's tea and appeared to be holding court in the living room, the center of many smiling women, Lydia firmly and proudly on one side and Mallory, red nosed and gazing vaguely about, on the other.

Piper drew closer to hear Jeremy regaling the group with a tale that unsurprisingly had to do with one of his successes in real estate. She paused near the doorway to listen. The story, she decided, was not all that interesting, but Jeremy's dramatic rendering had captured the rapt attention of those around him. His good looks and well-cut blazer over an open shirt and slacks didn't hurt, either.

"Quite the personality, isn't he?" a voice behind her commented softly, and Piper turned to see Emma Leahy lifting a crust-trimmed watercress sandwich to her mouth. "Mmm, this is good!" she soon pronounced, looking at the remainder of her sandwich speculatively. "I wonder if I could grow watercress?"

Having no idea, Piper instead said, "Thanks for rescuing me from Marguerite and Leona."

"You're quite welcome. Looks like you'll have to come up with something for the newsletter, though. Marguerite will be watching for it."

Piper drew Emma a few steps away from the crowd. "I just learned the history between Marguerite and Dirk Unger." She gave Emma a condensed version of Mallory's story as Emma polished off a raspberry-filled pastry she'd had on her plate.

"Add that to what Corinne Fortney told me and it sounds like Dirk had every intention of destroying Marguerite's business."

"Which gives Marguerite a pretty good motive for murder."

"Lydia didn't seem pleased that Mallory had told me what she did. Any idea why?"

Emma shook her head slowly. "Not a clue." She glanced back at the three Porters still surrounded by their admirers. "I get the impression Lydia doesn't like Mallory doing much of anything that hasn't been run by her first. She gives Jeremy more free rein, maybe because he's bringing home the big slabs of bacon. But I'd say she still has a pretty strong influence on him."

"I'd say so, too. I was sorry that Sugar got hurt but she probably was lucky to get away from that family."

"Apparently not everyone shares our opinion." Emma tipped her head toward the fawning group.

"And that might continue to hurt Sugar, or at least her business. Lydia's dropping Sugar as her caterer did some damage, which could increase if Lydia's influence around here grows."

"Well, we'll just have to see that it doesn't." Aunt Judy had joined Piper and Emma, her jaw set firmly. "I'm usually much more welcoming to newcomers but that woman seems to want to take over Cloverdale, and not for its betterment. If she badmouths Sugar in any way, I'll start a campaign that counteracts it. We'll see what happens then!"

"Ladies!" Jeremy Porter had left his group to—as Piper thought of it—spread his awesomeness around. "Great to see you. Enjoying my mother's tea?"

"Delicious food!" Emma managed, while Piper smiled as agreeably as she could. Aunt Judy, unfortunately, must have swallowed badly and struggled with a coughing fit.

Piper patted her back solicitously, helped by Emma. Jeremy, followed by several women from the living room, decided to quickly move on, as did Lydia and Mallory, who swept by without a sideways glance.

Which was perfectly fine with Piper, Emma, and Aunt Judy.

# 18

Piper declined an offer from Aunt Judy to follow her back to the farm after the tea and stay for dinner. She'd come up with what she thought was a brilliant idea that she'd already put in motion. From her car, Piper called Amy, who was on duty at A La Carte.

"I'm leaving the Porters' place now."

"It's ready," Amy said, and within minutes Piper had driven to the back of A La Carte, past the Dumpsters, and come to a stop at A La Carte's kitchen door.

"Here you are!" Amy held out a large bag holding two delicious-smelling packed dinners. There were advantages to knowing a chef in a top restaurant.

"Thanks, Amy. You'll put it on my bill?"

"All taken care of. Enjoy!"

Piper braced the bag carefully in her front passenge

well, then headed out of town toward the Burchett Christmas tree farm.

She was banking on Will being there, since her showing up would be a surprise, the idea having come to her at a free moment during the tea. So Piper crossed her fingers as she drove up the tree-flanked, graveled driveway, relaxing only when she spotted Will's green van parked in its usual spot. She continued on to the small brown house, set behind and slightly apart from the farm's outbuildings, then tapped her horn lightly as she came to a stop.

Will appeared at the doorway of the house, dressed in his usual jeans and flannel shirt. He looked both pleased and puzzled at her unexpected arrival, though Piper could see the scales tipped heavily toward pleased.

"Hope you haven't had dinner yet," she called, lifting out Amy's sumptuous concoction.

"Uh, no." Will ran a hand over his short blond hair, still perplexed but eyeing Piper's bag with great interest.

"Then you're in for a treat." Piper slipped past Will into the house and headed straight for his kitchen. "We can eat now, while these are hot, or wait and warm them up in your microwave."

"What is it?"

Piper pulled out one large Styrofoam box Amy had marked with a *W*, for *Will*. "Filet mignon medallions in cognac sauce." Removing the second box, marked *P*, she said, "Chicken in Provençale sauce. Both, I think, come with roasted potatoes and a vegetable." She peered back into the bag. "Looks like Amy threw in some rolls, too."

"Amy?"

"She was on the job at A La Carte. I was at Lydia

Porter's tea all afternoon or I might have whipped these up myself. Or," she said, grinning, "maybe not. So, what'll it be? Now or later?"

"I can't believe you did this," Will said, looking dazed. "It's terrific, and I'm more than ready to dig in. But what about you? Are you too stuffed with watercress sandwiches or whatever?"

"Uh-uh. I barely tried anything. Too busy snooping around. But I'll tell you all about that over dinner. Let's set the table."

Will quickly shifted a pile of papers and his laptop off the dining room table he'd once told Piper came with the house, along with a sagging but serviceable sofa and a few other odds and ends. He'd talked about wanting to replace most of it, but Piper suspected redecorating wasn't high on Will's priorities list, which put his farm—and maybe her?—near the top.

Piper found plates and cutlery and passed them to Will. "I guessed that you might like the medallions. Was I right?"

Will's near-rapturous expression was all the answer she needed. They quickly transferred the still-steaming food from boxes to plates and Will found a bottle of wine to complete the meal. "Sorry, I don't have any candles," he said, "except maybe fat red or green ones over in the Christmas shop. Shall I run and get them?"

Will's wry smile told Piper he was joking. "That's all right. Sit and start eating." He did.

"To what do I owe this generosity?" he asked, after taking one bite each of beef, potato, and carrot. He reached for a sip of his wine.

"Well, it might have been inspired by the hours spent surrounded by the elegance of the Porters' mansion. Who can go home to leftover pizza after that? And there's also the countless meals you've treated me to since last August, getting mostly pickles in return."

"But darned good pickles," Will pointed out.

"Agreed," Piper said, smiling. "But what man can live on pickles alone? I guess I mainly thought it would be a lovely way to end a not-so-fabulous day, despite all the polished silver, gleaming mahogany, and an endless array of pastries." As she sliced into her perfectly seasoned chicken, Piper told Will about her encounter with Marguerite Lloyd, her chat with Frances Billings, and the time spent with Mallory Porter.

"Jeremy Porter popped in near the end, I think as a special treat for all of Lydia's guests."

"Kind of him."

"I can see why Sugar was dazzled. He's quite charismatic, which obviously has served him well in his business. His sister, Mallory, on the other hand . . . well, I feel sorry for her. She seems to have had all the decision-making ability drummed out of her. Except for picking out colors for her new bedroom."

"Doesn't sound like Dirk's death has shaken any of them up." Will mopped a piece of filet through his cognac sauce.

"It doesn't. Of course, putting on a good face for guests might have been the order of the day. But some people would have canceled or at least postponed an event like that."

"You said Mallory claimed Jeremy didn't really like Dirk."

"She did. I can believe that after meeting Dirk myself. But Jeremy seemed to keep him close at hand. Why would you do that if you didn't like someone?"

"To keep an eye on him?"

Piper considered that. "Could Dirk have had something on Jeremy and Jeremy finally got tired of having to keep him around?"

"Possible. The trouble with someone like Dirk Unger is that there's no shortage of people who'd be happy to see him gone."

Piper nodded, then took a sip of her wine. "Tammy Butterworth said something to that effect. I thought at the time she might be exaggerating, but she was probably right. It doesn't make narrowing the suspect list easy."

To move away from the grim subject, Piper asked Will about his latest work around his tree farm. He told her about the work he and his helper, Tomas, had been doing the last few days out in the fields. As he helped himself to one last roll, Will mentioned he'd heard from his friend Matt Fleming, who Will and Piper had dined with recently along with his wife.

"How is he?"

"He's fine. He and Jen are on the verge of buying a house in Albany."

"Great! Wish it were in Cloverdale. I liked both of them."

Will smiled at that. "He said we should come visit once they're settled in."

"That'd be fun. And I could show you my favorite haunts from my time there." Piper saw a hint of a shadow cross Will's face and realized he might be wondering if those were places she'd visited with her then-fiancé, Scott.

Piper reached for Will's hand. "I had more friends than Scott in Albany, you know."

Will nodded. "I know. But he's the only one who's followed you here."

Piper took a deep breath. "This might be a good time to tell you I was with Scott last night. But," she hurried on, "it was because of Zach. I'd learned that Zach got into some trouble when he was at school and I thought Scott, as his lawyer, should hear his explanation. We had a quick dinner—the three of us—and that was it."

Will nodded several times, taking that in. "Is Zach's trouble going to affect his standing with the sheriff now?"

"I don't know. Scott will be talking with Zach and Sugar tomorrow."

"Well, let's hope for the best." He cocked an eyebrow at Piper. "Was last night another motivation for this fabulous dinner?"

"How could you think that?" Piper asked, feigning shock, then grinning sheepishly. "Did it work?"

In answer, Will rose from his seat and took Piper's hand, pulling her upward. He wrapped his arms around her and kissed her, gently at first, then more urgently. "You could say that," he murmured, finally releasing her.

Piper took a moment to catch her breath. "Then," she said, "definitely worth the price."

~~~~~~

Monday morning, all Piper's customers could talk about was Lydia's tea. *The house! The food! The decorations!* She'd agreed on as many points as she could but quickly grew weary of it. She found herself longing for Aunt Judy or Emma to drop in for a bit of relief. To her great surprise, the person who eventually showed up offering a change of pace was Mallory Porter.

Amy had arrived and was in the back room working on a pickled parsnip and carrot mix when Mallory walked in. She was dressed much more casually than the other times Piper had seen her, and the simple hooded sweater and jeans became her more than the expensive-looking dresses. Piper couldn't help wondering if Lydia had approved—or even seen—this outfit.

Though dressed comfortably, Mallory looked less than at ease as she glanced around Piper's Picklings. A casual observer might wonder if she'd just arrived from some far-off land where small shops of that sort didn't exist. Or perhaps, Piper thought, this was one of Mallory's rare ventures out on her own, without *Mother* leading the way. The idea was a disturbing one and Piper determined to smooth the way for the woman as best she could.

"How nice to see you, Mallory," she said. "All recovered from your busy day yesterday?"

Mallory's shoulders gave a little jump but she then smiled tentatively. "I think so. I had a good night's sleep."

"Great!" Piper waited but when Mallory didn't add anything more, she said, "Are you out getting to know the town?"

"No. I, um, we found this on one of the chairs. It must have fallen off someone's dress yesterday. I wondered if it was yours?" Mallory dug into her purse and held out a large, somewhat garish brooch in the shape of a butterfly. It was dotted with colored stones that might have been real or more likely were rhinestones and colored glass. Either way it was nothing near what Piper would have worn on her printed cotton dress. Even Mallory would have seen that. Had it simply been an excuse to stop by?

"It's not mine," Piper said. "I don't remember seeing it on anyone yesterday, either. Perhaps the owner will miss it and call."

"I guess so," Mallory mumbled and dropped the pin back into her purse. She looked around. "So, you make pickles here?"

"I do! We're in the process of making some right now. Would you like to come back and see?"

"Uh, no. I wanted to, that is, I wanted to find fabric for my bedroom curtains. There's a place in Cloverdale that has things like that. But I don't know it. Do you?"

Piper thought a minute. With what she'd brought with her from Albany, along with contributions from Aunt Judy, Piper hadn't needed to shop much for her apartment. But she knew there was a fabric shop a few blocks down off Beech. What was its name? Then she remembered. "Jeanine's?"

Mallory nodded. "That's it. Do you know the place?"

Piper was puzzled for a moment. Was Mallory asking for a reference? A confirmation of Jeanine's good service? Directions? Then it dawned on her. "I've never been to

Jeanine's shop. But I've always meant to stop in. Would you mind if I came along? I love looking at fabrics."

Mallory's eyes lit up. "Okay. Can you come now?"

"No problem." Piper began untying her apron and leaned into the back room. "Amy, I'm going out for an hour or so. Will you be all right?"

Amy gave a thumbs-up, and Piper reached under her counter to grab her purse. "We can walk there if you like. It's not far."

"Okay," Mallory said again, making Piper think it was the woman's favorite word. But once they got outside, Mallory came up with many more. It was as if the relief of having someone accompany her to the unknown and therefore frightening fabric shop—someone other than her mother—had unleashed a stream of chatter that had been held in tightly up until then. Since the chatter was mostly about decorating ideas, Piper just smiled and listened and indicated right or left turns as needed.

"Here it is," Piper said when they'd arrived at Jeanine's.

"Oh. It isn't very big. Do you suppose she'll have much of a selection?"

"Let's go in and see."

Piper led the way inside and they were greeted by a stout woman, a pencil stuck in her short white hair and a flip-packet of swatches in her hands.

Piper introduced herself and Mallory and explained what Mallory was interested in.

Jeanine quickly took over, asking Mallory a series of questions to narrow down her search. Mallory explained what she wanted articulately, showing a side of her that had not been at all apparent at the tea. Seeing the initial ice broken, Piper stepped back to wander around the shop, fingering an occasional upholstery swatch. Would Will's old sofa look better in a bright tweed, she wondered, then remembered the sagging springs. Will's living room would look better with a new sofa, period.

"And here's a white dotted Swiss that picks up your lavender very subtly," Jeanine was saying, and Piper glanced over to see Mallory draping the fabric for consideration over one hand.

"Possibly," she pronounced. "But maybe something heavier?"

The two debated over other choices until Mallory eventually called Piper over for an opinion on a pretty cotton floral. "What do you think of a duvet cover in this with a matching valence? I'd hang plain white sheers beneath the valence."

Piper could see that Mallory loved it. "I think that'd be beautiful," she declared, and Mallory beamed.

"I do, too." Mallory turned to Jeanine, who was also beaming. "Let's go with it."

Jeanine worked out the final details and Mallory placed her order, looking ecstatic.

"That went pretty quick," Piper said when she was ready to leave.

"I've been looking through lots of magazines. I knew what I liked and didn't like. Jeanine was great."

Piper checked her watch. "I have a few minutes to spare. Want to stop for a quick coffee?"

"Oh!" Mallory smiled. "That'd be nice."

"There's a place right around the corner." Piper led

the way to the Clover-Daily Deli, which offered good food and quick service.

"They have bakery things and sandwiches if you're hungry," she told Mallory as they went to the front counter to order.

Mallory apparently was hungry, adding a blueberry bagel to her order of chai tea. She let Piper pay and they carried their items to an empty table and sank into their chairs, Mallory still looking like a little girl who'd just gotten her first pair of patent leather shoes.

"How soon will your duvet cover and curtains come in?" Piper asked before taking a sip of her French roast.

"Jeanine thought it might be two weeks. She'll call and let me know."

"Think you can wait that long?" Piper asked with a smile.

Mallory smiled back. "It'll be hard. But exciting, too. I love decorating." She stirred cream into her tea, then bit into her bagel.

"You seemed very knowledgeable, back there. I probably wouldn't know a brocade from a batiste."

Mallory laughed. "Yes, you would. I've read a lot of decorating books, so I learned the names of all the fabrics and what works best for what." She stirred her tea. "I used to dream of being a decorator," she said, looking down at her cup.

"I'll bet you would have been good. What stopped you?"

Mallory shrugged. "Mother didn't like it."

Piper wanted to say *Mother wouldn't be the one doing it*, but instead said, "Your mother has strong opinions." She paused. "For a while, I was letting someone make decisions for my life, someone I thought I wanted to marry. But I finally saw that I wasn't as happy as I thought I'd be about that. That's when I moved here to Cloverdale and opened up my pickling shop."

"Was that scary?"

"Absolutely. I gave up a steady job and sank my savings into the shop. I didn't know if it would work out. But with a lot of effort—and a lot of support—it did. I've never been happier."

"Support," Mallory repeated softly, as though that were a new word to her.

They fell silent for a while, each sipping their own beverage. Then Piper said, "Your mother might not have liked the idea of you being a decorator, but she seems fine with Jeremy's career. That's a little surprising since she sounded so proud of an uncle who had been a member of Congress. I would have thought her preference would be for Jeremy to go into politics."

"She's okay with Jeremy being in real estate. She likes that he makes a lot of money in it."

*I'm sure she does.* "But what about Dirk? You said she pressed Jeremy to get rid of him. Was she very upset when he didn't?"

"Oh, she didn't like Dirk. But she put up with him. I guess she figured Jeremy needed Dirk."

"Needed him? For what?"

Mallory shrugged. "To do all the things Jeremy wanted done but didn't like to do himself."

"What, tedious or boring things?" Piper asked, hoping to draw out more details.

Mallory shook her head. "Like . . ." She bit into her

bagel and chewed. "Well, like, back when Jeremy was in high school, he had this friend who was kind of weird. Jeremy said he felt sorry for him. But when Jeremy didn't make first-string quarterback, which he *really* wanted, this weird friend, Clive, got into a huge brawl with the kid who *was* picked for first string. The fight wasn't over football, but something else—I don't know what—and it was dumb of Clive, who wasn't big or strong at all, to pick a fight with the bigger guy.

"Clive ended up pretty beat up but the other kid got suspended. That meant that Jeremy was moved up to first-string quarterback. He got pretty good, actually, with practice, and he ended up winning a trophy. And Chrissie Hagan, who never looked twice at him before, started dating him."

*Wow.* Piper's eyebrows shot up, but she said nothing.

"Dirk didn't pick fights with people," Mallory said.

"No, that wouldn't be his way of doing things. But he was, um, useful to Jeremy?"

"I think so. But," she said, shrugging, "I don't really know a lot about it."

Piper wanted to ask more but just then the deli's door opened and Sugar Heywood hurried in.

"I spotted you through the window," Sugar said. She appeared tense. "Zach and I just talked with Scott."

# 19

Mallory seemed surprised to see Sugar, and Piper wondered what Lydia might have told her to explain the sudden absence of Jeremy's girlfriend from their lives. Sugar slid onto a chair at their table.

"Scott advised Zach to go with him to talk to the sheriff. He thinks it might help Zach to give his explanation of what happened at that basketball game."

"That sounds like good advice," Piper said.

"They're on their way now. I thought it best not to go with them." Sugar rubbed at her eyes tiredly. "I wish Zach had told me about it when it happened. He said he didn't want to upset me. Hearing about it now, on top of everything else, is worse."

"Zach couldn't know what was going to come up with Dirk."

"I know. But I'm really concerned that his hiding this could make him look bad to Sheriff Carlyle."

"Why are you worried about Sheriff Carlyle?" Mallory asked, apparently clueless about Zach's situation.

Piper glanced at Sugar for an okay, then explained, "Zach is under suspicion for Dirk's murder. I don't know if you heard that Dirk was poisoned with a plant called bloodroot. Zach is a botany student and would know about it. He was also pretty upset with Dirk for, well, for being highly disrespectful to his mother, Sugar."

"Oh! But he didn't poison Dirk, right?"

"He absolutely didn't," Sugar said. "You've met Zach, Mallory. Did he strike you as someone who could commit murder?"

Mallory shook her head. "No, he didn't. I liked Zach."

"This is terrible for him, being under such suspicion," Sugar said. "He might not be allowed to leave Cloverdale to go back to school and finish his semester. Plus the stress."

"It's extremely hard on Sugar, too," Piper said to Mallory.

Mallory looked from one to the other. "I didn't know."

"We're all trying to find out what really happened to Dirk to put an end to this for Zach and for Sugar," Piper said. "If you—" she began, but Mallory suddenly stood up.

"I'd better go. Mother will be wondering." She took a final quick swallow of her tea and grabbed her purse. In a moment she was out the door, Piper and Sugar staring after her in surprise.

"Did we upset her?" Sugar asked.

Piper shook her head. "Not necessarily upset. She

just might not be used to hearing harsh truths." She took a sip of her cooling coffee and added thoughtfully, "It might actually have been good for her."

Piper came back to her shop to find Ralph Strawbridge there, waiting as Amy finished with a customer.

"I thought I'd catch Sugar here," he explained. "She said she might stop in after the meeting with Zach's lawyer."

"She found me at the Clover-Daily Deli." When Amy's customer left, Piper told Ralph about Scott accompanying Zach to the sheriff's. "You know about Zach's problem at college?"

Ralph nodded. "If it weren't for this Dirk Unger mess, the boy might have gotten away with not telling Sugar about it." He shook his head. "But it's too bad it happened. And hiding it can't help but make anyone wonder what else he might be covering up."

"College kids keep things from their parents all the time," Amy defended. "Not that it ever worked for me with a master interrogator for a father," she added with an eye roll. "What I mean is, keeping quiet about things you just feel stupid about doesn't automatically mean you're an evil person."

"I hope your father sees that," Ralph said.

Piper realized Ralph hadn't yet heard what she'd learned about Marguerite Lloyd, and she updated him.

"Now that sounds like a good motive to me," Ralph said. "When your livelihood is being threatened, and by an old enemy, I can imagine wanting to strike out."

"Marguerite is definitely not a person to take things lying down. And striking out is likely in her personality. But that's exactly why I'm having trouble with the idea of her choosing poison. A face-to-face confrontation seems much more her style."

"It's more Zach's style, too," Ralph said, "if, of course he were capable of it at all, which I don't believe he is. But that aside, poison has a lot going for it as a method of murder. No gunpowder residue to worry about or blood splatter on clothing."

"No weapon to dispose of," Amy chimed in.

"Or alibi needed," Piper said, "if the poison is consumed at a later time."

"And in the case of bloodroot, no record of purchase," Ralph added, "since it grows wild."

"And, at the moment, no actual murderer to name in place of Zach," Piper said with a grimace.

"We'll find him," Ralph said. "Or her. It's just a matter of time."

Piper nodded but wasn't as sure as Ralph sounded, or as comforted. Time could be just as destructive as productive. If Dirk Unger's murder became a cold case, Zach's once-bright future could be destroyed. With people's names so searchable on the Internet, what graduate school admissions board or future employer would choose a candidate whose name was still linked to an unsolved murder? Then there were friends, potential girlfriends, neighbors—the list of distrust and potential damage went on. It was a bleak thought.

From the moment Piper opened up shop the next morning, business bustled. For whatever reason, customers she hadn't seen for a while dropped in that day, and not just to hear or spread news but to buy. When Amy arrived, her first order of business was restocking the shelves.

"Your brandied cherries are popular today," she said as she returned from the back room with an armful of replacement jars.

"There's been a run on my hand-blended pickling spices, too. We might have to put up more, soon—when we have time." Piper had spotted another customer—Jody Norris—approaching and readied herself for another good sale. Mrs. Norris was a particularly avid pickler.

As Piper waited on Mrs. Norris, two more women arrived, and Amy left her jars of brandied cherries to take care of them. The rest of the morning continued in that mode, keeping both Piper and Amy jumping until at one particularly busy point Lydia walked in, Mallory in tow.

"Good morning, ladies!" Lydia called out as though the current gathering of customers had been arranged for her benefit. Most everyone returned the greeting enthusiastically, which told Piper that Lydia was fast becoming a Cloverdale Grande Dame, largely due, she supposed, to the success of her tea.

"Miss Lamb," Lydia said, interrupting Piper from a discussion with Lorena Hicks about the various ways to use pickled beets. "I just stopped in for a jar of mint jelly. Do you have it? Jeremy likes it with his roast lamb."

"It's right over here," Amy said, answering for Piper. "One jar?" she asked, reaching upward.

"That should do."

Amy took the jelly to the cash register to ring up but

Lydia continued addressing Piper, browsing idly, as she did, through the section of jellies and preserves.

"We're heading over to Jeanine's," she said, pulling down a jar of strawberry preserves, looking at it, and putting it back. "Mallory has had a change of heart on her order. We're going to choose something else."

Piper shot a look at Mallory, who was gazing expressionlessly at Piper's papier-mâché cat, tucked into a corner near the cookbooks. *Mallory* had a change of heart? Piper wondered what the real story was and felt sorry if Mallory had been bullied into giving up her own choice. She turned back to Lydia to see a disconcerting look of triumph on her face. *Don't interfere with my control of my daughter*, Lydia seemed to be saying, and Piper felt sure that the mint jelly had been only an excuse to send that message.

Mallory followed her mother to the cash register, stolidly avoiding eye contact with Piper or anyone else in the shop, and the two left soon, Lydia pausing on her way out to bestow a gracious word or two on Piper's other customers.

Amy caught Piper's eye and Piper made a subtle shrug before returning to her discussion with Lorena Hicks.

About an hour later, Piper was surprised to see Stan Yeager walk in, and, with a quick nod, begin his own search about her shop. Piper didn't remember Stan ever having come as a customer before and had assumed he just wasn't a pickle or preserve person. Eventually he brought over two jars of kimchi, a Korean mixed-vegetable ferment that Piper liked but whose strong taste had limited appeal.

Seeing Piper's look of mild surprise, Stan smiled somewhat awkwardly. "My daughter likes the stuff."

"Is your daughter visiting?" Piper asked, having a vague memory that Stan had a married daughter living somewhere other than Cloverdale.

"Um, no." He fumbled for his credit card and handed it over. "Maybe later."

"I see," Piper said, though she didn't. What she *was* seeing was an agitated man and knew that Sugar would want to attribute that to guilt over Dirk Unger's murder. Could Sugar be right? Was Stan showing signs of a troubled conscience?

"Oh, Mr. Yeager, I'm so glad to find you. I stopped at your office and . . ." A woman Piper didn't know grabbed Stan's arm and attention and slowly dragged him away with his bagged jars of kimchi as she prattled on about some question to do with house sales. Stan's place at the counter was quickly filled by another customer, so Piper temporarily shelved thoughts of murder and refocused on her work.

Business continued briskly enough for Piper and Amy to have to alternate break times instead of lunching together as they liked to do. Taking the first turn at the helm, Piper was pleased to see Tammy Butterworth open her door.

"One of my ladies gave me a recipe for radish pickles that she swears by," Tammy said with her usual cheeriness, referring, Piper figured, to a housecleaning client. "I had such fun putting up the beets, I thought I'd try this. What do you think?"

She handed Piper the recipe, which Piper scanned.

"Looks good. I think you'll love this on pumpernickel," she said. "What do you need?"

"Everything but the radishes," Tammy said, cackling. "Already picked up a big bunch at a farmer's market." So Piper went around gathering up jars of peppercorns, fennel seeds, and mustard seeds.

"Vinegar?" she asked, pausing at the row of jugs.

"Need it. And the kosher salt. Plus the jars and lids." Tammy laughed. "I do have the tablespoon of sugar that it calls for."

"Glad to hear it," Piper said with a grin. "Well," she said, looking over the small pile of items she'd gathered. "Anything else?"

"That should do it for now." As Piper began ringing up, Tammy asked, "Any luck looking into that problem between Dirk and the landscaping lady?" At that moment, the shop door opened and the landscaping lady herself— Marguerite Lloyd—walked in, followed closely by Mrs. Tilley.

"Oops!" Tammy said and mimed a tape-slap over her mouth.

Marguerite, back in her garden center clothes of jeans and rolled-sleeve shirt, scowled in their direction, though it seemed to be over Piper's being occupied rather than having heard Tammy's question. Marguerite, she knew, was not a person filled with patience but she seemed able to pull up enough at the moment to stop where she was and not interrupt.

Mrs. Tilley cheerfully stepped around Marguerite after twittering a greeting and picked up one of Piper's shopping baskets to load with whatever struck her fancy that day. Marguerite moved toward Piper's shelves, aiming her frown toward the collection of preserves and spices.

Tammy handed her credit card to Piper and shifted her conversation to her cleaning efforts at the Porter mansion following the tea. "Took me the full day to put the place back to rights," she said. "You'd be surprised how much ladies dressed to the nines can mess up a house. Spilt tea, squashed cakes on the hardwood. If you didn't know better you'd think a kindergarten class had made a field trip there." Tammy chuckled merrily and Piper thought how pleasantly Tammy would have livened up the event—if Lydia had deigned to invite her. That was probably a concept as alien as Marguerite Lloyd inviting those same kindergartners to run among her flowers.

Piper glanced at Marguerite as Tammy signed her receipt and wondered just a bit nervously what the landscaper had come for. Though Marguerite picked up the odd spice jar or two, Piper was sure she hadn't come for curry powder or turmeric.

Mrs. Tilley, on the other hand, had come for cinnamon, ginger, canning jars and lids, a jar of brandied cherries—which she'd reached around Marguerite to get—and two jars of pickled peppers, the kind of varied assortment that Piper had come to expect from the woman. Marguerite, who'd become distracted for a moment reading the ingredients of a jar of do chua, Piper's first attempt at the Vietnamese pickle blend, whipped around as Mrs. Tilley unloaded her shopping basket. She'd apparently reached her limit of patient waiting.

"Lamb!" she barked. "When is that article showing up in the newsletter?"

Piper gulped. She hadn't put a word on paper since she'd been out to Marguerite's gardening center. "I'm not sure. Emma Leahy handles the newsletter. I'll have to check with her."

"So it's not out yet? Good. I want you to put in that we'll have a sale on silky dogwoods, starting this weekend."

"I can do that," Piper said, her head bobbing.

"Great." Marguerite's manner warmed a degree or two. "I would have called but I was coming into town anyway and thought I'd come see your shop. It's not bad."

*Not bad?* Piper questioned, but said, "Thank you."

"Oh, it's a wonderful shop," Mrs. Tilley put in. "I'm here for one thing or another almost every day. Isn't that right, Piper?"

Piper nodded and smiled fondly at Mrs. Tilley, though she couldn't help picturing the woman's kitchen packed to the ceiling with unopened spices or preserves, unless she happened to gift her friends often.

"You seem to do a good business," Marguerite acknowledged, but with a definite tone of surprise. "Well, I'm off. Let me know about that newsletter," she ordered before pushing her way out the door.

Mrs. Tilley stood blinking after her. "She didn't buy anything!"

"She's a busy woman," Piper said, totaling up Mrs. Tilley's purchases.

"And a very brusque one," Amy said, coming out from the back room. She took over at the counter as soon as Mrs. Tilley left, giving Piper her welcome turn for a break. Piper trotted up to her apartment to slip off the shoes that had started to pinch. She then looked for the notes she'd scribbled during her "interview" with Marguerite, wondering when she would find the time to write up something printworthy.

As she was polishing off a hastily thrown together sandwich, Piper heard a familiar voice rise up from the shop. Recognizing it as Emma Leahy's, Piper's eyes lit up. She slipped back into her shoes and hurried down the stairs, a glass of iced tea and her notebook in hand.

"Emma, I'm so glad to see you. I need your help." Piper explained about Marguerite pressing her on the newsletter article. "Could you possibly write it up for me? I have plenty of notes."

"No problem at all. I'm sure I can add a few odds and ends to what you have, knowing the place as well as I do."

"Marguerite gave me the timeline of her business, which I wrote down. It might be interesting background to your club members. But she's more concerned about getting in mention of her silky dogwood sale."

"They're on sale?" Emma brows shot up excitedly. "Oooh. I . . . no, I really don't have the room. But . . . no." She shook her head, having apparently talked herself out of the purchase. "I just stopped by for a jar of curry. I'm making a chicken stir-fry tonight. But I'll write up this thing about Marguerite first and put your name on it."

Piper winced at the idea of taking the unearned credit but knew it had to be done. "That should settle any suspicions Marguerite might have had." She plucked the curry jar from its shelf and handed it to Emma. "No charge. Consider it a very small down payment on what I'll owe you."

~~~~~~

W hen it was time for Amy to leave for A La Carte, she wished Piper good luck managing on her own on that busy day. Piper wished *herself* good luck as two more customers walked in moments after Amy left. However, fortified with freshly brewed, strong coffee as well as the image of her sales total at the end of the day, Piper soldiered on, though she occasionally felt split in three as she answered questions from one person, found items for another, and listened to her phone ring insistently before the answering system clicked on.

By closing time, she finally had a few quiet moments, and she sank onto the tall stool behind her counter with relief. Piper was downing a long sip from the water bottle that had replaced her coffee mug when she spotted Scott out of the corner of one eye heading briskly toward her shop door. She set down her bottle, sensing urgency in her ex-fiancé's posture, and waited with some trepidation.

Scott threw open her door, setting the connecting bell jangling wildly.

"Have you seen Zach today?" he asked from the open doorway. His suit jacket was rumpled and the tie underneath hung askew. When Piper, bewildered, shook her head, he took a step forward, his shoulders sagging. "He's gone missing," he said.

# 20

"Missing!" Piper cried. "What do you mean? What's happened?"

Scott let the door swing closed behind him and took a few steps forward, bringing an air of gloom with him. "We talked to the sheriff this morning. Zach explained his side of the incident at college. The sheriff asked Zach to return this afternoon for more discussion. Zach agreed. But he never showed up."

"Sugar doesn't know where he is?"

"She hasn't seen or spoken to him since this morning at my office. The problem is . . ." Scott paused, causing Piper to hold her breath. "Zach's disappearance gives Sheriff Carlyle probable cause for a search warrant. He could get it and be over there within minutes. I've been trying to find Zach in hopes of heading it off."

"But . . . it should be okay, right? I mean, it's terrible to have strangers paw through your home, but there won't be anything to find, right?"

Scott looked at Piper for several moments. "I hope not," he finally said.

After Scott left, Piper got on the phone, acting on her first thought. Amy picked up right away and Piper heard busy kitchen sounds in the background.

"Sorry to call you at work," she said, then quickly explained the situation. "Would you or any of your friends know Zach's friends well enough to pump them for information?"

"I can try," Amy said. "But if Sugar doesn't know . . ."

"It's a shot in the dark. But it's the best I can come up with."

Piper closed up shop, then paced around her apartment, hoping to hear something positive. When the silence of her phone got to her, she called Scott's cell but only got voice mail. After downing a few bites of food, she could stand it no longer. She threw on a jacket and hurried down to her car and drove straight to Sugar's house.

Flashing lights bounced off Sugar's white siding as Piper drew near, signaling that Sheriff Carlyle and his team had started their search. Piper spotted Sugar standing outside on the sidewalk, Ralph Strawbridge beside her, and Scott next to Ralph, all staring grimly toward the house. Piper parked and approached the trio. Sugar, seeing her, reached out for a hug, and Piper could feel her friend trembling with anxiety.

"Any word from Zach?" she asked. Sugar shook her head.

"I'm worried to death. I can't believe he would just take off without saying a word! The sheriff should be out looking for him instead of poking through our things."

"You can be sure he has plenty others looking for Zach," Scott said. He looked at Piper. "I got your call. Just didn't have anything good to report."

Piper nodded and glanced around. The flashing lights had drawn the curious, which couldn't help Sugar's state of mind. There was nobody she recognized, and Piper wished she could shoo them all away. She could only hope the tedium of nothing much to see or learn would eventually scatter the crowd.

"I can't bear the thought of my kitchen being gone through," Sugar said, voicing the lesser of her worries.

"They'll start with Zach's room," Scott said. "They might not—" He stopped, and Piper finished the thought for herself. They might not search any farther if they found something incriminating in Zach's room. But what could they possibly find beyond normal college student things? Would innocent items suddenly take on sinister meanings? Piper squeezed Sugar's hand encouragingly but felt far from easy herself.

They saw sudden activity around Sugar's open front door, and Scott immediately headed over. Piper and the others watched him converse with the officers, straining to see any indication of what was happening. After what seemed like hours, he returned.

"They've found something in one of Zach's books." Scott's face was grim.

"What?" Sugar asked. "What did they find? Something he wrote?"

Scott shook his head. "It's a plant cutting pressed between the pages. They'll be checking with an expert to identify it." He paused. "But it was tucked among the pages that discuss bloodroot."

Back home, Piper returned calls that had collected on her voice mail. The first was to Amy. "Any results on Zach's whereabouts?" Piper asked.

"Afraid not. No one I've reached has seen Zach or knows where he could be. There's still hope, 'cause I haven't heard back from everyone. But I left the message on your cell because of the chatter some of our waitstaff have picked up. What's going on at Sugar's house?"

Piper told Amy what she knew but asked her not to spread around the discovery in Zach's book. "Nobody knows for sure yet what the plant is." Piper expected it was simply a matter of time before that news became public. Amy's father, Sheriff Carlyle, must have familiarized himself with bloodroot after Dirk Unger's poisoning. He was simply going through the proper procedures. Amy's glum response told Piper she understood that as well.

Piper's next call was to Aunt Judy, who'd been hearing from friends about the activities at Sugar's place as well and hoped Piper had a reassuring explanation. Piper was sorry not to have one and told her aunt about Zach's disappearance. She held off about the sheriff's discovery, figuring one upsetting piece of news was enough for the time being.

"Could he be hurt or in danger?" Aunt Judy asked worriedly.

"Scott seemed to think Zach was avoiding further interrogation."

"But that only makes him look guilty!"

"I'm afraid so," Piper said.

"He is, of course, very young," Aunt Judy said, struggling to hang on to anything positive. "He might have thought that removing himself from the scene was best for his mother, though it's truly the worst."

"Agreed." Piper remembered the anguished expression on Sugar's face as she waited outside her house and the pressure of her grip on Piper's hand. "I have Amy calling around to anyone she can think of who might know where Zach could have gone."

"That's good, dear. I'm afraid my contacts for Zach's generation are very limited. Please keep me posted."

Piper promised and sent her best to Uncle Frank.

Piper next spoke with Emma Leahy and Gil Williams, two more people she'd relied on and wanted to keep in the loop. She saved her last call for Will.

"How is Sugar doing?" was Will's first question after she filled him in.

"She's struggling. Ralph, I think, is a great help."

"Good. And you? How are you doing?"

Piper sighed. "I'm trying hard to keep my faith in Zach's innocence."

"Right. Disappearing wasn't a smart thing for an innocent person to do."

"As Aunt Judy says, he's immature and probably thinking less with his head than his emotions."

"It'll be bad if that plant turns out to be bloodroot."

"There must be an explanation," Piper said.

"If only Zach were around to give it."

"I know." Piper fell silent, then repeated, "I know."

"It's bloodroot." Scott stood across the counter from Piper. She'd spotted him lingering outside her shop window the next morning, apparently waiting to catch her at a quiet moment. He'd had a long wait, with many wanting to talk about last night's happenings at Sugar's. So far, the information of most was limited to the fact of the sheriff's search, and Piper hadn't added to that.

Piper sagged at Scott's statement, though she'd fairly expected it. "What now?"

"Now we have to find Zach. Before the sheriff does."

"I suppose he's stopped thinking of other suspects?"

"You can bet on that. Do you happen to know of anyone else having the poison that killed Dirk Unger on their premises?"

The discussion ended as two more of her steady flow of drop-ins pushed through the door. Scott excused himself and left her to her customers, though she'd had enough by then of others subtly picking at her brain, especially after what she'd just had confirmed.

"Did you hear about Ms. Heywood's house being searched last night?" Leah Harrison asked as the door closed behind Scott, and Piper bit her tongue and wished she could simply close up shop and pull down her shades.

Amy's arrival offered respite, though she still had nothing positive to report from her phone canvassing.

"It's like Zach dropped off the face of the earth. He doesn't have a car. How far could he have gone?"

"There's always hitchhiking, I suppose."

Amy shuddered. "Let's hope a friend gave him a lift but isn't talking."

"I'd rather hope Zach shows up claiming temporary amnesia."

"Then he'd better have a good bump on his head to back it up." Amy glanced toward the back room. "Anything to work on back there to keep my mind off things?"

"There's a bunch of strawberries you could help me turn into preserves. But if anyone comes in, I'd be glad if you'd run out to wait on them. I'm in dire need of downtime."

"You got it," Amy said, slipping on her apron and heading to the workroom. She had just begun to rinse the berries when the shop bell jangled, and she turned the job over to Piper, who willingly took it. Working on pickling or preserving would be a first-choice activity for Piper anytime, but that day it was her therapy, badly needed to counter the steady progression of terrible news.

By the time Amy needed to leave, the large batch of strawberries had been hulled, sugared, and slid into Piper's refrigerator to sit overnight. Piper felt reenergized by then—which snacking on a strawberry or two during the process hadn't hurt—and saw her assistant off without too much regret. The flurry of drop-ins had slowed, and she hoped it would trickle away to nothing before too long.

She'd had a few minutes of peace when she saw a

woman she didn't recognize approaching her door. The woman paused outside for a long time before coming in.

"That is the most amazing door I've ever seen!" she said as she came in, and Piper's mood rose several levels. It had been a long time since anyone had commented on Ralph's creation. Of course most everyone in town had already seen it, not to mention that people's thoughts were currently occupied by other, more pressing things.

The stranger's graying hair and crow's feet pegged her as mid to late fifties. A brown oversized sweater covered her roundish form from shoulders to knees followed by gray sweatpants that drooped over worn sneakers. "Really," she said. "That door is somethin' else."

"Thank you," Piper said. "Though the credit belongs to Ralph Strawbridge, who made it."

The woman grinned. "Can't take false credit, huh? I like that. Good for you."

She came closer, and Piper detected a faint odor of alcohol, causing her some uneasiness, though the woman appeared harmless. So far.

"I need a little help," the woman said, and Piper braced herself. "I'm looking for the Porter house. Jeremy Porter. And Lydia. And Mallory. Any idea how to find it?"

"Um," Piper hesitated. "Are you a friend of theirs?"

The woman made a loud, chortling laugh. "No, but they'll still have to take me in. That's what families do, right?"

"You're related?"

"Abso-posi-lutely! I'm Lydia's sister. Gwen Smyth."

She held out her hand and Piper shook it, offering her own name. "I went back to Smyth," the woman said. "It's spelled with a *Y*, by the way. Trips people up all the time, but it was better than my last husband's name, and the one before that—Russian, and loaded with *C*s and *Z*s. Never could remember how to spell it." She grinned, and Piper smiled back, though still grappling with Ms. Smyth-with-a-*Y*'s statement of being Lydia's sister.

"Is Lydia expecting you or is this a surprise?"

"Oh, I thought I'd just drop in and surprise them all. Heard Jeremy bought this nice, big house and that Lydia and Mallory moved in with him. Now he'll have his sister, his mother, and his aunt!"

Piper smiled again, this time a little wider as Gwen merrily sang a few bars of the familiar Gilbert and Sullivan tune with those words, her fingers waving in time to the ditty. Piper reached for a slip of paper and started scribbling. "Here's their address," she said, remembering it well from Lydia's tea. "And I wrote down a few directions. It's not hard to find."

Gwen glanced at the paper. "Thanks! I knew I picked the right shop to stop in and ask. Of course, that door of yours was truly beckoning to me."

*I'll bet it did*, Piper thought as another whiff of alcohol drifted her way. "Say hi to Lydia for me."

"Will do! Maybe we can all get together sometime," Gwen said as she headed for the door.

*That would be very interesting,* Piper thought as she waved good-bye.

"Who was that?" Lorena Hicks asked, entering as Gwen Smyth left.

"Lydia Porter's sister," Piper informed her. Lorena's brown eyes grew wide.

Later that day, Piper was waiting on an elderly gentleman who had stopped in to buy a large jar of bread-and-butters, when Emma Leahy walked in, her posture stiff and her face tense. Something was definitely up and Piper hurried through the sale to her customer—a kindly sort who didn't seem to mind being hustled along—to learn what was bothering Emma. As the man shuffled out, Emma hurried forward.

"Bad news," she said. "Joan Tilley's in the hospital. She's critically ill.

"Oh! I'm so sorry to hear that. What's wrong?"

Clearly struggling with her emotions, Emma took a moment to answer. "It was very sudden. Luckily her neighbor came by and called the ambulance." She swallowed. "She had the same symptoms as Dirk Unger."

"No!" Piper cried. "Mrs. Tilley? How could that be? And why?"

"I don't know. It doesn't make any sense at all. But there's something else you should know."

Emma paused, the strain of worry for her friend making her suddenly gulp. When she regained control, she said, "It might have been your cherries. She'd been eating from a jar of your brandied cherries."

Piper gasped, not knowing which was worse to hear—the illness or the cause. She stared, speechless for several moments. "I can't believe it! How . . . ?"

Emma shook her head, having no answer to Piper's

unfinished question. "I have to go," she said. "I just wanted you to know." She turned and hurried out.

A flood of questions filled Piper's head as she stared in dismay after her disappearing friend.

*Her cherries? It couldn't possibly be!* The thought made her physically ill—though not, she was sure, as ill as poor Mrs. Tilley.

# 21

~~~

"Sorry to have to do this." Sheriff Carlyle added one more jar of Piper's brandied cherries to the several he'd already boxed up. He'd arrived the next morning with the news that Mrs. Tilley was alive, though still in serious condition, and had confirmed that bloodroot was indeed found in her jar of brandied cherries.

"But it couldn't have been added during my cooking process," Piper protested. She'd studied up on bloodroot during her mostly sleepless night. "First of all, no way would it be put there by me or," she added significantly, "by your daughter. But besides that, bloodroot, I've learned, becomes harmless at high heat. It's only poisonous when it's eaten fresh."

The sheriff nodded. "I'm aware of that. Dirk Unger's was in his salad. A lot of it, and it was fresh. We're assuming his spicy Italian salad dressing smothered any taste.

The bloodroot in Joan Tilley's jar hadn't been cooked. It clearly had been added at some point afterward."

"But . . ." Piper sputtered.

"I'm not necessarily blaming you," he said, and Piper didn't much care for the *necessarily*. "Anyone could have slipped it into one of these jars after you'd finished with them. I don't see any safety seals on them."

"The lids are vacuum sealed to the jars as they cool. They become tight enough to actually lift the jar by the lid. Sheriff, if my jars had been opened, that vacuum would have been broken. Any knowledgeable person would notice that."

"You would hope so," the sheriff said. "It's been my experience that not everyone pays attention to things that they should. Now, tell me who has bought your brandied cherries."

Piper groaned. "I've had them in stock since last June. I can't possibly track down all the sales."

"All right, let's start with yesterday's sales and work backward."

At that point, and to Piper's relief, Amy walked in. "Daddy! What are you doing?"

"Sugarplum . . ." the sheriff began gently, but Amy was having none of it.

"I heard about Mrs. Tilley," she said. "You can't seriously think she got sick from Piper's cherries!"

"Bloodroot was in her jar of brandied cherries," Piper said. "Your father can't take the chance it might be in any more jars."

"But—"

"Amy," the sheriff said, "help Piper remember who bought any of these cherries lately. It's important."

"Oh gosh!" Amy sank onto one Piper's stools. "You sold a bunch of them yesterday before I showed up," she said to Piper, who agreed.

Piper ticked off several names, which Sheriff Carlyle wrote down. "Sugar Heywood bought lots of it lately," she said, which made the sheriff look up sharply. "But they were for Jeremy Porter's dinner of several days ago. Nobody got sick that I know of. And Lydia Porter picked up a jar. She said Mallory loved it, so probably that was okay."

The sheriff nodded but made a note of it. "Anyone else?"

"I'll go through my sales slips. But that'll take time." Piper had a thought. "Couldn't someone have simply walked off with a jar, then slipped it back on my shelf after doctoring it?"

"Yes!" Amy cried, jumping up from her stool. "The shop has been super busy lately. Piper and I couldn't possibly have kept an eye on everyone. Then there's your party, Piper. Think of all the people who came and milled around."

A look of pain flashed onto the sheriff's face. "That's a possibility," he admitted. "All the same, please get back to me with your sales records."

"I will," Piper promised, feeling that at least some pressure had come off her, personally. At the same time she sympathized with the enormous job the sheriff faced.

He carried off her boxed-up jars without further

discussion, and Amy turned to Piper after he'd left. "Does this eliminate Zach, since he hasn't been around?"

Piper thought about that. "Probably not. It could be argued that Zach had access to one of Sugar's jars of cherries and could have slipped it back onto my shelf anytime he was here."

"But it wouldn't make sense—unless he's suddenly turned into a psycho killer. There'd be no way he could know who would get that jar. Dirk Unger's food was poisoned to murder him, and only him. Putting bloodroot in one of your preserves would be a totally random murder."

"I know, and that could apply to whoever did it. I can't understand it myself."

As the day moved on, Piper began to understand the poisoner's intention.

"Business is so slow!" Amy said, having waited on only one person, and that occurring early in her shift.

"I've noticed," Piper said, turning to her ringing phone.

"Piper, dear," Aunt Judy said as soon as Piper picked up. "I've been hearing very upsetting things!" She went on to first say that she'd visited Joan Tilley at the hospital and had been dismayed at how wasted she'd appeared. "Joan could barely speak," Aunt Judy said. "They came terribly close to losing her! But I've been assured she's turned the corner, and that is very comforting. But Piper, dear, the talk is that it was from something in the brandied cherries from your shop. How could that be?"

"I'm afraid that's true," Piper said. She told her aunt about the sheriff's visit and that they'd agreed that bloodroot must have been added after Piper's cooking process. "He wants me to track down everyone who bought my cherries. I've been able to make a dent in that with business being very slow."

"That's why I called," Aunt Judy said. "Word is spreading about the source of Joan's illness, and people are throwing out anything they bought at your shop. Even the packaged spices. They're afraid to buy anything more from you. Piper," she said, her voice breaking, "your business could be ruined!"

"That's so unfair!" Amy cried, when Piper shared Aunt Judy's statement.

"Agreed," Piper said grimly, feeling as though she'd been punched. "But honestly, wouldn't you feel the same if you didn't know me?"

Piper could see Amy badly wanting to deny that, but she slowly and reluctantly nodded. "I'd probably think why take a chance? If I didn't know you like I do, that is."

"And how many people do?" Piper asked. "Who sees how carefully you and I work back there to follow all safety precautions? The problem is, once the jars are on the shelves or bought, they're out of our hands."

"But you offer so much more than your homemade pickles and preserves. There's the spices you order from around the world, and—"

"—and my pickling equipment—the jars and lids, canners, tongs, crocks. Totally safe, right? But don't you see? My shop's reputation has been tainted. Everything in it has become suspect."

"I heard," Gil Williams said, walking in from his shop next door and looking somber. "I'm sorry."

"Not your fault," Piper said with a weak smile. "I'd definitely like to know whose fault it is."

"The person who murdered Dirk Unger doesn't want you to get any closer to finding them out."

"I didn't feel close at all," Piper protested.

"Someone," Gil said, "apparently feared that you were. Your only way to fix this is to unmask them. This town needs to know who has been spreading poison around. Once it does, it can go back to normal life, and that includes patronizing your shop and buying your wares."

"You make it sound so simple!" Amy said, appearing on the verge of tears.

Piper rubbed Amy's arm soothingly. "It isn't, of course. But on the bright side, I now have much more time to work on the problem."

"You mean . . ."

Piper nodded. "I might as well close up shop. Don't you agree?" she asked, looking at Gil. To her surprise, he shook his head.

"Don't do it. It would be taken as an admission of guilt. You had nothing to do with Joan Tilley's poisoning. Another person somehow tampered with your wares. Show the town that you're mad as hell and won't put up with such atrocities."

"Right!" Amy cried, swallowing her tears and pumping a fist. "Show them!"

Piper looked from one to the other. "You're absolutely right, Gil. No way should I act as though I'm ashamed and hiding. I *am* mad. And if anyone happens to wander by, I'll tell them."

"They will, come by, that is. Little by little. Wait and see."

Piper hoped Gil was right, but either way she'd made her decision. She was going to fight back against the person guilty of these awful poisonings. "Actually, I don't think I want to sit and hope someone drops by. Amy, I think you can manage to hold down the super quiet fort. I'm going to go out to get my message across. And I'll start by visiting Mrs. Tilley."

"Good idea," Gil said.

"Yes!" Amy said. "And give her my best. She's such a sweet lady."

"Give her mine, too," Gil said, and Piper promised, not adding that she hoped she wouldn't be barred from approaching Mrs. Tilley. Piper grabbed her jacket and slipped her hands through the sleeves with crossed fingers—not the strongest way, she realized, to start off on a mission.

Piper walked down the hallway of the Bellingham Regional Hospital, having learned Mrs. Tilley's room number from the volunteer at the front desk. The good news was Mrs. Tilley was not in intensive care. The bad news, at least for Piper, was that many of the woman's friends had gathered in support, and a large group of them stood directly ahead.

As she drew nearer, Piper saw heads turn and whispers shared. This would be a trial by fire, and she was determined to project the innocence that was rightly hers of having had any part in Mrs. Tilley's situation. A few of the well-wishers began to back away, their gazes aimed everywhere but at Piper, though she caught one or two glances before they flicked away. She was beginning to grow desperate when Emma Leahy suddenly broke through the ranks.

"Piper! I'm glad you could come. Joan will be so happy to see you." She enveloped Piper in a hug, and Piper saw, over Emma's shoulder, some of the uncertainty of the others begin to fade.

"How is she?" Piper asked.

Emma's face was serious. "Still pretty bad but, I think, improving. She's gone through a lot."

"I can imagine. I was horrified that something like this could happen to her. And nearly as horrified to learn where the poison came from."

"We all were. Whoever did this is truly evil, and I'm so sorry that person involved you."

At that, Lorena Hicks stepped forward. "I'm sorry, too, Piper," she said, taking Piper's hand. "We know you had nothing whatsoever to do with it."

Piper saw a few heads nodding and heard murmurs of agreement, though they were subdued. It was encouraging for her, personally, though she knew it still meant her shop's wares remained untrustworthy.

"Come say hello to Joan," Emma said, drawing her toward the door. "We've been taking turns, not wanting to tax her."

Piper followed Emma into the room, her heart sinking at sight of the once-lively woman appearing to barely cling to life, her breaths shallow and her skin nearly transparent. Mrs. Tilley's eyelids lifted halfway and she smiled weakly. "Piper." One palm rolled upward and Piper laid her own in it, pained at the total lack of strength she felt. "So . . . good," Mrs. Tilley breathed out.

Piper covered the dry hand with her own second one, wanting to somehow pump warmth and energy into the older woman's wasted body. "It's good to see *you*," she said. "We all want you to get over this and be back with us soon."

Mrs. Tilley smiled. She drew a long breath. "Trying."

"I know you are. Mrs. Tilley, I'm so sorry it was my brandied cherries that made you this sick. I don't know who put something in them, but I'm going to try my best to find out."

Mrs. Tilley made a slight nod, more with her eyelids than her head. "Not . . . your fault," she said. She drew another breath. "Find . . . who."

"We will, Joan," Emma said. "We'll find who did this. Won't we, Piper?"

Piper's impulse was to admit how difficult that might be. But she saw Joan Tilley's pale blue eyes brighten at Emma's promise. How could she not keep that spark alive?

"Yes, we will," she agreed. "The person who did this

to you is going to pay. I promise to do my best to see that nothing like this will happen again."

At that, Mrs. Tilley's eyes slowly closed, but her lips had curled into a smile. Piper gently squeezed the woman's hand, then tucked it under the sheet. She followed Emma out of the room, thinking that she'd made a promise and had meant it. She'd better get busy at keeping it.

## 22

The following day was just as deadly quiet at Piper's Picklings as the previous one, and Amy's cell phone ring was the only bright interruption to the gloom. Amy chatted a few minutes, her comments making it clear that it was her long-time friend, Megan, on the other end. When the call ended, Amy turned to Piper.

"Megan said a strange woman stopped her a couple of days ago, asking where Franklin Street was. And by strange, Megan didn't mean that she didn't know her. She meant *strange*."

"I think I know who she means," Piper said. "Gwen Smyth. She stopped in here, too, wanting to know where the Porters' house was. I thought I gave her good directions but she might not have been, um, able to absorb them very well."

"Why was she going to the Porters'? Who is she?"

"She said she's Lydia Porter's sister."

"What? Megan described her as looking like a homeless person."

"She might well be." Piper retied her apron strings, which had loosened. "Or she might just be someone with a very, um, casual lifestyle. Either way, she seemed to expect Lydia and Jeremy to take her in."

"Well, that should be interesting."

Piper thought so, too, but she had other things to think of besides Porter relatives. She had told Amy about the lukewarm reception she got from Mrs. Tilley's friends at the hospital. She was grateful to Emma Leahy for standing up for her, and she knew Aunt Judy would do the same. But Piper also knew it would mainly be up to her to salvage what she could of her shop's reputation.

Piper eyed the rows of jars on her shelves surrounding the large gap left by the brandied cherries Sheriff Carlyle had carried off. "I may have to destroy all my handmade pickles and preserves to convince my customers it's safe to shop here again."

"Don't!" Amy cried. "I checked all the vacuum seals on the lids. Every lid is absolutely tight. Absolutely nothing out here or in the back room has been tampered with."

"Good to know, and thank you for checking. We can be just as sure that the spices I bought from dealers are sealed and safe. But will my customers be as certain? I'm afraid nothing other than a total replacement of my inventory will convince people who worry about poisoning."

"But . . . can you afford to do that?" Amy asked. "I mean, that must be thousands of dollars' worth of merchandise."

Piper knew she couldn't, really. But she said, "Let's worry about that later. I promised Mrs. Tilley I'd find the person who caused all this, so I'm going to concentrate on that first."

When it came time for Amy to leave for her restaurant job, she did so reluctantly, clearly more concerned about Piper and her predicament. Piper appreciated the sentiment but shooed her assistant off, doing her best to appear upbeat. She managed that until Amy was out of sight but quickly felt the realities of her situation come crushing back down. That was not good.

She'd agreed with Gil that keeping Piper's Picklings open was the smarter thing to do. But sitting alone in the empty store, feeling unfairly shunned, was more difficult than she'd expected. For the first time in her life she didn't want to put up any pickles or preserves. The thought that others would look at the jars with suspicion was just too defeating. But she had to keep busy or find herself sinking into self-pity.

Amy had already given Sheriff Carlyle a list of buyers of the brandied cherries, going back to December. Piper decided she might as well search the purchases for the weeks before that, time-wasting though it felt. She herself was convinced the bloodroot had been added to the one jar that Mrs. Tilley ended up with. But if the sheriff wanted the full list, she'd give it to him. The tedious, mind-numbing job might actually help free up her thoughts for identifying the person responsible for it.

Piper sighed and pulled out a stool to get to work, opening up her laptop and her charged-sale records. She'd been at it for possibly ten unhappy minutes when rescue appeared in the form of Tammy Butterworth. Anyone at all would have been a welcome reprieve, but Tammy, with her unfailing cheeriness, was like being handed a glass of ice water while dragging through the desert. Piper hopped off her stool and managed to keep from wrapping her arms around the woman.

"How did the radish pickling go?" she asked once Tammy had breezed through the door.

"Great! At least, so far. We'll see how they taste later on." Tammy's megawatt smile dimmed a few units. "I heard about your problem, the tainted cherries and all. I wanted to say don't worry too much. Sure, you'll lose business for a while"—her glance swept the quiet shop—"but I think you'll find people have short memories. That's been my experience, anyway." Her grin turned slightly wicked at that, making Piper smile while wondering what this model cleaning lady's experience might have involved.

"Thanks, Tammy. How did you hear?"

"From Lydia Porter. I was polishing silver in the kitchen when she and Jeremy came in looking for coffee. Jeremy wanted toast, too, but couldn't find any jam to go with it. I know he really likes jam, so I said I wouldn't mind running over here to get him some, that yours was the best in town. That's when Lydia reared up and said in effect *no way*, then explained why. I stood up for you, which didn't go over well. Lydia doesn't like being crossed, in case you haven't noticed."

"I've noticed," Piper said. "I hope you didn't put your job at risk."

Tammy shook her head. "That's one thing Jeremy

insists on—keeping me on the job. I moved to Clover-dale at his request, if you remember."

Piper nodded. "So that's worked out for you, huh? I mean, you picked up enough other cleaning jobs to make it worthwhile?"

"Oh, sure," Tammy flapped a hand. "No problem there. Word spreads fast in my line of work, especially in a small town." She chuckled softly. "Just like it's going to spread about Lydia's sister."

"You met her?"

"In a way. I had finished up at the house and was loading up my car when she came by. She asked me if that was the Porters' house, and I said yes but warned her they weren't good for soliciting. I really thought that's what she had in mind. But she said, 'That's okay. I'm family.' Of course, I didn't rush off after hearing that."

Piper smiled. Neither would she. "Who answered the door?"

"Lydia herself. I'm betting she spotted who was head-ing up the walk and rushed to pull the woman in and out of sight. All I heard was the stranger cry, 'Sis!' before she was hustled inside."

"Well, I guess her claim of being family was true. Her name's Gwen Smyth, by the way. She stopped in here, looking for directions."

"And in a few other places, too, from what I'm hear-ing. If Lydia hoped to keep her out of view, that ship has sailed."

"She might be a perfectly nice, respectable person, of course."

Tammy grinned. "Could anyone be respectable enough for Lydia?"

Piper thought about Lydia's immediate hints to Mrs. Tilley and other Cloverdale Women's Club members concerning her impressive ancestry and her not-so-casual mention to Piper of a high-ranking congressman-uncle. No, no sister below a Nancy Reagan was going to be good enough for Lydia, and Nancy herself might have had a struggle, considering her Hollywood background. Gwen Smyth, from what Piper had seen, was a goner.

"Well," Tammy said, giving a brisk tap to Piper's counter, "I've got to be going. Don't forget: Keep that chin up!"

"Will do. Thanks, Tammy."

Tammy took off, leaving Piper in a much better mood than before. So much so that she had a sudden inspiration. She put aside her depressing sales search and locked up her shop, painfully aware that closing for a few minutes wasn't going to make a whit of difference to her day's sales. She trotted down to the office supply store a couple of blocks away, where she bought a large sheet of posterboard and a set of markers, among other things, and carried them back to the shop.

She got to work, and within minutes Piper was taping the finished sign in her front window:

"Get well soon, Joan Tilley!

Sign our card and leave any gifts here

We will deliver them daily"

Piper set a large wicker basket beneath the sign, then stepped outside to judge the placement of both. She then went inside and waited.

Nothing happened for the first hour. Then one by one, people dribbled in.

"How is Joan?" the first woman—unknown to Piper—asked. "I can't get over to the hospital, but I'd love to sign the card and send my best wishes."

"Joan is very weak but getting better." Piper slid forward the super-size card she'd made on the office supply store's card stock, decorating it with ribbons and glitter. She was quite proud of it.

The second person—Patsy Morris—arrived a few minutes later. "I saw your sign and wrapped up this little book of inspirational quotes that I thought Joan might like to read when she's feeling better. Do you think that's okay?"

"It's perfect," Piper said, and waved toward the basket into which she'd previously set a pickling cookbook, to prime the pump, so to speak.

Two more ladies came in a few minutes after that to sign the card. "That's a great idea," one said, nodding toward Piper's sign. "Getting to the hospital is such a long drive." She scribbled her name and a greeting on Piper's card.

"We should take up a collection from the group for something nice," the second woman said to her companion. "All right if we bring it by tomorrow?" she asked Piper.

"Absolutely. Mrs. Tilley would really appreciate that."

"That's so nice of you to do this!" the second woman said, adding her name to the card.

Piper smiled modestly. "Not at all. Please spread the word."

The two promised to do so and left—of course without

buying anything, but that didn't concern Piper. Just getting people into her shop in a positive way was enough at that point, and Mrs. Tilley, she was sure, would be thrilled with all the remembrances.

Piper's handmade card and basket slowly filled with signatures and small gifts or promises of gifts to come. One or two drop-ins broached the subject of Piper's tainted brandied cherries but did so delicately and with obvious sympathy for her as well as Mrs. Tilley. No one showed up with any of Piper's pickles or preserves asking for a refund—which Piper would have agreed to. She suspected, though, that none of those jars were being opened, either, if they still actually remained in cupboards.

Talk of Lydia Porter's sister, whose appearance in Cloverdale was surprising in more ways than one, began cropping up. Apparently, Gwen Smyth had spent a good amount of time wandering about Cloverdale before finally arriving at her destination. If Lydia had hoped to keep her sister's visit private, those hopes were definitely quashed. *Had that been Gwen's intention,* Piper wondered? It did seem an odd way to start a visit.

"She came into Niki's while we were having lunch," one customer told Piper. "Frankly, we wondered if she'd be able to pay. Imagine our shock when we learned who she was!"

Another of Piper's customers, Nancy Phillips, mentioned having chatted briefly with Gwen at the park off the town square. "I was walking Oliver, my little Yorkie, and she came over to pet him. She seemed perfectly nice, but"—Nancy lowered her voice—"I think she might have been drinking. In the *afternoon,*" she added.

Gil Williams stopped in and seemed to be one of the very few who hadn't encountered Gwen Smyth. He did, however, approve of Piper's Tilley Project, as he called it.

"I've been hearing about the gift collection from my own customers and brought something she might enjoy." He held out a paperback copy of Carolyn Hart's latest mystery. "I happen to know Joan is a fan."

"Who isn't?" Piper asked with a smile. "Like me to wrap it for you?"

"Would you mind? All I had were my shop bags."

Piper found a sheet of pretty paper and began cutting it to size. She was taping it over the book when Ralph Strawbridge came in looking very much like he had something to tell.

"News of Zach?" Piper asked hopefully.

"No, I'm afraid not. We still don't know where he could be."

"Then what?" Piper's fingers had halted midtaping. Gil had straightened up in concerned anticipation.

"It's the Realtor," Ralph said. "Stan Yeager. Now he's missing."

# 23

$\sim\sim$

"Stan!" Piper cried, shocked. "Missing? Are you sure?"

"Nobody knows where he is." Ralph ran a hand through his gray-speckled hair. "As you know, I've been trying to keep an eye on Stan's comings and goings as much as I can. When I walked over to his office today, I saw it was locked up. I checked with the woman who works for him part time. She said she hadn't heard anything from him in two days and couldn't get in when she showed up this morning. I went to his house. There was no answer when I knocked and no car in the driveway. I talked to his neighbors, but nobody knows a thing."

"But that's crazy," Piper said.

"Also worrying," Gil put in.

"Sugar is convinced it confirms his guilt," Ralph said. "She doesn't, of course, feel the same about Zach's disappearance."

"Have you told the sheriff?" Gil asked.

"I did. I don't know what he thinks of it, though. As far as I'm aware, we were the only ones suspicious of Stan."

"But the sheriff should be, too," Piper protested, while at the same time feeling her loyalties waver. She wanted Zach to be exonerated, but she didn't particularly want it to be by Stan Yeager. However, Stan's going off like that was very odd.

At that point Scott came in. Taking in the three serious faces, he asked, "You heard?"

"About Yeager? I already notified the sheriff," Ralph said.

"What effect do you think this will have on Zach Heywood's situation?" Gil asked.

Scott shook his head. "Hard to say. It certainly complicates things. We need to find Zach. He should know about this."

"Sugar and I are trying our best," Ralph said. He turned to Piper. "Do you think Yeager might be your cherry preserves poisoner?"

The shop door opened, and one of Piper's customers, Mrs. Anderson, came in, a small parcel in her hands. She paused to look at the others inquiringly, then said, "I'll just drop this in your basket, Piper. It's for Joan Tilley."

"Thank you, Mrs. Anderson," Piper said. "I'll see that she gets it." The woman smiled and left.

Scott stared after her, then at the gift basket in bewilderment. "Joan Tilley?" he asked Piper.

"You didn't know?" Though surprised, Piper wasn't sure if she should be gratified that there was something major going on in her life that Scott didn't know about.

"Of course, you've been focused on Zach, as you should be. But something's happened that's probably connected." She explained about the poisoned jar of brandied cherries that had landed Mrs. Tilley in the hospital.

"Holy . . . !" Scott swallowed hard. "Why didn't you call me?"

"To do what? The sheriff doesn't seem to be blaming me. It probably helps that his daughter takes a large part in my pickle production."

"But . . . your shop? Your business?"

"In trouble, yes, but I'll handle it, one way or another. I've thought about who could have tampered with my jar and left it on the shelf. Unfortunately, the list includes everyone we've been looking at along with probably half the town."

"Was Stan Yeager in recently?" Ralph asked.

"He was, and that surprised me. He isn't normally a customer."

Ralph nodded, as did the other two men, taking in all the possible implications of that.

Piper's phone rang and she excused herself.

"I just heard," Will said as Piper picked up. "Tomas and I have been busy all day in the fields. What can I do?"

Piper smiled. No *Why didn't you call me*, just a simple offer of help. "Thanks, Will. Can I get back to you in a bit? Got a few people here right now."

"You're still getting customers? Great!"

"Well . . ."

"I've got to run, Piper," Scott called out. "I'll be back later."

"Wait, was that Scott?" Will asked.

"Um, yes."

"And he's coming back later?"

Piper sighed. *Simple*, it seemed, just flew out the window.


As Piper was ready to close up, Aunt Judy walked in. "I decided calling wasn't enough. I wanted to see you in person." She took Piper by the shoulders and looked at her searchingly. "How are you holding up?"

At sight of her aunt's loving, sympathetic face, all the emotions Piper had been holding in rushed to the surface, and to her chagrin she began tearing up. Aunt Judy pulled her close and hugged.

"Uncle Frank and I will help you out in any way we can," she murmured. "You can get through this."

"I intend to," Piper said, sniffing. "But not by imposing on people I love if I can help it."

"There's no shame in accepting help. We all need it from time to time." Aunt Judy patted Piper's back, then let go as a woman entered the shop to drop a small package in the wicker basket. Piper turned to grab a tissue and Aunt Judy stepped forward and thanked the woman. After the woman left, Aunt Judy said, "I heard about your gift collection for Joan Tilley. A perfectly lovely thought. Would you like me to take it to the hospital? I'll be going there tonight."

"Would you?" Piper blew her nose. "I was going to drop them off before meeting Will at the Elm Street Café, which meant a lot of extra driving. I'd love to grab a few minutes of downtime before dinner."

"It looks like a lot of small things in the basket that shouldn't be any trouble at all."

"Let me load them into something easier to carry," Piper said, and trotted up to her apartment for a tote bag.

As she helped Piper pack up the gifts, Aunt Judy said, "I'm so glad Will's taking you out for a nice evening."

Piper smiled, feeling much the same. After Will's initial spark of jealousy at hearing Scott's voice in the background, he'd returned to his usual terrific self when they'd talked later. She was looking forward to spending time with him.

"Think you can handle all this in one bag," she asked, "or should I divide the load in two?"

Aunt Judy tested the weight. "This is fine. I haven't lived most of my life on a farm without developing a few muscles," she said with a grin. "By the way, did you know Frances Billings is still in town? I thought she'd gone back to Florida, but she's still at the Cloverton. I should give her a call and see if she'd like to get together."

Piper remembered the older woman she'd spoken with at Lydia Porter's tea. Considering she was essentially saying final good-byes to her childhood home, Frances Billings had been remarkably upbeat. "Why is she still in town?" she asked.

"I don't really know. Maybe catching up with an old friend or two? I know she doesn't have family here anymore."

"She and I met, if you remember, in the Porters'

library." Piper smiled at the memory. "She wasn't impressed with the books that had been stocked in it."

"Well, she used to be a librarian. I'm sure that gives her strong opinions on the subject."

"Was she? She didn't mention that."

"It was at a private school, I believe, in Albany. She told me the name. What was it? Treyburn?" Aunt Judy waved a hand. "Something like that, not that it matters. Her family's fortune, you know, had declined, so Frances needed to support herself. That may have been where she met her husband," Aunt Judy said, then shook her head. "I'm really not too clear on that, either," she said, and laughed at herself.

"I'm sure Frances would love to meet with you," Piper said. "And give my best to Mrs. Tilley tonight. I hope you'll find her doing much better."

"I do, too." Aunt Judy took the handmade card filled with signatures and greetings and slipped it into the tote bag. "All these good wishes can't fail to help."

They hugged good-bye, and Piper finished closing up shop, which didn't take long with no sales whatsoever to total up. *It can only get better*, she told herself, and went upstairs to get ready for her date.

Will had suggested the Elm Street Café, a quiet, out-of-the-way place, which was exactly what Piper needed. They slid onto vinyl-cushioned seats at a booth that had paper place mats on a bare wood table, then studied a menu full of comfort foods. After giving a grandfatherly waiter their order, Piper updated Will on the status of her shop and how she'd been distracting herself from the lack of business with her Tilley Project.

"It's a good indication that your old customers are taking to it. If they blamed you for the poisoned cherry preserves, they wouldn't come near your shop."

"I think so, too, and that's encouraging. A few even sounded sympathetic to my plight. Nobody was buying, though."

"Give it time."

Piper nodded but didn't mention that her funds for running a shop that brought in no income wouldn't last long, not to mention the astronomical cost if she had to replace all of her stock. The troubled look in Will's eyes, which he couldn't quite hide, told her he knew.

To move away from her own problems, Piper told him about Stan Yeager's apparent disappearance. "That's raised Sugar's hopes, since she's been focusing on Stan as Dirk Unger's murderer."

Will shook his head. "The idea of Stan murdering someone just doesn't work for me. I know you said he'd lost business because of Unger stealing clients away, but I still can't see him reacting with violence."

"I'm struggling with that, too. Unfortunately, experience has proven that the nicest-seeming person can have a dark side."

Their food arrived, their waiter hovering solicitously to make sure everything was to their liking, and they suspended their talk of murder and suspects for a while.

They were halfway through their meal when Piper noticed a surprising new arrival to the café.

She leaned closer to Will. "Don't look now, but Jeremy Porter and his sister, Mallory, just walked in."

Will's eyebrows rose. "Without Lydia?"

"Ah, you don't know about the family's possible black sheep." Piper explained about Lydia's sister Gwen. "I have a feeling Lydia might be keeping her close to home. That would explain why Jeremy and Mallory are here on their own."

"Sounds like the cat's out of the bag about the sister's existence."

"I know. Lydia might not know that, though. I'd love to have been a fly on the wall when Gwen walked in."

Will grinned. "What do you suppose she showed up for?"

"I doubt it was for sisterly affection. Those two are clearly such polar opposites that I can't imagine any close bond. Money? She seemed a bit down on her luck. Or maybe"—Piper glanced at Jeremy and Mallory's table—"maybe she has real feelings for her niece and nephew. I'd like to think that was her reason."

Their genial waiter came over again to refill water glasses and fuss over them. By the time he'd left, Piper's thoughts had moved on. "Aunt Judy was telling me about Frances Billings, the older lady I met at the tea who sold Jeremy Porter her house. Aunt Judy said Ms. Billings had been a school librarian in Albany. She thought the name might have been Treyburn. The friends of yours we met with for dinner—the Flemings? Didn't Jen

Fleming say she'd worked at a private school in Albany? Was that the name?"

Will thought a moment. "Tedbury. I'm fairly sure it was Tedbury Academy."

"I'll bet it's the same one. I remember Jen mentioning that Lydia had been on the board because her two children had gone there. I wonder if they, or Mallory in particular, knew Frances Billings?"

Will shrugged, though Piper had only been thinking aloud.

"If Mallory did," Piper said, "she might like to see Frances again while she's still in town. I mean, to see her without Lydia beside her and doing all the talking. Mallory recently made a brief stab at independent action. A little more might be good for her. I'd like to encourage that."

"Sure." Will glanced back at the two Porters. "Worth a try."

Their coffee arrived, and between sips Piper checked Jeremy and Mallory's table. There seemed to be little conversation going on, with Mallory looking down at her food or beyond Jeremy at the wall most of the time. Perhaps feeling somewhat anonymous in the small café, Jeremy had left behind his life-of-the-party persona and appeared glum. Piper couldn't help but think how much improved his life would have been if he'd kept Sugar Heywood in it.

Mallory either hadn't seen Piper or was pretending not to, but Piper wasn't going to let that stop her. When she and Will had finished and Will dealt with the bill, Piper headed over to the Porters' table.

"Nice to see you both again," she said as Jeremy instantly rose. "I hope you're enjoying your dinner?"

Jeremy's public face flashed back into place and he raved about their meals, then held out his hand when Will joined them and was introduced. As Will and Jeremy engaged in small talk, Piper turned to Mallory.

"Mallory, I enjoyed our stop for coffee after the fabric shop the other day. We should do it again sometime, or maybe a lunch."

Mallory's lips curved in a tentative smile. "I'd like that."

"I also just found out something interesting about Frances Billings—the woman who used to own your house? Turns out she had been a librarian on the staff at your school, Tedbury Academy. Did you know her?"

Mallory looked at Piper as though she'd suddenly lost her mind. "Our school librarian was Miss Lucas!"

"Oh. Well, I guess Mrs. Billings must have been there at another time." Piper smiled. "I don't want to hold you up from your meal. Good to see you."

Piper and Will took their leave, Jeremy acting as though they were the best of friends, but Mallory simply nodding and picking up her fork. Piper sighed. Coaxing Lydia's daughter out of her shell was going to be two steps forward followed by one step back and would require patience. But with all that Piper had on her plate right then, any Mallory project would have to be put on hold.

## 24

Saturday morning, Piper opened her shop again with faint hope of customers. She did, however, put the "gifts for Mrs. Tilley" basket back in place and hoped it and her sign would continue to draw people in. Within a few minutes, Aunt Judy called to report on her hospital visit.

"Joan was so pleased and touched by all the remembrances you gathered! Emma and I helped her unwrap them—she's still terribly weak—and we set your card on her table where she could see it."

That reminded Piper to make a second card for that day's get-well wishes, and after they'd hung up she got busy on that, cutting and folding her card stock, then decorating it with colored pens and pencils. She had sprinkled a bit of glitter and was holding her finished product out to judge the effect when out of the corner of her eye she saw two figures approaching her door. *Just in time*, she thought, setting her card in place as she anticipated old customers or perhaps a couple of Aunt Judy's friends walking in.

To her surprise, one of the pair was Lydia Porter. But the other wasn't Mallory. Instead Piper saw another very well-dressed and coiffed woman. She stared for a moment, thinking that the second woman seemed vaguely familiar. Then recognition dawned. It was Gwen Smyth, Lydia's sister!

The transformation was nothing short of amazing. Gwen's straggly hair had been trimmed and styled, makeup glowed on her face, and either she'd been loaned one of Lydia's spring suits or they'd gone shopping in a hurry. The only thing that remained of the bag lady who'd been in her shop three days ago was the mischievous look in her eyes. Gwen, Piper saw, was greatly enjoying her astonishment. Standing half a step back from Lydia, she raised an index finger to her lips as her eyes danced.

"Miss Lamb," Lydia said, "I'd like you to meet my sister, Gwendolyn. She's surprised us with a visit, coming all the way from San Francisco."

"How do you do?" Piper said, avoiding a direct look at Gwen in an effort to keep a straight face.

"Delighted to meet you, Miss Lamb. What a charming shop you have!"

"Thank you. Will you be in Cloverdale long?"

"She's just here for a few days," Lydia answered, "much to our disappointment, of course. But her many duties in San Francisco are calling her back."

"Yes," Gwen said. "My many duties."

"I've been showing Gwendolyn our little town. At the gift shop over on Maple, we learned about your collection for that poor lady in the hospital and brought a little something to add." Lydia pulled an elaborately wrapped box from the shopping bag she carried and plopped it on top of Piper's newly made card. "What a shame she got so sick from one of your homemade preserves," Lydia added, though she didn't look terribly concerned.

"Yes," Piper said. "It was from a jar of my brandied cherries." Then she couldn't resist saying, "I do hope that you didn't get ill from your jar."

"Fortunately, Mallory had only tasted it. I, of course, disposed of the jar the minute I heard."

"Really?" Gwen piped up. "I love brandied cherries. Do you have any more?" she asked Piper.

"I'm afraid not."

"Then"—Gwen headed over to Piper's shelves—"let's see what else looks good. Ooh, Lydia, we should get the blueberry jam."

"I don't—" Lydia began, frowning, but Gwen cut her off.

"And these bread-and-butter pickles. Don't they look great! Oh, she has sweet red pepper relish. That sounds yummy!" Gwen scoured through Piper's shelves, loading her arms with as much as she could and bringing all to Piper to ring up.

"You're sure?" Piper asked, and Gwen nodded brightly.

"You have your credit card, Lydia, don't you? I left mine at home."

Lydia, after a significant pause, reached stiffly into her

purse and handed Piper her credit card. Piper made the transaction and pulled out a bag for Gwen's purchases.

"I ran into your son and daughter last night," Piper told Lydia as she began wrapping protective paper around the jars. "At the Elm Street Café."

"Really? Neither of them mentioned seeing you."

"I thought Mallory might have known Frances Billings from the Tedbury Academy."

"Frances Billings? At Tedbury?"

"I understand she ran the school library, though I don't know exactly when. I guess that didn't come up when you spoke with her?"

"There was no reason for it to come up." Lydia sniffed. "Our interaction with Mrs. Billings was totally house-related during the very brief time she was here."

"Actually, I hear she's still in town," Piper said. "Staying at the Cloverton."

"Ah, those happy golden days at Tedbury," Gwen put in. "Remember the headmistress, Mrs. Walters?" she asked Lydia. "She—oh, wait, that was after your time, wasn't it? Hilda Walters took over as headmistress when I was there, *six years* later."

Lydia shot a steely glare at her sister. "We'd best be going. There's so much more of Cloverdale I want to show you, Gwendolyn, dear."

Piper handed over the jars—packed in a large bag with "Piper's Picklings" in bright, bold letters on both sides for all to see—and thanked them for coming, looking mainly at Gwen as she said it. The two left, with Piper sure that Lydia's face ached from all the forced smiles she must be pulling up that morning. The woman

was surely counting the seconds until her "dear" sister
would take off.

A couple of ladies dropped off gifts for Mrs. Tilley
and hurriedly signed Piper's card before leaving
empty handed. *At least I'll have had one good sale for
the day, thanks to Gwen Smyth*, Piper thought, and bus-
ied herself with dusting her shelves until Amy arrived.

"Hey, that's my job," Amy protested smilingly as she
walked in.

"I probably should have told you not to come in,"
Piper said, setting a steel canning pot back in place.
"There's nothing much to do."

"No pickles to make?"

Piper sighed. "I didn't pick up the sugar snap peas I
was going to. Frankly, I just can't bring myself to do
any pickling. I'd be just going through the motions.
Pickles should be made with joy."

"Things will get better," Amy said, doing her best to
look optimistic, and Piper nodded without really believ-
ing that oft-repeated encouragement.

She was telling Amy about Lydia's visit with her sister
when she spotted Sugar Heywood heading toward the
shop, wearing the same drooping gray sweater she'd had
on during the sheriff's search of her house, her once-
lovely silver blond hair appearing unwashed and straggly.
Piper reflected how less than two weeks earlier Sugar had
been happily planning to cater Jeremy Porter's dinner
and Piper had been anticipating the installation of Ralph's
beautiful door with excitement. How drastically things

had changed in that short time. Would either of them totally recover? At the moment, that seemed highly questionable.

As Sugar walked in, Amy greeted her brightly with, "Hi, Ms. Heywood," clearly doing her best to add a bit of cheer.

Sugar smiled gamely, though her eyes remained sad. "Hi, you two. I got tired of sitting in the house and worrying and decided I could worry just as well here."

"Ralph hasn't been with you?" Piper asked. The two had seemed inseparable since Zach's troubles first began.

"He's off somewhere. I told him he should look after his own affairs once in a while and I guess he took me up on it." She smiled wanly. "I miss him."

"Ralph's been amazing," Piper said. "Stepping right in to help."

"I don't know what I would have done without him," Sugar said, agreeing. "You heard about Stan Yeager disappearing?" Sugar asked, and as Piper and Amy nodded Sugar's voice rose in frustration. "I'm positive that man has something to hide! Why isn't *his* house being searched? That's what I'd like to know." She glanced at Amy and took a deep breath. "No offense."

Amy waved off the half apology as Piper said, "I'm sure Sheriff Carlyle is doing exactly what the law allows him to do. He must not see any probable cause for getting a search warrant on Stan's place. What's going on with Stan's wife? She's been away since before all this began."

Sugar's eyes flashed. "She probably knew what Stan did—which was to murder Dirk Unger—and she either left Stan or took off first with plans for him to join her in hiding."

Piper wasn't so sure about that somewhat dramatic scenario, though she'd already admitted—to herself and to Will—that people weren't always what they seemed.

"Coffee?" Amy asked, offering the only comfort she could, and Sugar nodded.

As Amy hurried back to get it, Sugar pulled out a stool, taking in the signs of Piper's Tilley Project. "Ralph told me about Mrs. Tilley and your brandied cherries. I'm so sorry. How is she doing?"

"Recovering."

"And you?" She took the steaming mug Amy brought back, Piper gratefully accepting a second one Amy held out to her.

"I'm hanging in there," Piper said. "It's about all I can do—for the shop, that is. The drop in business at least gives me more time to work on the murder."

Sugar covered Piper's hand with her own. "We'll get through this. The truth will come out and your shop and my catering business *will rise again*." She smiled weakly. "As I believe someone named Scarlett O'Hara once said."

"She might have been talking about the South," Piper said.

"Well, she was right, wasn't she? The South got back on its feet, and so will we." Sugar's face crumbled again. "But first Zach needs to come home."

Piper silently squeezed Sugar's hand, having no idea what to say. They sat, each sipping their coffee as Amy looked on unhappily, until Amy's friend Megan breezed in, a gust of wind sending her blond hair flying along with some of the surrounding gloom. "Hi there!" she cried, reminding Piper what a contrast Megan's lively personality was to that of her brother, Ben, who took all things, especially his auxiliary police officership, extremely seriously.

"Have you seen Lydia Porter's sister today?" Megan asked. Seeing Sugar's questioning look, she launched into a gleeful description of Gwen Porter's jaw-dropping transformation from when Megan first encountered her outside the library. "She was double-checking her directions to the Porters' place. It turned out she was dropping in unannounced on her sister, Mrs. Porter. I'll bet *that* was a surprise!

"Jeremy's aunt?" Sugar asked. "I hadn't heard. You say she appeared down-and-out?"

"Definitely not up to Lydia's family standards, presencewise," Piper said, "though I found her very likable. The two stopped in here this morning. Gwen was enjoying herself—and I'm sure it wasn't because of her fashion makeover. It's hard to believe they're sisters, though Lydia would probably be the first to deny it if they weren't."

Sugar actually chuckled, the first Piper had heard from her in a long time. Unfortunately, Scott chose that moment to stop in, which instantly turned Sugar's thoughts back to her worries.

"No word from Zach?" he asked, and when Sugar dejectedly shook her head, said, "I've contacted a few people I know from my time as an ADA. They've promised to do what they can to help locate him."

"It's getting to the point," Sugar said, "that even if Zach ends up being arrested, I'll be glad to at least have him back. Not knowing where my son is or *how* he is, is horrible."

"I'm sure he doesn't realize what he's putting you through," Piper said, while at the same time wishing heartily that Zach *did* realize and put an end to it.

"He's twenty," Megan said. "Guys that age have mush for brains. Some," she said, "still have mush at thirty. Present company excepted, of course," she added, glancing at Scott.

"What Megan means," Amy said, "is Zach is bright—we all know that—but like most guys his age he's probably letting his emotions blot out any clear thinking."

Piper saw Scott wince at Amy's well-intentioned words, which might describe exactly what Amy's father—Sheriff Carlyle—had in mind: that Zach had acted emotionally and overridden his normal good sense to murder Dirk Unger.

Piper didn't want to believe that herself, though Zach's continued disappearance made that more difficult by the hour to hang on to.

# 25

Aunt Judy came to the shop later that afternoon, and the sight of her lifted Piper's sagging spirits. She'd collected more gifts for Mrs. Tilley, along with a few more encouraging words of support. But when it came to her old customers trusting Piper's pickles and preserves enough to buy, well, that was apparently for someone else to do.

"For goodness' sake," Aunt Judy said, exasperated, "you'd think people would at least realize that your pickling *equipment* is perfectly safe."

Piper shook her head. "It wouldn't matter. There's a ghostly skull and crossbones hanging over my entire shop because of that one jar of poisoned cherries."

Aunt Judy tsked worriedly but moved on to less distressing things. "I talked with Frances Billings," she told Piper. "It turns out she's stayed in town because of a sudden attack of nostalgia. She's been visiting the few places from her childhood that are still around, like the grandstand in the park and the old Majestic theater, which used to be *the* place to go for all the big movies. Your Uncle Frank took me there on our first date. It's rather run-down, now, though I did hear there are plans to refurbish it for a community theater group. Won't that be nice?

"Anyway, that's what has kept her here. I offered to take her around tomorrow, then bring her to the farmhouse for dinner, but she said she'd had an unexpected invitation to lunch and at her age she wasn't up to doing too much in one day. Frances sounded a bit regretful that she had to pass on my offer."

"Who wouldn't?" Piper asked, meaning it, but Aunt Judy laughed and waved that off.

"I meant that she wished she could do everything. I'm sure that lunch with whoever she's meeting will be very enjoyable." She glanced at the Tilley gift basket. "Shall I take those with me? I won't see Joan tonight but I plan to stop at the hospital after church tomorrow."

"Thanks, but I'll run these over. I'd like to visit Mrs. Tilley again."

"You're not seeing Will tonight?"

Piper knew her aunt was thinking of it being a Saturday night and therefore an automatic date night. Perhaps like a movie at the Majestic with Uncle Frank had been.

"Will and I enjoyed a very nice dinner together last night. But he's gotten behind on some of the business side of his work, things like confirming standing orders for his trees and reaching out for new outlets that he needs to do this time of year."

"Tree farmers must have to do like the rest of us farmers—fit in all kinds of work whenever they can. Give my love to Joan Tilley when you see her, and try"—Aunt Judy glanced around the overly quiet shop—"try not to worry about your shop too much."

Piper thought she could say the same to her aunt, who looked as though Piper's troubles weighed just as heavily on her as they did on Piper, but she dredged up as positive a smile as she could. "I won't," she said and waved a reasonably cheery good-bye.

Emma Leahy caught Piper as she was heading down the hospital corridor to Mrs. Tilley's room.

"She's sleeping," Emma said, beckoning Piper toward the patient lounge. "A few of her visitors this afternoon stayed a bit too long, so I'm glad to see her rest. More gifts for her?" she asked, nodding toward Piper's tote bag.

"They keep coming. A lot of people really care about her. How is she?"

"Much better. If all goes well, they'll be releasing her tomorrow."

"I'm so glad."

"Of course, she'll still need help. Hospitals don't keep you a minute longer than they have to, you know, and someone her age doesn't just bounce right back into taking care of herself. But I'll stick with her. Others will pitch in, too, I'm sure."

"She has good friends," Piper said. "Would you like me to start a sign-up sheet for shifts once she gets home?"

Emma considered that. "Let's see how it goes. There's

some who make good nurses, then there's those who have good intentions, but . . ." She shrugged. "Then again, Joan might surprise us by perking up once she's back in familiar surroundings."

"That'd be great. How about you, Emma? If Mrs. Tilley is out of the woods, maybe you should go on home and catch up on your own rest." Piper had noticed dark shadows under Emma's eyes and wondered how many hours she'd been spending at the hospital.

Emma drew a weary breath. "You know, that doesn't sound like a bad idea." She glanced hesitantly at Piper's bulging tote.

"I can stay until she wakes up," Piper said. "I'll help her handle these."

Emma brightened. "Would you? I know she'd be pleased to see a new face. If you're sure?"

"Go," Piper said, grabbing Emma's jacket from the green, vinyl-covered sofa where it lay, handing it to her, and turning her by the shoulder toward the door. "Enjoy a hot meal and put your feet up."

"You'll call if . . . ?"

"I'll call." Piper patted the purse that held her phone. "Get a good night's sleep."

"Thank you," Emma said as Piper guided her, one hand on her back, into the corridor. Emma's pace quickened as an elevator door opened up ahead.

Piper smiled as the kindhearted woman hurried off, then slipped off her own jacket to make herself comfortable, figuring she'd check on Mrs. Tilley in half an hour or so. She picked up a well-thumbed magazine from one of the tables and sank onto the sofa—which gave off a soft whooshing noise—then flipped idly through the pages, finding little in the months-old celebrity gossip rag to catch her interest. Setting the publication aside, she pulled out her phone and checked for messages, then began browsing the Internet.

*What does one do for a living when one's business venture goes bankrupt?* she wondered, trying to keep an unemotional and practical approach to the problem that faced her. Return to her old job at the state tax office in Albany? The thought was deeply depressing, first because she'd left that unfulfilling job with relief, but mostly because it meant leaving Cloverdale. How could she leave Will, Aunt Judy and Uncle Frank, and all the people she'd come to know and care about in Cloverdale?

Cloverdale, though, she reminded herself, was turning its back on her to some extent. Not those closest to her, of course, but the people on whom her livelihood depended. Memories of the looks on the faces of Mrs. Tilley's friends as Piper approached her hospital room that first visit still stung. If Emma hadn't been there to stand up for her, would accusations of *poisoner!* have been thrown at her? A grim thought and one she hastened to sweep away. Better to look ahead, rather than back. Except, ahead loomed debt and tough decisions.

Thankfully, before Piper could sink further into gloom, an excellent distraction appeared in the form of Gil Williams.

"I ran into Emma Leahy in the parking lot," Gil said, holding a bouquet of spring flowers wrapped in a cone of green tissue paper. "She told me you took her place watching over Joan Tilley. Very considerate of you."

"Poor Emma badly needed a break, though it was hard for her to admit it."

"This was my first chance to come by," Gil said. He glanced down the hall toward Mrs. Tilley's room. "It never occurred to me that our patient might not be ready for a visitor."

"She'll probably be awake in a little while. If you don't mind waiting, I'd be very glad for the company."

"Well, that's not something I hear every day!" Gil joked, then headed toward one of the vinyl-covered chairs opposite Piper. "I hope her room isn't packed with these," he said as he laid his flowers on a nearby table. "I already added a book to your gift collection, and I didn't think a fruit basket, under the circumstances, would be entirely appropriate."

Piper smiled. "I think you made a good choice." Her smile faded. "I'm still appalled that someone—whoever it was—did that to her, of all people."

Gil's face darkened. "As am I. I suspect poor Joan was simply collateral damage and that our killer is quite cold blooded."

"If so, then that, to my mind, at least, eliminates the most obvious suspects: Zach and Stan Yeager."

"Quite probably," Gil said, nodding. Piper noted Gil's *probably* but said nothing since she knew she'd left the door open on those two, at least a crack. Human nature never being completely predictable, it was the realistic thing to do, though she'd never say so to Sugar.

"Excuse me." A young nurse's aide in flower-printed scrubs appeared at the lounge doorway. "I'm looking for Emma Leahy. Mrs. Tilley was asking about her."

"Oh, she's awake! Emma went home but we're here in her place," Piper said. "Can we see Mrs. Tilley now?"

"Absolutely." The aide glanced at the clock on the wall. "But keep it to half an hour, if you would."

"Of course," Gil said, pulling himself out of his chair and reaching for his flowers. "Will it tire Joan too much to stay longer?"

The young woman dimpled at that. "Not really. She's doing a lot better. Enough to know that her favorite show—one of those British comedies on PBS—will be on in half an hour. She'd hate to miss it."

Gil and Piper grinned and jointly promised not to overstay their welcome.

Mrs. Tilley's face lit up when they appeared in her doorway and Piper was very happy to see the significant improvement in the older woman.

"Oh! Flowers for me?" Mrs. Tilley cried, reaching out for a sniff of Gil's bouquet. "There's a vase for them on the windowsill, if you wouldn't mind," she said, handing it back. "People have been so kind," she added as Piper explained about Emma's absence and then held up the latest batch of gifts she'd brought.

Gil took one of the visitor's chairs while Piper got started unwrapping each present for Mrs. Tilley to examine. Piper noted the return of color to her older friend's cheeks along with other improvements, though she agreed with Emma that Joan Tilley probably still had plenty of recovery ahead of her. She spoke much more heartily than she had at Piper's first visit and definitely smiled more, but the movements of her hands were slow and fairly weak.

"Well," Mrs. Tilley said, once they'd opened the last package. "I believe I'll have enough reading material to last me a good while. And chocolates and perfumed soaps. I love it all!"

"Anything you'd like close at hand?" Piper asked before setting the latest haul to the side.

Mrs. Tilley shook her head. "I've been reading the book Gil sent and it's right here where I can reach it. Thank you so much, Gil. And for the flowers, too! And Piper, for the, the . . ." She struggled to remember exactly what Piper had sent her and Piper jumped in to help.

"The pickling cookbook."

"That's right! I'm so sorry. My brain has been a bit addled lately, I'm afraid."

"If I'd gone through what you did," Gil said, "I'd probably have trouble remembering my own name."

Mrs. Tilley laughed, saying, "There's been times . . . But Piper, thank you so much. I can't wait to try those new recipes. Hopefully it won't be long before I'm back in your shop for more jars and seasonings."

Piper smiled but suppressed a wince as she wondered if her shop would still be open for business when Mrs. Tilley felt up to pickling again. Searching for a less painful subject, she grabbed at the first thing that popped into her head. "Did you know Frances Billings?" she asked. "The lady who owned the large house that the Porters bought? Aunt Judy said she's been staying a while in Cloverdale to revisit a few places she remembered from years ago."

"Oh, yes, I knew Frances. Or rather, I knew *of* her. She was a bit older. And a Kingsley. In those days, that

meant she traveled in a different sphere. But she was a
lovely lady. I imagine she will have gone to see the War
Memorial near the courthouse. Her grandfather, Herbert
Kingsley, put that up, you know, at his own expense to
remember our Cloverdale fallen soldiers. That was
before the family fortune dwindled, of course."

Mrs. Tilley glanced at the wall clock and Piper realized it was time for her television show. Gil, apparently,
caught that, too, as he rose from his chair.

"We should get going and let you get some rest," he
said.

Mrs. Tilley twittered a polite protest, which Piper and
Gil easily overrode, and they said their good-byes, making sure the television remote was near at hand. As they
closed the door gently behind them, sounds of the show's
theme song followed them and they smiled at each other.

"She looks much better, doesn't she?" the aide whom
they'd spoken to before said as she came toward them
in the hall.

"Much better," Piper agreed. "Her friend, Emma,
hated to leave her tonight, but I think I can assure her
Mrs. Tilley will be fine."

"Absolutely!" the young woman said. "And we'll
keep a good eye on her, don't you worry."

Piper thanked her and put through a call to Emma
as she and Gil made their way to the elevator. "All is
well, Emma. I'm leaving now so Joan can watch her TV
show in peace, which is a very good sign, wouldn't you
agree? Relax and get a good night's sleep yourself." She
pressed *end* as the elevator doors opened and rode down
with Gil to the first floor.

"I'm going to follow you home, if you don't mind," Gil said as they stepped out into the hospital lobby.

"But . . ." Piper began, knowing that Gil, who didn't live above his shop as she did, would be driving much too far out of his way. Then she recalled the harrowing ride home she'd had several months ago from another visit to the hospital and realized he'd thought of it, too. That ride had also been late at night and Piper had been closing in on another murderer, as she could only hope she was now—though it didn't feel that way. She nodded, knowing that Gil's offer was a sensible precaution.

"Just try not to go too far over the speed limit," Gil called as they parted. "My aging car, remember, will be driven by an ancient driver."

Piper laughed and promised, then waited near the parking lot exit until she saw Gil's not-so-ancient white Buick pull up behind her. She waved, grateful for the worry-free trip home she would have—worry-free, that was, of immediate danger. Her multitude of other worries still lingered closely, just waiting for a quiet moment to tiptoe out.

When Piper got home, she noticed the message light on her shop phone blinking and clicked it, expecting to hear a question from one of her customers. To her surprise, it was a message from Jen Fleming, wife of Will's friend, Matt, asking Piper to call her back, which she did immediately.

"I hope you don't mind me calling your shop," Jen said. "Matt's out, and I didn't know the best way to reach you, so I just looked up your shop number."

"That's fine," Piper said, curious to know what Jen wanted to talk to her about. "As a matter of fact, your name came up just the other night, in connection with Tedbury Academy."

"That's a coincidence because that's kind of what I'm calling about," Jen said. "When you mentioned Lydia Porter during our dinner with Matt and Will, it got me thinking about why she decided to leave the academy board, so when I lunched with one of my old co-workers today, I brought the subject up." Jen paused. "And I learned something you might want to know."

Piper was all ears but had to wait as Jen suddenly excused herself to tend to her ten-month-old, who'd started fussing.

"Sorry about that," Jen apologized, back on the line. "As I said, I'm on my own right now, and Dylan's teething."

"No problem. You were saying about Lydia Porter?"

"Right. Well, there'd been rumors flying around about why Lydia left, particularly since she wasn't that well liked. I learned a long time ago not to pay much attention to such talk. But my co-worker, one of the school secretaries and someone I've always considered very reliable, told me about a phone call she happened to partially overhear shortly before Lydia resigned."

Jen paused as Piper heard distant cries from her son. They stopped, and Jen went on. "My friend said she didn't know who Lydia was talking to at the time, but that she definitely sounded tense. She remembered hearing Lydia loudly demand, 'How could you possibly have found out about that?' Then, 'You got it from someone who was here at the school, didn't you?' which caught my friend's attention. Then Lydia asked, 'Who have you told this to?' in a tone that my friend said was enough to chill anyone's blood. Lydia seemed to realize at that point that her door was slightly open and slammed it shut, so my secretary friend didn't hear anything more."

"Your friend had no idea who Lydia was speaking to?"

"Right. But she said when Lydia came out a few minutes later, her lips were pinched nearly white. And it was a very short time after that, like, within a couple of days, that she announced her resignation from the board, saying she'd decided to take her son up on his request to move closer to him. That family was so important, and blah, blah, blah."

"But most people didn't believe that?"

"Not really. Lydia was giving up a position of power that she obviously relished. To do what?"

"To interfere in a lot of people's lives in Cloverdale, for one," Piper said. "Including her son's."

"That sounds like her, but still a greatly reduced position, wouldn't you say? She loved wielding the power she had as head of the board. I guess I just thought you might like to know that Lydia's reasons for moving to Cloverdale might not be as pure as she pretends."

"Thanks, Jen. I've already seen sides of Lydia Porter that I don't like very much. I'll keep an eye out for—"

The sounds of Dylan's wails stopped her as Jen said, "I'm sorry, Piper. I'd better go." Jen hung up, leaving Piper with one more thing to mull over, among the dozen or so others already milling about in her head.

# 26

~~~~

Piper, not surprisingly, had a restless time that night, though she tried everything she could think of to turn off her brain and sink into sleep: counting sheep, warm milk, flipping through a car magazine that had inexplicably shown up in her mailbox—though that last effort was worse than nothing as her thoughts continually left the glossy pages to wander back to her concerns.

In desperation, she turned to television and flipped through the channels, finding a glut of old movies. Piper skipped past a few westerns as well as a 1950s sci-fi filled with cardboard scenery and bad acting.

The shopping channel almost caught her. *Could I sell my pickles and preserves there?* she wondered briefly before deciding their *poisoned* reputation would continue to haunt her, what with the relentless and vastly reaching Internet and social networks. Continuing her search, late-night Saturday seemed to be high school movie night, as *Sixteen Candles*, *Dead Poets Society*, and *Mr. Holland's Opus* popped up, none of them interesting her. Then she found *The Prime of Miss Jean Brodie*, a movie she'd heard of but had never seen. It was just beginning, and she plumped her pillows and settled in to watch.

An impossibly young Maggie Smith and the others in the cast offered great acting, and the plot was intriguing enough to pull Piper away from her own problems. With her mind finally relaxed, her tired self eventually followed suit, and Piper drifted off, waking late Sunday morning to the sound of an overly peppy commercial promoting, of course, a breakfast cereal.

Piper rose on one elbow and clicked off the set, grateful to have grabbed a few hours of sleep but wishing it had been in less of a cricked-neck position. A hot shower helped, and she let it run extra long, feeling in no hurry to start a day that promised only gloom.

Coffee worked its wonders as well, and as Piper sipped she heard distant church bells and realized she could make the last Mass at All Saints if she hurried. A few prayers couldn't hurt, she figured, and she immediately downed the coffee, changing quickly into more appropriate Sunday morning church garb than the gray sweats she'd originally thrown on, though she skipped the dressier shoes and chose comfortable flats. Church in Albany might have called for heels. Cloverdale, not so much.

Piper slipped into a back pew as the first hymn was winding down. Two more latecomers arrived after her, and she slid over to make room, exchanging smiles and passing over hymn books. The familiar rituals were soothing and Piper recognized a few faces here and there, including, to her surprise, Aunt Judy's and Uncle Frank's. They were early risers by nature and necessity, and she knew they usually caught the eight o'clock Mass, so they were the last two people she'd expected to encounter at this hour. Seeing her was apparently as startling for Aunt Judy, as her aunt double-blinked when she happened to turn. Piper waggled her fingers in silent greeting, then turned her attention back to the service.

At one point, just after the sermon, members of the youth group were called forward. The teens had worked together to collect canned goods for the church food pantry and they were called up to have their efforts applauded by the congregation. Piper scanned the lineup with interest, picking out the kids who seemed the most enthusiastic and the few who were likely there from parental prodding. Because of the students and their ages, the movie titles she'd flipped through the night before came to mind, and as the little ceremony droned on a bit too long, her mind followed another route that took increasing twists and turns, so much so that by the end of the service, as the final hymn began, Piper squeezed past the others in her pew apologetically and hurried out the door. She pulled out her phone and turned it back on, wishing she'd thought to put Jen's number into her cell phone contacts the night before.

"Will," she said as she stepped to one side outdoors. "I need to talk to Jen Fleming. Do you have a number where I can reach her?"

Will, picking up Piper's urgent tone, didn't ask questions.

"I have Matt's cell but not hers. Here's their home number."
He read off that number. "You might be able to catch Jen
at the house."

"Great! I'll explain later. Wish me luck." Piper rang
off and called the Flemings' home, praying silently as
she heard it ring. To her delight, Jen picked up.

"Jen, it's Piper. I'm in a bit of a hurry and don't have
time to explain. Can you confirm that Frances Billings
had been the school librarian at Tedbury Academy? It
would have been several years ago."

"Billings?" There was a pause. "No, that name doesn't
ring a bell at all."

Piper's heart sank until Mrs. Tilley's words from the
night before came back to her. *She was a Kingsley.*
"What about Kingsley?" Piper asked. "That would have
been her maiden name. Frances Kingsley."

"Oh! There was a Frances Kingsley there ages ago.
I only know because there are photos of past staff
members—the more outstanding ones—hanging in the
school library. I remember Frances because she looked
very much like my mother at that age. I used to say 'Hi,
Mom' sometimes when I passed her photo. I even asked
my mother if they could have been related—they
weren't—but that's why the name sticks with me."

"Excellent! Can you give me a time frame?"

There was a pause, as Jen considered. "Late sixties
through early seventies, I believe."

Piper would have whooped if she weren't standing
in a crowd of exiting parishioners by then. "Thank you,
Jen! I promise, I'll get back to you soon and explain
everything." She had spotted Aunt Judy and Uncle

Frank strolling out of the church as they chatted with another couple. Piper caught Aunt Judy's eye and waved her over with some urgency.

"How nice to see you here, Piper! We don't . . ." Aunt Judy began before Piper stopped her with an arm squeeze.

"Aunt Judy, I'm sorry, but this is important. You said Frances Billings was going out to lunch with somebody today. Did she give any hint at all as to who that would be and when?"

"Why, no," Aunt Judy said, looking puzzled. "All she said was that she'd been invited out." She glanced at her watch. "Since she said *lunch*, my guess would be right about now. It's just past noon."

"Then I'd better get busy. I don't suppose you reached Frances on her cell phone, did you?"

"No," Aunt Judy said, "I reached her through the hotel." She pulled out her phone and made a few taps before handing it to Piper. "Maybe you can catch her there."

Piper took the phone and put through the call on the number Aunt Judy had brought up.

"Cloverton? I want to speak with Frances Billings, please. Room . . ." She glanced at Aunt Judy, who held up her fingers, and said, "305."

"I'm sorry," the Cloverton desk person said, "but Ms. Billings just left."

Piper grimaced. "Did she say where she was going? This is Piper Lamb. It's very important that I find her."

"Why yes, she did," the receptionist said. "Ms. Billings said she was meeting someone at a place she was unfamiliar with. She wondered if she needed to call a cab. I told her the White Swan was only two blocks away and she decided it was a nice enough day to walk."

"The White Swan? Thank you!"

Piper handed the phone back to her aunt.

"She's lunching at the White Swan. I'm heading over."

"Who with? Is she in danger?" Aunt Judy asked. "Should the sheriff be involved?"

Piper thought for a moment. Was she sure enough to bring in the sheriff? She could be wrong. But if Piper was right, Frances's life could be at risk. That settled it.

"I'll call him on the way," she said and turned to hurry off.

"Who is it?" Aunt Judy called after Piper but several people had moved between them by then and Piper simply waved. Right or wrong, Aunt Judy would find out before very long.

As she crept along in the long line of cars heading out of the church parking lot, Piper put in a call to the sheriff's office. A young-sounding female answered and told Piper Sheriff Carlyle was not in the office.

"Can you reach him?"

"It's his day off," the voice told her firmly, then asked, as though suddenly remembering the protocol, "Is this an emergency?"

Was it? Piper couldn't say it definitely was. All she had was her theory. She explained her thoughts as best she could, inching forward at the same time toward the main road.

The person on the other end sounded doubtful.

"Please," Piper begged, "just pass my information on to the sheriff or send someone to the White Swan. We can work it out once we're there." She'd reached the cross-road and set down the phone, her attention required for driving. She grabbed an opening in the traffic to turn, not knowing if her call would bring a deputy to the tearoom or not and feeling the urgency for getting there ratchet up.

Winding through Cloverdale streets—once running a red light that had no traffic flowing against her—Piper, after one wrong turn, pulled up outside the White Swan. She scrambled out and hurried through the doorway to scan the patrons at the scattering of white-cloth covered tables.

"May I help you?" a gray-haired hostess at the desk asked politely.

"Frances Billings. She's supposed to be here, but I don't see her."

"Billings?"

Piper gave the former librarian's description. "I know she was coming here and I know I didn't pass her on the route from the Cloverton. Was there a reservation?" Piper gave the other name a reservation might have been made under.

The hostess studied her reservations list and shook her head. "Nothing under either of those names. I'm sorry." She thought for a moment. "Now that I think of it, I did see a lady similar to your description approach us when I happened to look out the window during a slow period."

"But she didn't come in?"

"No, she didn't. A car pulled up on the opposite side of the street and the driver appeared to call to her. After a moment, your friend, if that were she, climbed in on the passenger side and the car drove off."

"Did you see the driver?"

"It was too far away, I'm afraid, and the car was in the shadows."

"What kind of car? Did you see a license plate?"

The older woman shook her head and smiled. "All I can tell you is it was black and a sedan. Beyond that, I really don't know one car from another. I hope you find your friend," she added pleasantly.

Piper thanked her and left the tearoom to stand outside and wonder what to do. No sheriff's car had shown up and she wasn't sure what to do about that, either. Had she been wrong, she asked herself? No, Frances Billings had been taken to another location for an ominous reason, of that Piper was increasingly sure. The problem was where and how could Piper find them.

She pulled out her phone and looked up the number she wanted. She heard it ring twice before a woman answered—an older woman. Piper hesitated, surprised for a moment, then realized who it must be.

"Gwen Smyth?" she asked.

# 27

<u>~~~~</u>

"Yes, this is Gwen," Lydia Porter's sister said cheerfully into the phone. "And who are you?"

"This is Piper Lamb. I own the pickling shop?"

"Yes, hi! How're you doing? What can I do for you?"

"I need to know where Lydia is right now."

"Lydia?" Gwen paused. "She's gone out."

"Yes, but do you know where?"

"I haven't the faintest, sorry." Gwen paused, possibly picking up on the urgency in Piper's voice. "Want me to try Lydia's cell? I can do it while you're holding on."

"Yes, please do." Piper waited, shifting her weight as Gwen apparently used her own cell phone to call her sister.

After a few moments she heard, "No luck. It went to voice mail. Or *the black hole*, as I call it."

Unsurprised, Piper asked, "What kind of car does Lydia drive? Do you know the license number?"

"License number? Good grief, no. I do know it's a Lexus, though. And it's black."

Piper heard Gwen speak to someone else.

"Mallory doesn't know the license number, either," she said, coming back on the phone.

"Mallory's there?" Piper perked up. "Would you put her on?"

Piper heard a muffled discussion, as though Gwen needed to persuade her niece to take the phone. After what seemed like hours, Mallory finally said, "Hello?"

"Mallory, it's Piper."

"Yes, I know. Hello, Piper." Mallory sounded hesitant and Piper knew she needed to tread slowly. Frustrating though that was, it was her only hope of getting anything from Lydia's daughter.

"Mallory, I'm really hoping you can help me."

"Me? With what?"

"Remember that person I told you about who once worked as librarian at your old school? Frances Billings?"

There was an excruciatingly long pause, then Mallory said, "Yes, I remember."

"Did your mother mention her at all? Maybe yesterday? Or today?"

Another pause dragged on until Mallory finally said, "Yes."

*O . . . kay.* "Can you tell me what she said?"

"I don't know if I should tell you."

"Mallory, this is very important. Ms. Billings's life could be at stake. I know you've always done what your mother wanted you to do, but I'm just as sure that you're ready to think for yourself. Your mother may have made some very bad decisions and it's time to put a stop to it all. Will you help me do that, please?"

Piper waited for what seemed like an eternity. For a horrible moment she feared Mallory had put the phone down and walked away. Had Lydia irreparably broken her daughter down? Then she heard Mallory's answer.

"Yes."

It was a single word but Piper grabbed at it. "You'll help?"

"Yes. My mother was very upset. She said Ms. Billings had lied. That she'd hidden who she really was."

*Exactly what Piper had expected!*

"Thank you, Mallory. Did your mother say she was going to see her?"

"No, she didn't say that."

"Your mother did go out today, though. I think she planned to see Ms. Billings. I don't know where that would be. Do you have any idea where your mother would have gone with Ms. Billings?"

Piper waited, assuming Mallory was thinking. What were the chances she would come up with something? If Lydia were planning murder, how likely was it that she'd mention to anyone where that would be? But it was all Piper had to go on.

"Wait a minute," Mallory said. "Mother was on her laptop this morning. I think she might have been checking a map."

Piper heard the phone clunk as Mallory dropped it. Piper caught herself holding her breath and quickly sucked in air. This was not the time to pass out. She waited, phone held tightly to her ear, and paced in circles, barely aware of patrons of the White Swan entering and leaving the tearoom only steps away. Finally she heard scrambling noises as Mallory picked up again.

"She was checking directions to the Birch Café. That's probably where she went. It's in Bellingham on Birch Street near Tenth."

"Thank you, Mallory!"

"You're welcome, Piper."

Piper heard a new tone of confidence in Mallory's voice and knew what it meant. She also knew what it might cost Mallory but that was something to think about later. Piper said good-bye and called her shop assistant next, instead of the sheriff's office.

"Amy," she said, "is your father there?"

"Dad? No, he's off fishing."

"Can you reach him? I don't think the person answering calls at his office is taking me seriously. You're my only hope for getting through to your dad." She explained what was going on. "I'm heading over to the Birch Café right now. I hope you can convince your father to have someone from the Bellingham police meet me there."

"Absolutely. Assuming I can get through to his cell. Sometimes service is sketchy where he goes."

"Try." Piper thought a moment. "And if you can't get your dad, call Ben Schaeffer." An auxiliary police officer, Piper reasoned, was better than no one, and she might need any help she could get. "Also, pass on that Lydia Porter is driving a black Lexus but I don't have the license number."

"Will do."

Piper was in her car by then. She ended the call to look up Tenth and Birch Streets in Bellingham on her phone app, then drove off, keeping the screen at hand for last-minute checks. She wound her way through Cloverdale, fighting an urge to hurry that would only put others at risk. Once she made it to the highway, she picked up speed, though traffic and limited passing opportunities continued to frustrate her.

Piper's mind moved faster than her car, running over all the possibilities as she drove—at times convinced she was right, at others worried that she could be very wrong—and that everything she had set in motion, including herself, could end up as one huge embarrassment. Bad as that might be, it was nothing compared to what the result would be if she was right—and too late. Piper pressed harder on her accelerator at the thought.

Signs for Bellingham appeared and Piper watched anxiously for the turnoff, her eyes flicking often from road to clock. Twenty minutes had passed since she'd left the White Swan. How many had gone by since Frances Billings climbed into that black Lexus?

The exit arrived and Piper took it, glancing at the small screen on her older-model phone for help but getting none. Why hadn't she invested in a decent GPS? Or downloaded a newer app for her aged phone? One that spoke to you? Because, she answered herself, she always thought she had time to study the way to unknown places. Who knew she'd someday be making a life-or-death trip to an obscure café in the middle of Bellingham, a town she knew only for its hospital and shopping mall? Piper scanned signs at the end of the ramp and made a quick decision to turn right.

Hating to do it, but unsure of what to do next, she pulled over to study her digital map. The Birch Café was tucked in the center of a horror of a maze of streets. Had Lydia chosen it for that reason? Piper did her best to memorize the complicated route, then pulled back onto the road. The first part of her drive, on main highways, was easy. It very quickly became mind-boggling.

Pulling over twice more during the process, Piper feared Frances Billings's only hope would be if Amy reached her sheriff father, who would then set the Bellingham police into motion. Barring that, would Ben Schaeffer be of help? Piper had no idea if Ben would be able to zero in on the Birch Café any faster than she was. The pile of unknowns began pressing down with crushing weight but Piper pushed on, aware that she might end up being the only hope of rescue.

A series of wrong turns, one oblivious pass of the unobtrusive café, and a circle back brought Piper—amazingly—to her target. The Birch Café sat tucked between a tiny grocery store and a beauty salon, its sign visible only to the few who searched carefully. Piper pulled into the single open space—at a fire hydrant—and was out of her car in an instant. Would the women be there? Or would the crafty Lydia have changed locations once again? She couldn't hope to string along Frances, who was nobody's fool, for too long, Piper told herself as she took off toward the café at a run.

She pushed through the café door and paused. The café was deeper than she'd expected and apparently popular, with many tables filled, making it difficult to locate who she was looking for.

"Can I help—?" a hostess began, but Piper suddenly spotted Frances Billings, sitting alone at a table set for two against the far wall. Her face was flushed and she clutched at her throat as though gasping for breath.

"Call 911," Piper cried. "That woman in the purple dress needs help!"

# 28

The hostess of the Birch Café looked where Piper pointed. "Oh! Oh, my goodness!" she cried, and spun toward the desk.

"Is there a doctor here?" Piper called, weaving rapidly between the tables to reach Frances. "Anyone?"

"I'm a nurse!" A woman seated near the front of the café jumped up and followed after Piper.

When they reached Frances, she was gasping. The people at nearby tables scattered to make room as Piper and the nurse helped Frances lie down.

"I think she's been poisoned," Piper told the nurse, whose face registered shock. "The desk is calling 911. Make sure they take her food with them to be tested. It might seem like a heart attack, but it could be bloodroot. Possibly something else."

The nurse nodded, though still stunned, and took

charge at that point, leaving Piper able to scan the café. Where was Lydia? She scrambled up, leaving Frances with the nurse, and hurried back to the hostess.

"There were two people at that table. Where did the other person go?"

The hostess looked at Piper blankly, clearly struggling just to process all that was happening. Piper left her and ran to the door. She leaned out to scan the street in the direction of her car but saw no one. She looked the other way and spotted a woman in a dark suit walking rapidly, closing in on a black Lexus at the end of the block.

Piper rushed out, but before she got more than a few feet, Lydia had jumped into the Lexus and was taking off. Piper raced back to her own hatchback, praying that Lydia wouldn't disappear from sight before she could get behind the wheel.

Piper screeched out of her spot, barely missing a red Ford coming from the opposite direction, and turned right at the intersection, as she'd seen Lydia's Lexus do. She soon spied the black car up ahead, hampered by the congested, narrow street, as was Piper. Two cars separated them but Piper was able to keep Lydia in sight, though aware that could change at any moment.

She watched as the Lexus turned left on a green light up ahead. The car behind it slowed as the light changed to yellow, then red. "No!" Piper cried as both cars ahead of her stopped. But each then turned right after the required pause at the intersection. Piper, now first in line, looked to the left to see Lydia's Lexus disappearing in the distance. She checked cross traffic and decided to chance it, swinging left in front of an approaching white van whose horn blared and whose driver no doubt cursed as he braked to avoid collision. Her heart racing, Piper saw the tail end of the Lexus turning right up ahead. She pressed down on her accelerator to close the distance between them enough to see Lydia take the ramp leading to the highway.

Piper raced to pull onto the ramp herself, appalled to see heavy traffic flowing. *Didn't anyone stay home anymore?* She eased onto the congested roadway, struggling to keep moving safely while watching for the Lexus. Then she spotted it. Unable to close the gap between them, the best Piper could do was keep the black car in view, thankful that the traffic at least kept Lydia from taking too far off.

Had Lydia seen her give chase outside the café? Piper couldn't be sure, though if she had, Lydia would know her plan to get away with an attempt on Frances's life was shattered. Lydia had probably picked the Birch Café as a place she would be unknown and where the busy staff would be unlikely to come up with a description. With Piper able to place her at the scene, any attempt to manufacture an alibi would be useless. Was Lydia instead hoping to escape altogether? If that were the case, Piper intended to put a stop to that as well, though exactly how was still up in the air.

The Lexus changed lanes, then took the exit for Cloverdale. Piper, working her way through the traffic, was able to follow suit. Though several cars behind, she still had Lydia in sight. Was Lydia heading home after all, she wondered? Perhaps ready to give up altogether? Piper wanted to hope so. But then the Lexus suddenly turned off onto a side road. Where was Lydia heading? Puzzled, Piper continued to follow. Then it hit her. That road led straight to Sugar's place!

Piper scrambled for her cell phone. Deciding her best bet of direct contact to the sheriff would again be through his daughter, she called that number.

"Amy! Did you reach your father?"

"Yes, but it took a while. He informed the Bellingham police. Did they get there?"

"Not in time." She gave Amy a quick rundown of what had happened and her current location.

"Tell your father to send someone to Sugar Heywood's place. Lydia is heading there. I don't know what she has in mind, but it can't be for anything good. I'm right behind but I'll need help!"

"I'll get him," Amy promised and immediately disconnected.

Piper drew a deep breath, confident that aid would come. But how soon? She pressed down on her gas pedal to close the gap between Lydia and herself. *She*, at least, had Lydia in sight.

# 29

Lydia knew she was being followed. That became obvious to Piper as the Lexus wove down the middle of the narrow, shoulderless road as if to block any attempt by Piper to pull ahead and block her—a scheme that only a mad person would try, what with all the twists and turns they were navigating. Heading to Sugar's, then, could mean only one thing. Lydia, Piper feared, had given up any thought of getting away with murder and had decided, as some demented form of satisfaction, to strike at one last person while she could.

Piper had tried to warn Sugar, calling both her landline and cell phone, but got no answer. Did that mean she wasn't home and that her cell phone wasn't on? Maybe, but though she hoped that was the case, Piper couldn't count on it.

The road finally opened up, and Piper recognized

Sugar's white house up ahead. Lydia apparently knew it, too, as she picked up speed. Her Lexus swerved onto the driveway, tires spraying gravel, and Lydia was out of the car in seconds. Piper pulled up behind the Lexus within moments and blocked her in as Lydia raced to the front door. She pounded Sugar's door with her fists and rattled the doorknob, but the door, thankfully, must have been locked. Piper jumped out of her car, hoping again that nobody was home. Then she saw Sugar come around the side of the house from the backyard, drawn by the racket.

Piper tried to wave her back, but it was too late. Lydia caught sight of Sugar, too. *Where was the sheriff?*

"You!" Lydia cried.

Sugar stopped, looking stunned into immobility at the sight of Lydia on her front stoop, skirt twisted, blouse hanging loose, and hair in disarray.

Lydia flew at her, fingers curled into claws. "You'll never have my son!" she screamed. Lydia wasn't a large woman, but the momentum of rushing at Sugar, along with the element of surprise, pushed Sugar off balance and to the ground. "You'll never be a Porter! I'll see to that! I'll kill you first."

Lydia had both hands at Sugar's throat and was pressing down hard enough that Piper could see Sugar struggling for breath. She rushed up and tried to pull Lydia off, yanking at her arms. The woman was surprisingly strong, plus the tangle of legs kicking out—both Sugar's and Lydia's—made it difficult for Piper to brace. There wasn't enough of Lydia's silvery, short-cut hair to grasp, so Piper swung one arm around Lydia's neck, grabbed onto her own wrist, and squeezed.

"Get . . . off . . . !" Lydia gasped, but Piper held firm until she saw Lydia's hands leave Sugar's throat.

Lydia fell sideways to the ground and Sugar rolled away, breathing hard.

"Help me hold her," Piper cried, quickly grabbing Lydia's hands and pulling them behind her back. Sugar scrambled over and plopped onto Lydia's legs.

"What . . . ?" Sugar started to ask until the sound of sirens pulled her attention to the road.

Piper sighed with relief. Sheriff Carlyle was on his way. She felt Lydia's struggles slow, though Piper continued to hold on to her tightly. No way was this murderer going to slip away from justice.

Before the sheriff's car appeared, a tan pickup drove up behind Piper's hatchback. Two people jumped out from each side of the cab.

"Mom?" Zach cried, frozen for a moment before running toward them. "What the heck? What's going on?"

Sugar looked up in astonishment to see her son standing over her, with Ralph Strawbridge coming up from behind.

"Found him," Ralph announced, calmly, just as Sheriff Carlyle's flashing lights rushed down the road.


Lydia sat, handcuffed and nearly unrecognizable in her current state, in the back of the sheriff's car as Sheriff Carlyle continued to interview Piper and the others. Sugar was smiling from ear to ear as she held on to Zach's arm and looked like she had no intention of letting go for quite a while.

"He was at his girlfriend's," Ralph said early on, and when Sugar looked puzzled, Zach explained.

"Her name's Lauren. My friends don't really know about her, yet, but I mentioned her to Ralph, when we were talking, one time. I was going to tell you about her, Mom, but then all this stuff happened. She's really special and she didn't know about any of this," he said, waving toward the sheriff. "Lauren thought you and I were having problems and I needed a place to cool down."

"If she's really special," Sugar said, "you'd better start being more honest with her."

Sheriff Carlyle had enough to charge Lydia with for the time being—her assault on Sugar—but wanted the rest of the story.

"All I know for sure at this point," Piper said, "is that Frances Billings had worked at Tedbury Academy when Lydia was a student there. She must have known something that Lydia wanted hidden badly enough to try to silence her. Is Frances okay?"

"She's alive and apparently recovering. Thanks to you, they knew exactly how to treat her at the hospital."

"Thank goodness."

"We'll get her story as soon as she's able to talk with us." The sheriff turned to Zach. "As for you, young man. We need to talk more, too." His stern expression relaxed a smidgen. "That can wait until tomorrow. I imagine your mother has a few words for you, first."

"Yes, sir," Zach said, looking relieved.

They watched the sheriff drive off, Lydia facing stonily ahead. Then Sugar urged them all to come inside. "I haven't been able to cook for days. Now I have an amazing reason!"

Piper excused herself. This was family time. And from the looks of it, Ralph would be sharing that title before very long. Sugar was extremely grateful for his actions in finding Zach, of course. But the looks of affection Piper had seen flowing between them came from much more than gratitude. She gave and received hugs all around, then headed on home. There were plenty of people who were waiting for news.

And she could hardly wait to tell them.

# 30

~~~~~

"Well," Emma Leahy said Monday morning at Piper's Picklings, "between Joan Tilley and Frances Billings, there's been plenty of mileage put on cars running between Cloverdale and Bellingham Regional Hospital." She handed Piper the two jars of spiced apple butter she was picking up for Joan Tilley.

Piper nodded agreement. "At least Mrs. Tilley is home now."

"Yes, and her appetite for your preserves has returned. Frances has a ways to go yet, but she's getting there. Tell me exactly why Lydia wanted to get rid of her, would you? When Judy called me, I was so astonished I wasn't able to take it all in."

Piper finished ringing up the apple butters and reached for a bag. "Frances was the librarian at Tedbury Academy years ago, when Lydia was a student. She was Frances

Kingsley, then, so Lydia didn't make the connection when they met again all those years later. And, of course, besides the name, Frances herself had changed."

"So what clued Lydia in?"

"I did, I'm afraid. I told Mallory about Frances having been on the Tedbury staff. Then for good measure, I told Lydia, too, when she came here the next day with her sister, Gwen." Piper grimaced at the memory, though she'd done it quite unwittingly at the time. "I'm sure Lydia had heard the Kingsley family name mentioned as the original owners of the house, and she finally connected Frances Billings as having been Frances Kingsley from Tedbury.

"When I started putting all the pieces together—that Lydia had something so important for her to hide that she resigned from her prestigious position at Tedbury, and that Frances must have known Lydia in her student days—I became very afraid for Frances, though I didn't know the full story yet. I got that later from Frances.

"Lydia, it turns out, left Tedbury under a cloud during her third year as a student there. She was pregnant. The school kept that very quiet. In those days, I'm sure you know, and at that school, particularly, a student being pregnant was not something to be talked about. But Lydia was certain that Frances must have known about her condition, that she must have been Dirk Unger's source of that information when he informed Lydia that he knew, and that she would also let it out to others in Cloverdale. Lydia couldn't stand the thought of what that would do to the perfect image she'd so carefully built up. The sad thing is that Frances, once she realized who Lydia was, wouldn't have said a word about Lydia's past. Gossip about former students was unthinkable to her. She told me when I saw her at the hospital that if Lydia had spoken to her about it, she would have assured her of that. Lydia, unfortunately, acted on her own assumptions."

Emma nodded. "People tend to believe others will behave the same as they would." She thought about Piper's revelations for a moment. "So Jeremy was born out of wedlock?"

"No, not Jeremy. He was born a few years later, after Lydia married. She didn't keep her first baby. These things happen, and I'm totally sympathetic to teens who find themselves in that situation. But I can't forgive Lydia for being so hypocritical regarding Sugar. Lydia, of all people, should have understood. Instead, she denounced Sugar for being a single mom and pronounced her unworthy of any connection to the exalted Porters."

"Sugar's lucky she got away from that family when she did."

Piper spotted someone at her shop door. "You're not the only one who feels that way. Hi, Ralph!" she called as Ralph Strawbridge walked in.

Ralph looked much more relaxed than he had the last several days. He greeted both women, then said, "I thought you might like to know what was up with Stan Yeager's sudden disappearance."

"Absolutely!" Piper cried. "With everything else, I'd almost forgotten about Stan. Is he okay?"

"He's fine, and both Stan and his wife are back home. Neither of them had a clue that anyone was concerned about their absence."

Sugar, of course, in her anxiety to see her son cleared of suspicion, had been convinced that poor Stan was a murderer, but Piper didn't bring that up.

"Where were they?" Emma asked.

"In Cleveland." Ralph grinned at the *huh?* looks he got back from that information. "His daughter was going through a high-risk pregnancy. Stan's wife went first, to be with her and help out. Stan followed later, when the delivery seemed imminent."

"So that's why he seemed so anxious the last several days," Piper said. "He was worried about his daughter!" She thought about Stan's last visit to her shop. "He bought kimchi and said it was for her."

"Kimchi?" Emma asked. "For an expectant mother?"

"He said she liked it. He didn't say anything about her condition."

"Some people," Emma said, "especially men, don't like to talk about things they're worried about—particularly female-type things. Did she have the baby yet? Is everything okay?" she asked Ralph.

"She did—a boy—and all is well. Stan is back at his office and has blue 'It's a Boy!' balloons in the window. That's how I found out."

"That's terrific," Piper said, delighted for the Realtor. "I remember we had wondered where Stan was when Dirk Unger was poisoned. Stan had closed his office at five thirty but didn't show up at the party here at the shop until seven."

Ralph nodded. "We may never know what he did in that time frame, unless . . ." He looked from Piper to Emma. "Either of you feel like asking?" Ralph grinned as both firmly shook their heads. "So, we'll just assume he went somewhere by himself to deal with his worry over his daughter and leave it at that."

"Good thought," Emma said, then smiled broadly. "A new grandson! I'll have to run over and congratulate Stan."

"I'm heading back that way if you'd like a lift," Ralph offered, and Emma readily took him up on it.

"Oh, but before I go," she said, "there's one more thing I was wondering about. That bloodroot leaf that Sheriff Carlyle found in Zach's book. Did Zach ever explain why it was there?"

"It's only a guess," Piper said. "But Zach thinks Lydia put it there. He said he spotted Lydia at the library the day before. He kept his distance from her, but he remembered leaving his backpack unguarded at his study table, when he went in search of another book. Zach thinks Lydia could have planted the leaf in one of his own books—one he seldom referred to that he kept in his backpack—at that time."

Piper paused, thinking. "At Lydia's tea," she said, "I browsed through the books on the house's library shelves. I came across one called *Healing Plants* and checked the index for bloodroot and I didn't find it listed. But Frances had told me most of those books had been bought by Dirk Unger from an estate sale, so I didn't think it mattered, one way or the other. Lydia wasn't really on my radar, then, as a suspect.

"The sheriff found that book when they searched the Porters' house. It turns out it hadn't been part of the bulk sale but was Lydia's own book, which she'd hidden in plain sight. Bloodroot was definitely discussed in that book—how it can be medicinal if used properly—but it was listed under its Latin name. Lydia apparently was interested in how it could be used in a deadly way." Piper grimaced. "I wish I'd figured her out much sooner."

"Lydia fooled all of us," Emma said. "We never thought to wonder where she was when Dirk Unger was poisoned."

Piper nodded. "She could have added bloodroot to his salad very easily. She knew when he'd be with Jeremy and away from his house, and she surely knew about his habit of misplacing his keys and therefore leaving his doors unlocked. Dirk somehow discovered Lydia's secret and was using it for his own selfish ends. I'm sure it's the reason Lydia left her prestigious position on the Tedbury Academy board and came to Cloverdale. Although she claimed it was to be close to her son, it was more likely to keep an eye on Dirk and to watch for a chance to get rid of him."

"She must have been responsible for Joan Tilley's poisoning, too," Emma said, showing more anger over that than over Dirk Unger's poisoning.

"I'm sure she was. Lydia had bought a jar of my brandied cherries the first time she was in my shop and she later claimed that Mallory loved it. But Mallory told the sheriff she never even saw the jar. She simply backed her mother's claim out of her habit of obedience."

"So when Lydia realized you might be getting close to finding her out," Ralph said, "as well as possibly for interfering with her control of Mallory, she must have poisoned the jar she already had and slipped it back on your shelf, hoping to derail your efforts."

"Evil woman," Emma said. "She didn't care who she

hurt, did she? You were very clever, Piper, to put things together when you did." Piper shrugged, still badly wishing she'd been quicker.

Emma turned to Ralph. "On to Stan's, now, to congratulate him on his new grandson!"

Piper smiled as the two took off, highly pleased that Stan's life had taken a happy turn instead of the kind she'd once feared for him. They'd barely left, when Tammy Butterworth walked in, glancing over her shoulder at Ralph's truck disappearing in the distance.

"That was Ralph Strawbridge, wasn't it?" she asked Piper. When Piper agreed it was, she said, "I heard about him figuring out where Zach was all that time. Clever man!"

"He certainly is. There's a lot more to Ralph than expert woodworker."

"Oh, I knew that." Tammy's eyes twinkled mischievously.

"You did?"

Tammy glanced back at the street Ralph had just driven down. "He doesn't know me, but I know him."

Piper waited, and, when Tammy only grinned, cried, "Well? Are you going to tell me?"

Tammy laughed. "The cat's going to be out of the bag soon, so I might as well. Ralph's a millionaire. Maybe billionaire."

"What!"

Tammy nodded vigorously. "He was one of the developers of that social networking site, Frendz. Are you on it? Seems like everyone in the world is, nowadays."

"How do you know this?" Piper asked. "I mean about Ralph being the developer?"

Tammy smiled, clearly enjoying her tale. "My mother was his nanny. It was years ago, of course, but she was very fond of him and liked to keep track of things he did as he grew up. She talked about him so much and was so proud of him—Mum liked to claim it was her proper potty training that set him on the right path—and after she died I kept an eye on his comings and goings, too. It wasn't hard. He was in the papers a lot, mostly the financial pages. He made a bundle when he finally left with all the Frendz stock options he'd held on to."

"He did? Then why is he making doors and bookcases? I mean, I'm glad he is doing his woodwork, but . . ."

"Well, I'm sure he has more money than he could ever use and doesn't need to make any more. My guess is he's just decided to live the simple life and do what makes him happy."

"Oh my gosh!" Piper sank down on one of her stools as she took in that information. "I remember him giving Amy some pretty thoughtful business advice about setting up her restaurant one day, but I never dreamed . . ."

"He's a crafty one." Tammy cackled. "Sugar Heywood's going to be pretty surprised, wouldn't you say?"

"Whoo! You got that right." Piper thought about Sugar's initial, single criticism of Ralph, that he wasn't ambitious enough. She'd obviously long since put any concern of that sort aside but Sugar was still going to be bowled over when the full story came out. Which it surely would. Piper remembered Sugar's admonishment to Zach about being honest with the girl he cared for. Ralph was going to have to fess up. Piper wished she could see Sugar's reaction when that happened.

"Well, what I came in for was some of your lemon curd," Tammy said. "I'll be going over to Jeremy's and wanted to take him some. It's small comfort, I know, for what he's going through. But it's something."

Piper went over to her shelf and reached for a jar. "That's very thoughtful of you, Tammy," she said. "It must be hard on all of them."

Tammy nodded. "On second thought, give me two jars."

As Piper rang them up, Tammy said, "I'm sure your business will pick up again, now that everyone will know the source of your poisoned preserve."

"I have seen a couple of regular customers come in who'd stayed away. They might have come to hear more details of what happened yesterday but they left with purchases."

"See! Didn't I tell you? Things will be back the way they used to be before long."

Piper hoped so, at least for her shop. But some things would never be the same. Jeremy and Mallory were in for a pretty rough time, for one thing. Dirk Unger wouldn't spring back to life but at least Mrs. Tilley and Frances Billings had survived, though who knew with what possible health repercussions down the road. At their age, recovering from such critical illness didn't come easily, Piper was sure. But Zach was cleared and free to resume his education and things were definitely looking up for Sugar, so several changes were for the better.

Piper smiled, thanked Tammy for her purchases, and decided to be as optimistic as this extraordinary cleaning lady.

~~~~~~

t wasn't too much later that Piper got a call from Marguerite Lloyd. Expecting a question concerning Lydia Porter, she instead heard, "Lamb! Is that newsletter out?"

Piper had completely forgotten about the women's club newsletter for which she'd promised to write an article about Marguerite's landscaping business.

"I'm not sure, Marguerite. Can I get back to you on that?"

"I need to know. I can't keep my silky dogwoods on sale forever. You did put in that they're on sale, didn't you?"

Since Piper had turned writing of the article over to Emma, and Emma had been occupied with looking after Mrs. Tilley, Piper had no idea what was or was not in the newsletter.

"Marguerite, things have been pretty busy around here," she said, aware of her extreme understatement.

"Oh, right. The Porter thing." Marguerite's tone changed. "So she's the one did in Unger?"

"It definitely appears that way."

"Slimy thing—Unger, I mean." Marguerite huffed. "Lydia, too, I suppose. I worked with him, you know, some time ago."

Piper did know, but she simply said, "Oh?"

"Back in Ohio. Backstabbing snake of a man. I wouldn't have minded bumping him off myself. I should thank Lydia for doing it for me. Why did she, by the way? Did he have something on her?"

"Most likely." Piper knew what Unger had found out about Lydia—her illegitimate baby—but didn't say so.

Nor did she mention how high on the list of suspects Marguerite herself had once been. Instead, she said, "I imagine it will all come out, eventually."

"Right. Well, let me know about that newsletter as soon as you can." Marguerite had moved back to what she considered more important things.

Piper promised, then heard the click as Marguerite hung up. Must be nice, Piper thought as she set down the phone, to be so focused and able to easily shut out any and all things that didn't directly affect oneself. She wished Marguerite well—and hoped she'd have little to do with her from then on.

# 31

~~~~

A month had gone by since Lydia Porter's arrest and the news came out that Lydia Porter had pleaded guilty to the murder of Dirk Unger and the attempted murders of Frances Billings and Joan Tilley, thus avoiding a lengthy trial that would be highly stressful for her children. Rumor was she'd gotten a plea bargain.

Aunt Judy, who'd stopped by Piper's Picklings, tsked. "Very sad about Lydia. Of course, she made her own bed."

"She did," Piper agreed, "and hurt plenty of people in the process. I don't think she'll be terribly missed."

"How is Mallory taking it all?" Aunt Judy asked.

"It's been a roller coaster of emotions for her. But overall, I think she's proud of herself for finally standing up for what was right. She's come out of it all with a sense of strength and freedom she's probably never experienced before."

"Poor thing. To be treated like a twelve-year-old for so long by her mother." Aunt Judy tsked again and looked about to say more when they suddenly spotted the subject of their conversation heading toward the shop.

"Piper!" Mallory cried as she burst in looking super excited. "I got the job! Jeanine hired me to work in her fabric shop."

"That's wonderful, Mallory," Piper said, and Aunt Judy clapped her hands. They both gave Mallory congratulatory hugs. "I know you'll be fantastic at it," Piper said, stepping back.

Mallory beamed. "You think so? I'm a little scared. I never had a job before. But Aunt Gwen's been walking me through all the things I should know, like getting my own checking account and stuff. I might even get my own apartment! Then I could decorate the whole thing myself."

"First things first," Aunt Judy said, laughing. "I'm sure Jeremy wouldn't mind letting you do a little redecorating at his house while you save up your salary."

"Well . . ." Mallory's lips curved upward in a kind of secretive smile. "Maybe, but I should probably leave that up to . . ." She stopped.

"Up to who?" Aunt Judy asked.

"I'm not sure I should say yet," Mallory said, still smiling oddly.

Emma Leahy had walked in to catch the last of the conversation. "Why not?" she asked. "It's all over town."

"What is?" Aunt Judy asked.

Amy, who'd been in the back working on a batch of pickled fennel, appeared, wiping her hands on a towel and looking interested as well, always somehow able to keep up with anything going on at the front of the shop, no matter how busy she was.

"So you haven't heard yet?" Emma asked slyly.

"No, Emma!" Aunt Judy cried in good-natured frustration. "Now, will you please tell us!"

Emma looked at Mallory, who nodded, then said, "Jeremy and Tammy Butterworth have run off and got married."

"What!"

Emma thoroughly enjoyed the shock on all three faces.

"Is that true, Mallory?" Piper asked.

"Yes!" Mallory cried, bouncing on her toes by then, with a full grin on her face.

"Oh, what a hoot!" Amy cried, throwing her towel toward the ceiling and collapsing on a nearby stool. "Won't Lydia—" She glanced at Mallory and stopped herself from finishing that, saying instead, "That's just terrific!"

"I . . . I'm surprised," Aunt Judy said. "I didn't realize they . . ."

"I'm surprised, too," Piper said, "but I think I can understand it. Jeremy likes to be fussed over and Tammy likes to fuss. He'll be well looked after, I guarantee."

"Yes, but . . ." Aunt Judy was still struggling.

"Jeremy probably felt free to finally make such a decision with his mother not there to interfere," Emma said. "Don't you think, Mallory?"

"Oh, yes," Mallory said. "Absolutely.

"Who knows," Emma added, "how long he might

have had leanings in that direction but never dared to
act on them. They've known each other for quite a while,
from what I understand. Then again, Tammy . . .
well . . . never try to understand the ways of the heart,"
Emma said, patting Aunt Judy's arm. "Speaking of
which," she turned to Piper, "I happened to see Scott
Littleton browsing through the gift shop over on Maple.
You don't suppose . . ."

She looked at Piper significantly and Piper felt Aunt
Judy's and Amy's eyes turn on her as well. She shrugged,
though aware of a growing uneasiness. "Maybe he was
picking out a wedding present for Tammy and Jeremy?"

Emma shook her head firmly. "He didn't even know
until I told him."

"Sugar and Ralph?" Aunt Judy asked tentatively.

"Nothing's been announced there," Piper said, adding, "yet. I imagine they're taking things slowly. But
wasn't that a surprise about Ralph's former career?" she
asked, more than happy to steer the subject in another
direction.

"Absolutely!" both older women cried.

"I can't imagine hiding something like that," Amy
said. "Most people would be bragging about what they'd
accomplished."

"Ralph Strawbridge isn't the bragging type," Aunt
Judy said. "Maybe he wanted people to like him for himself, not for how much money he'd acquired."

Emma nodded and Piper thought about how much
pleasure Ralph clearly got from the praise of his hand-
carved door. Surely that meant more than buying an

expensive car you didn't need or moving into an over-sized mansion. Some people figured things out a lot sooner than others.

She suddenly spotted Scott heading toward her shop, carrying a package.

Apparently Aunt Judy saw him, too. "I just remembered," she said, grabbing her purse. "I was going to stop at the library for a book. Walk with me, Emma," she said, turning her friend firmly by the arm toward the door. "You, too, Mallory."

Amy, picking up on the reason for the others' hasty departure, withdrew to the back room and her pickled fennel, leaving Piper alone to brace herself, unsure exactly what for. But knowing Scott . . .

There was a flurry of greetings outside her shop, as Aunt Judy, Emma, and Mallory met up with Scott. Then the women continued on, Emma looking back a bit longingly as Scott leaned on the door of Piper's Picklings, pushing it open with one shoulder as he clutched his package with both hands. Piper eyed the box nervously.

"Hi, there," he said as he let the door close behind him.

"Hi. Looks like you've been shopping." Piper picked up a duster and began flicking it rapidly over her shelved jars.

"I have." Scott carried his package over to her counter and set it down. "I saw this and couldn't resist."

Piper set down her duster and stared firmly at him. "No, Scott."

"No, what?"

"No gifts."

"But—"

"We agreed, remember? And you promised not to do this anymore."

There was a long pause, then Scott cleared his throat. "Piper," he said. "This isn't for you."

"Oh!" Piper felt her cheeks warm. "Okay. Sorry. Um, who is it for?"

"It's for Sugar." Scott began untying the string that secured the top. "She's been sending me new clients and I wanted to thank her somehow, some way special. Then I spotted this." He flipped off the lid and began flinging out wads of tissue paper as Piper watched, catching one or two wads. Scott grasped an object wrapped thickly in Bubble Wrap and carefully pulled it out. He set it on Piper's counter and began peeling away the wrap.

Piper let out a soft *ohhhh* as Scott's gift was gradually revealed: a lovely porcelain statue of a mother and child, the child young but clearly a boy.

Scott looked at Piper, gauging her reaction. "Well?" he asked. "What do you think? Will she like it?"

"She'll love it, Scott." Piper felt her eyes begin to tear and rapidly blinked them clear. "It's a perfect gift for Sugar. That was very perceptive of you."

Scott smiled. "There was no missing their love for each other the whole time I worked for those two."

"Can I see?" Amy's voice called from the back room, and both Piper and Scott grinned.

"Absolutely," Scott said, and Amy stepped out, her towel slung over one shoulder.

"Nice!" she proclaimed after a careful study of the statue. "*Very* nice."

Scott smiled, then suddenly looked worried. "Do you think, coming from me, it would become a reminder of a bad time in their lives? I wouldn't want that."

"I think," Amy said, "all things considered, it turned out to be a *good* time. Don't you, Piper? I mean, everything worked out, Ralph came into their lives and I've never seen Sugar looking so happy."

Piper thought that Scott even asking such a question was a sign of how much he had changed from their time back in Albany, when he had focused too much on what was good for *him*. "Sugar is a very positive person," she said. "She'll certainly treasure this gift as something that was thoughtfully chosen."

Scott seemed satisfied with that and began rewrapping his statue. Amy helped him pack it back up in the box and then he carefully retied the string. "There!"

"When will you give it to Sugar?" Piper asked.

"I thought instead of just running it over, that it'd be fun to meet for dinner. Sugar and Ralph, me and . . ." He looked meaningfully at Piper, who caught his drift and took a step backward.

"I'd better check on my fennel," Amy said and quickly disappeared.

Scott was clearly asking Piper to join him for dinner, along with two other people she would certainly enjoy being with. She had dined with Scott when they met Zach at Niki's to get his explanation of the bad incident at school. But she'd thought of that as a working dinner.

Would this, considering how hard both she and Scott had worked on Zach's behalf, be so different?

She knew it was. But she also knew Scott had changed during the time he'd been in Cloverdale. She liked the change. He'd become much more concerned about others and she'd been impressed with his caring attitude toward Zach and Sugar, something that showed with this gift. Many of her old feelings for Scott had resurfaced since his move to Cloverdale. Will had been amazingly understanding about that, giving her time to work it all out. But Piper couldn't expect him to wait around forever. It was decision time.

Her shop phone rang.

"I'll get it back here," Amy called.

"Scott . . ." Piper hated seeing the look on his face, hopeful and, yes, loving. It was hard to bring the words out that she knew she had to say. "Scott," she said softly, "it's time to move on." She watched his face fall and felt her own stomach clench. Breaking her engagement months ago to the old Scott had been so much easier.

He swallowed hard, then brought up a shaky smile. "Not what I wanted to hear," he said. "But . . . okay."

"I'm sorry."

He nodded, his smile firmer. "Me, too. But can't blame a guy for trying." He picked up his box, started to turn, then set the box back down to look hard at her. "Good-bye, Piper." Piper matched the gaze for several moments, then stepped out from behind her counter. She reached up to give Scott a hug. He held her tight for a moment, then pulled away. "Take care."

Piper watched him go, knowing she had done the right thing but still feeling a mess of emotions. After the door had closed and she'd watched him disappear from sight, all while drawing many deep breaths, she heard Amy step out from the back room.

"That call was from Will," Amy said. "I told him you'd get back to him."

Piper smiled, then, and turned toward Amy. "Amy, that was absolutely the perfect thing to say."

"Huh?" Amy asked, looking puzzled.

Piper grinned. "Never mind."

She clapped her hands briskly. "Well! How's that pickled fennel coming? Almost done? Maybe we should put up another batch of pickled carrots. Those are always popular, and business has been picking up. We'll need to have more on hand. Strawberries! I should pick up strawberries for jam. Will loves strawberry jam. Yes! That'll be next, after the carrots. Something really good for Will."

Piper realized she was babbling and Amy smiled. "I think you've already got something for Will, something good to tell him, that is."

"I do," Piper said, returning the smile. "But it'll wait." Will, after all, had been waiting for several months to hear what she was finally ready to tell him. A few more hours wouldn't hurt. And she wanted it to be in person, not over the phone.

Piper headed back to her pickling station, feeling that her life had just turned a corner, excited, a little anxious, but happy. As she checked her carrots and lined up her canning jars, she began to hum and realized she was grinning widely. For the first time in what seemed like forever, things were looking pretty darned good.

With that thought, she slipped a clean apron over her head, reached for her peeler, and got to work. First things first.

# Recipes

## BRANDIED CHERRIES

### MAKES ABOUT 6 HALF-PINT JARS

1 cup sugar
2 cups brandy
1 cup red wine
Zest of one orange, removed in large strips with a
    vegetable peeler
3 pounds sweet cherries, pitted

Combine the sugar, brandy, wine, and orange zest in a 6- to
8-quart preserving pan, bring to a boil, stirring to dissolve
the sugar, and boil for 5 minutes.

Add the cherries and lower the heat to a simmer, stirring occasionally, until the cherries are tender (about 5 minutes).

Ladle the syrup and cherries into prepared, hot jars, leaving ¼" headspace and wiping the rims clean. Top each jar with a flat lid and ring, tightening to finger-tight.

Put the jars in a canning pot and cover with at least 1" of water. Boil for 5 minutes, then remove the jars and let sit undisturbed for 12 hours. Check that the lids have sealed (can't be pushed down). Any jars that have not sealed properly should be refrigerated immediately.

## SPICY CARROT PICKLES

2 pounds carrots
5½ cups cider vinegar (5% acidity)
1 tablespoon pure kosher salt
3 tablespoons sugar
3 cinnamon sticks
3 bay leaves
8 dried hot chiles, stemmed
4 cloves garlic, sliced
4 sprigs thyme
1 to 2 teaspoons crushed red pepper flakes, to taste
½ teaspoon whole black peppercorns
½ small white onion, thinly sliced lengthwise

Scrub, trim, and peel the carrots; cut into sticks ½" thick and 4" long. Let sit in ice water.

Combine the vinegar, salt, sugar, cinnamon sticks, bay leaves, and 1 cup water in a wide, 6- to 8-quart preserving pan, and bring to a boil. Simmer for 5 minutes.

Add the carrots and cook for 8 to 10 minutes until tender-crisp.

Prepare jars and lids. While still hot, divide the chiles, garlic, thyme, red pepper flakes, and peppercorns among the jars.

Add the carrots to the jars, using tongs or a slotted spoon (don't pack too tightly), and loosely fill spaces with slivers of onion.

Ladle the pickling liquid into the jars, leaving ½" headspace, and remove any air bubbles with a chopstick. Wipe the rims clean, then top each jar with a flat lid and ring, tightening to finger-tight.

Put the jars in a canning pot and cover with 1" of water. Boil for 15 minutes, then remove the jars and let sit undisturbed for 12 hours. Check that the lids have sealed (can't be pushed down). Any jars that have not sealed properly should be refrigerated immediately.